BOSTON LUST

WOL-VRIEY

Other Books By Wol-vriey:

The Bizarro Story of I

Meat Suitcase

Chainsaw Cop Corpse

Vegan Zombie Apocalypse

Boston Posh (Bud Malone #1)

Vegan Vampire Vaginas

Vagina Mundi

Melanie Nemesis Catchpole

Bizarro 101: A Basic Primer

Boston Corpse (Bud Malone #2)

Dr. Orgasm

**Novellas and Short Stories By
Wol-vriey:**

Big Trouble in Little Ass
A novella featured in
Westward Hoes

Forever Ago Sunshine
A short story featured in
The Big Book of Bizarro

BOSTON LUST

WOL-VRIEY

Boston Lust
By **Wol-vriey**

Burning Bulb Publishing
P.O. Box 4721
Bridgeport, WV 26330-4721
United States of America
www.BurningBulbPublishing.com

Cover designed by Gary Lee Vincent.
Author Photo: Lolade Akinsowon © 2014

First Edition.

Paperback Edition ISBN: 978-0692574270

Printed in the United States of America

DEDICATION

To everyone who likes weird fiction.

ACKNOWLEDGMENTS

Major thanks to Gary Lee Vincent and Rich Bottles Jr. at Burning Bulb Publishing for supporting my writing.

Thanks too to my lovely wife Victoria for all her love and support.

And, last, but definitely not least, thanks also to you the reader for reading my work and permitting me to entertain you.

Peace, Everyone!

Wol-vriey.

11/14/2015

PART 1:
NIGHT CREATURES

CHAPTER 1

Jayne

It was a hot August night; really hot outside. Seated at a table in XX, a 'ladies only' nightclub on Essex Street, Jayne Howman was relieved to be out of the heat. Earlier, while entering XX's double doors, she'd felt like a roast leaving a furnace. The club's air-conditioning units were so far proving adequate to the challenge of keeping everyone cool. At least for the moment. Later was anyone's guess, Jayne figured; the units could stage a bulk collapse and they'd all die of heatstroke.

Her gaze floated around the expansive space that formed the club's main hall, past the grouped tables and chairs, over to the dance floor, all glitzy with wriggling female bodies and sparkling neon. *Ooh, yeah, girls do just want to have fun!* Amidst the wrigglers, an elevated stripper was halfway through her act, her body undulating like theirs.

Jayne grinned. The stripper had a great body; she knew how to work it too. Jayne watched her a for a while, growing steadily warmer in the crotch, then returned her attention to her glass of 7-Up. She took a sip, then checked her phone for the time: 8 p.m.

She sipped more of her drink. It was early hours yet in XX. Wednesday nights were always a little slow, hanging as they did like wet laundry midway between weekends. The partying only picked up by, say, 10 p.m. and was dead again by 1 a.m. Nothing like Fridays, for instance, but that was usual.

This evening still had potential.

Jayne Howman was smallish and blonde. Twenty-three years old. Pretty enough, with gray eyes, a largish mouth, and a snub nose. Her jeans were baggy, her gray cotton shirt somewhat too tight—it was squeezing her chest, letting everyone see that her breasts were quite big.

Her clothes were still slightly damp from the outside heat, but she felt good.

Across the room the stripper finished her act, gathered up her tips and panties and departed the raised stage. Another barely-clad female in high heels strode out along the pencil-thin walkway and wrapped herself around the silver pole. A romance of flesh and glitter. A new song began; she began resolutely losing her clothes to its pulsating beat.

Jayne licked her lips when the stripper, blonde like her and equally busty, peeled off her bra and struck a pose that pushed her crotch forward.

Jayne was here looking for someone . . . anyone. Once done for the day at her job as a Robopol receptionist she was on the prowl. Dammit, she was on the prowl even at work, but practically no one ever visited Robopol HQ except robot cop machines and hoodlums headed for lockdown.

Across the room the stripper turned, bent forward and shook her ass in Jayne's direction. She began sliding her buttocks up and down the pole. Each time she paused in a crouch, several of the dancing women stuck dollar bills in her waistband. A few slapped her ass. As if stung by the intrusive contact, the stripper leapt up and spun around again, synthetic smile plastered across her face like she was being forced to have a public orgasm against her wishes.

Jayne felt the woman's coltish body like a magnet summoning her across the darkness. The warmth between her legs intensified, became entangled with moisture.

Jayne realized she'd begun sweating despite the air-con; if she'd been a man she'd have been sporting a raging hard-on by now. She quickly gulped down the rest of her 7-Up and signaled a waitress, ordered a whiskey and soda.

It was time to step her drinking up a grade. Cold sober, she'd shortly start fantasizing about the stripper or growing depressed if she didn't hook up with someone tonight. Drunk, she'd likely become obnoxious, but no way would she remember what she'd done or said (or regret it—which was more important) come morning.

Now where's that hottie I'm dying to spend the night with?

"May I join you?"

She looked up. The speaker was a slim woman with long black hair down to her ribs. She wore a black dress and high boots. Her face was long and thin and utterly pale, her eyes large and black, her lips glazed with darkness. She was very good-looking, albeit in a starved way.

A Goth chick, Jayne realized. *The kind that cream themselves silly over snaps of Marilyn Manson.*

She smiled at the new arrival, gestured at the three chairs around the table. "Please do." Then laughing, she added, "Just don't block out the pole lady."

Laughing back, the woman sat on Jayne's right then extended her hand. "I'm Lily," she said. "I saw you sitting alone and felt you might like some company."

"Thanks." Jayne shook Lily's hand. It was slim and bony. Delicate and soft too, like she did very little housework. A faint perfume Jayne couldn't place wafted up from the dainty digits.

Lily pointed at the stripper, who now, her back to them, was shimmying out of her panties. "You think she's good?"

"She's great eye candy. As for her moves? I wouldn't mind having her dance in bed for me."

Lily stifled a giggle. "I wouldn't either; she's got the curves I like." She winked at Jayne, her gaze falling to Jayne's straining chest and lingering on her breasts just a second too long before rising back to her face and staring brazenly into her eyes, her black lips curling in a suggestive smile. "You know what I mean; I'm certain you do." She had very white teeth.

Jayne hid a grin. *At least false modesty ain't a problem here; she's definitely hitting on me. Curves she likes?* She realized Lily had noticed that her own ample mammary endowment was comparable to the stripper's.

Looking into Lily's black eyes, Jayne nodded demurely back. She tensed as wetness flooded her crotch. Imagining Lily could read her arousal on her face, she gulped at her scotch, then smiled at the Gothic-themed woman. She focused a moment on her pale companion's dark lips, imagining what they'd feel like pressed against her flesh, tongue lapping between her legs like sea waves against a beach.

From the quickened rise and fall of Lily's diminutive chest, Jayne determined she was aroused too. She placed a hand over Lily's as it rested on the table. Lily smiled back. Jayne made eyes at her. Lily pouted a kiss. The pair giggled.

A waitress brought Lily a beer. She left. Hand in hand, Jayne and Lily sat watching the dancers, while the strippers changed places like skittles being replaced in a human bowling alley.

After a while they kissed in the neon dark.

***

At 9:45, Jayne and Lily left XX.

"Your place or mine?" Lily asked. "My AG's in the lot. It's a white Jaguar, a speed thrill; we'll be at my apartment in next to no time."

"Mine," Jayne replied, her voice trembling with lust. "It's just around the corner on Bedford Street, right up by Church Green. Five minutes walk."

***

Once through her front door, Jayne kicked her pumps off, then she and Lily spent a long moment staring out of her living room window at the One Boston Place skyscraper, where she worked 9 to 5.

"So what's it like working for Robopol?" Lily asked. (Jayne had noticed that, oddly, though they'd drank equal amounts at XX, Lily hardly seemed addled at all. Her eyes and mind still seemed crystal clear. *Or maybe I'm imagining it?* Jayne, however, was now quite tipsy; she wavered on her feet almost in sync with the curtains as the wind fluttered them. In her fleeting moments of perfect lucidity, she also imagined she felt a creepy vibe coming from her companion, but then she'd shrug it off as being just the woman's 'darkside' getup.)

"It's weird, you know, being surrounded by robots all day long," she replied the query. "Has benefits though."

Lily made a face. "Benefits?"

Jayne nodded. "Well, for one thing, the pay's fantastic."

6

"Yeah?"

"Oh yes. And there's very little human competition—practically no office politicking and bitching—which I'm delirious over." That emphatic statement, however, accompanied by a fierce nod, reminded Jayne of how horny she was. *Oh, hell, we can talk later.* She turned away from the window and stepped up close to Lily, pressing against her so their breasts compressed like marshmallows, so their hot breath mingled.

"Fuck work," she growled, her voice rumbling deep in her throat. Her eyes fastened like clamps on Lily's face. "And you . . .*fuck me.*"

Then, pressing her lips hard against Lily's, she dipped her hand between the other woman's legs and squeezed the crotch of her dress, imagining she felt vaginal wetness through the black fabric.

"Oh, yes," Lily enthused, coming up for air, black lipstick smeared across her chin. "Where's the bed?"

* * *

They retired quickly to the bedroom. Got naked even quicker.

Jayne gasped as Lily peeled her black dress off over her head. *Holy shit!*

Lily's body was incredible: she was slim, but her figure whistled with perfection. Her small breasts sat just right over her ribcage, a seductive blend of cone and hemisphere; her waist dipped in just so, her hips spreading like a wasp's; and the revealed ass . . .

Her skin was bleach-pale, almost translucent, with blue tracings of surface veins. Jayne's gaze dropped to Lily's crotch, where her sex nestled amidst neat and glossy black hair, then swept outward and down the shapely thighs and legs to the petite feet.

Damn, this is one classy chick! Jayne thought. Then she realized that Lily was staring at her too, her gaze seemingly riveted on Jayne's chest. She was suddenly worried: Lily's gaze didn't seem one of lust, rather, it seemed predatory, like she was hungry. The pale woman licked her lips, her tongue a pink snake flicking over her smudged black lipstick.

Oh, shit, Jayne thought, equally worried and aroused. *I've not made a mistake tonight, have I? If she's a psycho, I've already drank too much to . . . where's my can of mace? Did I remember to put it in—*

"I love your rack," Lily interrupted Jayne's thoughts, then advanced on her. "Your tits are out of this world."

She grabbed Jayne's large breasts, then, using them as levers, pushed her back onto the bed and fell on top of her. Jayne began giggling. Lily dropped her face to Jayne's nipples and began sucking.

As pleasure flowed from her breasts to her body, Jayne shed her worries. She'd been wrong, after all. Lily just wanted some ass too. And as for Jayne herself? This was exactly what she needed. The jackpot at the end of her countdown to ecstasy. Moaning encouragement, she grabbed her lover's shoulders and urged her lower, pushing her down between her split legs to her pleasure point.

Once Lily's tongue hit Jayne's wet spot, Jayne really began moaning.

Lily was a skilful lover. Gasping and writhing beneath the thin, pale woman, bathed in her flowing black hair, Jayne felt completely overpowered. The nipping teeth on her nipples, the wet mouth on her vagina, the fingers and thumb penetrating her both back and front, sliding back and forth . . . she felt glorious.

Lily loved and loved her. She made Jayne come over and over again till Jayne, her ecstasy-tormented form writhing with delight, felt like she was floating, a buoy adrift on an ocean of pleasure.

Once or twice between dizzying bursts of sensation, Jayne noticed Lily staring at her hungrily, but when she attempted pleasuring the other woman, slipping fingers into Lily's also-dripping vagina, she encountered resistance. After she'd doggedly coaxed Lily to a single orgasm that doused her digits in the woman's sexual cream, Lily pushed her hands away. "Don't worry, darling," she gasped. "Just let me take care of you. I'll get mine later."

She dipped her mouth to suck on Jayne's clitoris again. Stuck dripping fingers back up her anus. The pleasure recommenced.

Night sweat spread wet on bed sheets.

Finally, Jayne had had enough. "Stop, please!" she moaned. "You're going to kill me."

Lily raised her mouth from Jayne's crotch. (Her lips were pale now, her dark lipstick completely vanished into Jayne's saliva-slick crevices.) Pearls of vaginal secretion dripped from her white teeth. A strand of blonde hair bisected her tongue.

She giggled. "Kill you, baby? How weird that you should put it that way."

Something in Lily's voice alerted Jayne to the fact that she was in danger. But how? She regarded her lover of tonight, focusing on the woman's dark eyes. Yes, that scary feral hunger was back in them. She felt cold now, drenched in icy sensation.

"Y-you . . . you're not going to hurt me, are you?" she queried. Her voice was tremulous—she was utterly scared. "Don't do it, I'm telling you. Don't. My friends all know I'm with you; people saw us together at the club; they saw us leaving. I work with the cops . . . you'll never get away with it . . ." Oh, but she was so weak, too weak from all the glorious sex they'd just had—all those orgasms that had felt like she was dying—to even move. Too weak to even reach her can of mace, which she'd just now noticed sitting on the dresser.

"It's just time for me to get mine, baby," Lily replied. "Sorry. And hey—just so you know before you go—you're a great fuck."

Then Lily laughed, spreading her lips wide like she was yawning. Jayne stared paralyzed as a sudden horrible change came over Lily's face.

Lily grinned down at the prostrate Jayne. Jayne began whimpering like a baby.

Then Jayne stopped whimpering and the liquid sounds of drinking started.

CHAPTER 2

Malone

Bud Malone swung open the car door.

Despite the street being devoid of life, the five steps from his black BMW to the entrance of Fuzzy Joe's pawn shop seemed to take forever to complete. His blaster was in his hand, his eyes and ears alert for danger. Here in the Abstracta, peril dogged one's every step. Let down your guard for even the thinnest slice of a moment and you might become food for something, or worse yet, simply be killed by a thrill seeker who wouldn't even bother to rob your corpse afterwards.

Unsure why he felt so oddly apprehensive over a simple retrieval, Malone warily pushed open the pawn shop's front door.

He made it inside alive.

Malone stuck his gun back in its hip holster.

Fuzzy Joe's was, like pawn shops the world over, full of clutter and litter: shelves, racks, and displays coated with bric-a-brac. The smell of must mixed with that of recent polish. Once through the door, Malone—a handsome fortyish man with brown hair and eyes—took a moment to look around. Like on each previous visit here, he was impressed by the sort of stuff people parted with when they needed fast cash: an assortment of weapons, china, old radios and record players, two autographed guitars (one a Les Paul signed by Vivian Campbell of Def Leppard), leather jackets, jewelry, stuffed animals, assorted unidentifiable curios . . . An array of gleaming samurai swords hung on one side of the display window, two theremins sat in the other. Close to the counter there was another display for old jewelry.

Yes, jewelry . . .

He looked across to the sales counter. Fuzzy Joe sat atop it, beady eyes regarding him with an indecipherable rodent expression.

Fuzzy Joe was a mutated rat. Black and big as a rabbit. It waved to get his attention.

Walking toward the counter, Malone winced; the rat stank.

"Ah, Malone," it said in its squeaky voice once he was headed its way, "you're late. Trouble?"

He shook his head. "Where is it?"

Fuzzy Joe produced a little dark object from a leather pouch at its waist and handed it to Malone.

He examined it. It was a small ring of dull black stone. About the only thing that impressed him about it was the blood on it. Seeing the blood brought back his previous unease.

He looked at Fuzzy Joe. "Where'd you get this, Joe? And are you certain it's the right one?"

The big rat looked pained. It stood on all fours, shook itself. "C'mon, Malone, have some faith in me. You know me better than to think I'd pull a fastie on you. Sure it's the real deal. As for *where?* A guy named Jackson calls me up; he wants to flog the ring on his girlfriend's behalf. I've done biz with Jackson before; he's legit, so we fix a rendezvous for his place. I go over there and meet a complete bloodbath—something got them both. Something real big—there were deep tooth marks in the bodies and intestines strewn everywhere. Blood was splashed all over the walls; on the ceiling even. The blood was still wet too." Sniffing the air with 'ten-minutes-earlier-and-that-could-have-been-me' nervousness, Fuzzy Joe stared its beady gaze at Malone. "Jackson always was a bit careless. Some guys never learn, you know? And his girlfriend must have been equally careless—they do say like attracts like." The huge rat sniggered. "Not like you, eh, Malone?"

Frowning, Malone said, "Nah, not like me." He weighed the black ring in his palm for a moment. "So you grabbed it and got out. No one saw you?"

Fuzzy Joe sat back down and spread its forepaws wide. "Yes to the first: whatever got Jackson missed eating his left hand—the ring was on his finger. But . . . I've no way of knowing for sure 'bout the second. You know here in the Abstracta, the walls occasionally do have ears . . . some even have eyes too."

Malone nodded. "Okay, I'll take my chances on that."

"Me more than you."

"Yeah, that's right. But I'm paying your ass for the risk, Joe. So, how much?"

The rat's black lips creased into a greasy smile and its whiskers twitched. "Thirty grand . . . and it's cheap at that price."

Malone rolled his eyes. He'd expected this. It was quintessential Joe, the rat trying to make as much profit as possible on the deal, despite in this case not having paid a cent for the ring. Still, Adrienne Lake, Malone's client, was rich. She'd told him he could pay up to fifty thousand dollars for the ring. He hid a smile at Fuzzy Joe's determined expression. This time the rat was selling itself short and didn't even know it. *Joe, you should have started bargaining at a hundred!*

He put on his best deadpan face and growled in a tough voice, "Joe, it's just a damned ring. Fifteen."

"What?" In pained indignation, Fuzzy Joe pulled itself up to its full two feet two inches height. It began strutting across the countertop. "I went through a lot of pain to get that . . ." It paused, gestured around the shop, then glared at Malone. "How am I ever gonna make ends meet if you lowball me, huh? Okay, 'cos I like you, Malone, twenty-nine thousand."

"Joe . . ." Malone began, then reconsidered. He still felt uneasy being in here (though a glance outside the shop revealed nothing suspicious) and felt it best to get this over with quickly. Adrienne Lake wouldn't miss the money, but . . . it now occurred to Malone that while Joe wouldn't deceive him over the ring's genuineness, it might itself have been deceived. What if Jackson had been trying to swindle the rodent? He peered at the black ring in his palm. Maybe, just maybe this was a fake. Only Adrienne would know for sure though.

Fuzzy Joe had in the meantime mistaken Malone's thoughtful expression for reluctance. "Okay, Malone, you drive a hard bargain. Twenty-eight grand, and that's my—"

Next moment, Fuzzy Joe exploded into a mess of rat entrails. A rain of meat and black fur filled the air.

Where Fuzzy Joe had been standing, the wooden countertop now sported a large round hole with glowing edges. Behind the counter, something big was coming through another just-burnt hole in the wall.

12

Malone reacted on instinct. He tucked the black ring into his shirt pocket and pulled his gun.

The creature that had killed Fuzzy Joe stepped into the pawn shop.

Malone gaped at it. It was a berserker.

Oh, crap!

The berserker was huge: a sasquatch—a 'bigfoot'—carrying an energy rifle. Its hairy brown bulk was covered with dust from the destroyed wall. Except for two ammo belts crossing its torso in an 'X' it was unclothed. And yes, it had a lot of teeth, was clearly the 'something' that had eaten Jackson and his lady.

The berserker saw Malone, trained its gun on him, and began shooting.

Malone ducked and ran. Covering his eyes, he flung himself through the store's glass front display. The pawn shop's shelves exploded into debris as the berserker swung its gun after him.

Glass pattering like rain around him, Malone landed on the sidewalk.

He looked back, saw the sasquatch sighting on him again, and dashed across the empty street, winding up in the doorway opposite both Fuzzy Joe's pawn shop and his car. At the far end of the street to his left stood the Soft Wall—the Abstracta's boundary. Off-white unpolished stone, it rose to merge with the clouds.

The Soft Wall was two hundred yards away; on its other side lay safety. Getting there alive, however . . .

In a follow-up shower of glass, the berserker crashed out through the shop display. Malone winced at the size of the thing—it had to be close to eight feet tall. Shaggier than any dog alive, the massive hairy creature had a face that was neither human nor ape, yet which somehow managed to be way uglier than both. It towered over Malone's car, its head swiveling to and fro as it searched for him.

The berserker sighted Malone. It leapt over his car and headed for him, a rush of teeth and murderous intent.

Malone shot it, aiming for the head.

His first shot missed, chipping stone off the wall behind. The second shot hit the berserker in the head. A portion of the creature's skull blew off, revealing pink bloody brain. It came on, however, stamping holes in the road, still raising its gun to kill him. Malone fired twice more, scoring two direct hits that sliced off the top of its head.

The giant sasquatch collapsed face-forward into the road.

Heaving a sigh of relief, Malone ran past its bleeding corpse, across the street to his parked BMW. It was time to be far gone from here. He glanced into the pawn shop, winced at the patches of bloody fur that had recently been Fuzzy Joe. Gun at the ready, he quickly unlocked the car door.

Then, about to pull the door open, he heard the patter of running feet to his right.

He turned quickly. Looking like an animated hillock of spiky brown fur, another berserker (this one even larger than the first) was loping along the sidewalk towards him on all fours. Seeing Malone had noticed it, it leapt up to its feet, swung its energy rifle forward from its back and began shooting.

Malone flung himself hard over the car's hood as two energy blasts streaked past its door. Crouched on the BMW's other side, he decided there wasn't any use hanging around to fight. Cars were easily replaced, and besides, he'd already got what he'd come for. No point dying for no reason.

The berserker paused in its firing. Malone leapt up into the calm and sent several blasts of his own its way.

It ducked through a shop door.

Once the berserker was out of sight, Malone sent several more energy blasts after it to keep it in concealment. Then he tiptoed back into Fuzzy Joe's shop.

He made his way quickly through the mess in there, walking around behind the sales counter and then out through the hole in the wall made by his initial attacker. The door of the next room led out back. Malone ran up the street towards the Soft Wall, then because this new street ended in an L-junction, he was forced to cross back to the one that housed Fuzzy Joe's pawn shop.

The detour had been worth it. He was now much farther up the street, the Soft Wall just forty yards ahead. Back by his car, the berserker was looking around for him, its subnormal intelligence perplexed that he'd vanished. Malone pressed himself against the wall and waited till it had entered the pawn shop, then he turned and sprinted for the Soft Wall, here a white stone barrier that turned the road into a dead end.

An illusion, he knew.

Then, fifteen yards from safety, a circular ring of fire appeared in the middle of the sidewalk and a berserker sprouted from it like a weed, blocking off Malone's exit.

Malone winced. He had no idea if this was a new attacker or simply the previous one activating a teleport circle.

This bigfoot stretched a massive clawed hand toward Malone. "Hand ring over." Its guttural voice sounded like a lion chewing meat. It stank almost as badly as Fuzzy Joe had.

Malone hedged, unsure how many unused bullets remained in his gun. The weapon was a 'dual' model—its bullets could function either as normal projectiles, or if 'blast mode' was activated, they detonated/decompressed inside the gun, which then projected their energy at the target. Only thing was, this latter mode used up thrice as much ammo as the first and burnt through bullets faster. While fleeing he'd reset the gun from 'blast' to 'projectile' to conserve ammo. But how many blasts had he fired? He thought hard: *This bigfoot's gun will likely have a full charge . . . and the Soft Wall is just behind it. What do I do?*

"So I give you the ring," he said. "And then what?"

The berserker laughed, its hairy body heaving with mirth. "Then I let you go." Its deep-pitched words dropped into the empty street and echoed like bouncing balls.

A long strand of raw flesh dangling between its teeth fell loose to the ground. The sight increased Malone's lack of confidence in the creature. The berserker kept on laughing. Malone suddenly realized that if it was waiting for reinforcements they'd have arrived by now. So clearly, it was alone.

He decided to go for broke. He swung his gun up and shot the berserker.

The sasquatch-mercenary's body jerked back and it stopped laughing. Blood spurted from its shoulder, dribbled red through its overabundant fur.

Malone fired again. His gun clicked empty.

Fuck!

The berserker growled in pain, hurt in its yellow eyes.

"Should just have handed ring over, punk," it said. It raised its gun, then, about to pull the trigger it changed its mind and lowered the weapon. Even wounded, Malone was clearly no longer a threat to it; it towered over him by at least two feet.

It strode towards him. "Can't melt or damage the ring . . . hand it over, punk human."

Malone stared past the approaching berserker (which was now regarding him hungrily) at the white expanse of the Soft Wall. Over there was safety; no way would the berserker let him live once it had the ring. He grimaced. *This bigfoot son-of-a-bitch is blocking the way! And I need a weapon!*

"Give fight up!" the berserker growled. "Give me ring!"

Malone smirked at the sasquatch. *All I need to do is shoot it one more time and it'll die . . . maybe with its own gun . . .*

"Ah, this wasting time. Ring must be in your pockets! I'll shoot your head off and search!"

Malone lunged at the berserker. It stumbled back to avoid him, firing as it did so. The blast flashed over Malone's head.

Malone leapt at the berserker again. It was still off balance and he grabbed its arm before it could fire again. Unable to shoot, it instead began clubbing at him with its massive fists and trying to rake him down the back with its claws. It head-butted him twice, slamming its chin down hard on the top of his head, partly dazing him.

No match for the giant in the punching arena, Malone fought to wrestle its gun from it. But he was weakening fast as he swam in the sea of its pungent hair. Another chin-butt almost knocked him unconscious. Any moment now, he'd be too mentally fuddled to fight at all.

Sensing victory, the berserker raised both hands to deliver a skull-crushing blow to Malone's head.

Then, in a whoosh of heat that doused Malone like shower water, the berserker's head exploded off its shoulders. For a moment its body wavered and twitched, then it collapsed flat to the floor, freshets of blood seeping from its cauterized neck.

Malone fell on top of it, which felt like being thrown onto a spiky wet carpet. Then he leapt up again. *Who in the world just helped me?*

"Over here, Malone."

The voice had come from behind him. He spun towards it.

A woman stood by a nearby lamppost caressing a smoking energy pistol. She was good-looking, with crimson hair and lips and emerald eyes. She wore a brown leather jacket over a white T-shirt, blue jeans, and brown boots.

She was smiling at him with something like gentle mockery in her eyes.

"Thanks," he said, pointing to the sasquatch's corpse. "I owe you my life. Who are you?"

She laughed. "Trudi Carmen at your service, Malone." She jerked a thumb toward the Soft Wall's white expanse. "I think you were about leaving?"

"How do you know—?"

"Look, Malone, it's been really nice saving your life, but I gotta run, okay? I've business to handle in the Abstracta."

He watched her walk off, her hourglass figure slinking away from him. "Hey, Trudi, how do I see you again?"

She turned back, her smile both teasing and demure. She laughed. "C'mon, Malone, business before pleasure. What's important is that you take very good care of that ring you've got with you."

With that, Trudi Carmen vanished down a side street.

"Thanks," he mouthed after her.

Then, bemused, he returned his thoughts to her last statement. *Take very good care of that ring.* He patted his shirt pocket to ensure he still had it. *Okay, time to return you to your owner.*

For a moment Malone considered walking back down the street to retrieve his BMW.

He shrugged the thoughts off. It wasn't wise: there might be other berserker's waiting for him at Fuzzy Joe's . . . and those bigfoot boneheads were hardcore.

Nah, best to quit while I'm ahead. I'll pick it up later—if it still runs.

Malone scanned the street to ensure there was no danger in sight, then walked up to the Soft Wall and into it.

The white mass absorbed him, his body entering the seemingly solid rock face like it was sinking into milk. The Soft Wall spat him out its other side into Boston Normal. Behind him, it resumed its seamless aspect.

Outside in the 'real world' again, it was early evening. Malone got out his cellphone and dialed.

17

"Hello, Adrienne? . . . Yes, it's Malone. . . . Yeah, I've gotten your ring. . . . Yeah, it's undamaged. . . . Say, is it okay if I bring it round tomorrow? . . . No, I can't come over right away; I need to get back to my office urgently, some paperwork to see to. . . . Alright, thanks, say about noon tomorrow? . . . That's cool? . . . Okay, see you then."

He hung up. That was fixed then. Adrienne Lake had sounded ecstatic.

He pocketed the phone, checked the flow of traffic, then struck out left along Beacon Street towards the Arlington intersection.

Malone suddenly felt totally winded. It was time to find a cab and get home; have a shower, get some rest. He'd definitely had enough excitement for one day.

CHAPTER 3

The Abstracta: Lucy's Legacy.

Six months ago, as part of her bloody vendetta against Golden Dragon Casino owner Sookie Ling, Lucy Tang had thrown four nightmare pods into the Beacon Hill Hotel and Bistro, thereby opening a space-time rift that linked directly to a part of Hell.

Monsters had poured out of the rift and massacred Sookie's men.

Lucy Tang had since died. The monsters she'd released, however, had remained and proliferated . . . and spread.

Everyone had expected the nightmare pods' influence to in time extend along the whole of Charles Street, where the Beacon Hill Hotel and Bistro was located. Add or take a few blocks either side of it too for good measure. But . . . no one had expected the pods' corruption of logic and reality to spread across the entirety of Beacon Hill.

And it spread rapidly. Within two weeks after Lucy's death, the entire area bounded by Cambridge Street in the north and east, Beacon Street in the south, and Embankment Road in the west was a nightmare realm, as Hell came to Earth to play with insane abandon.

As the transformation threatened to corrupt the whole of Boston, Robopol—Boston's robot police force—moved to halt its spread. The robot cops had quickly grown tired of constantly battling those Beacon Hill nightmares that threatened to escape the confines of their zone (which in theory shouldn't have been possible but *was* happening) as it took away from their regular crime prevention duties and they were already understaffed.

So . . . they opened up an OD sinkhole. Boston, MA thronged with OD's—otherworld doors—space-time portals that led to just about everywhere in the conceivable universe, from right next door,

to Alpha Centauri, to the deep prehistoric past, to the far flung future
. . . and to an almost unimaginable number of parallel universes
where just about everything was possible.

Most important/relevant in this case? Lots of OD's led to empty
void-like realms that seemed the perfect place to dump an overflow
of Hellish crap and creatures that everyone in Boston wanted to see
the last of.

The Robopol robots weren't being careless. They (backed by the
best USAcme scientists and technology—USAcme owned
Robopol) had already cleaned up a similar nightmare pod mess from
Sookie Ling's 'High Tower' high rise in her Golden Dragon Casino.
In that case the affected hotel suite (on the fourth floor) had been
restored to normal. So they went ahead.

But in this case, something went wrong. Very wrong. Either the
OD they linked to was too large, or maybe the area they were trying
to clean up was, but what happened was, instead of the sinkhole
leeching away Boston's unwanted oddity, it flooded the Beacon Hill
area with an influx of something even stranger than what everyone
wanted gone.

Enter the Abstracta: a white 'rock' mountain with a 'soft wall'—
a solid-seeming barrier that one could nonetheless walk or drive
through into a realm of miraculous impossibility, and then
walk/drive back out of again.

Boston's designation as the 'Hub of the Universe' just might
have come true: the Abstracta seemed a mingling of everywhere—
real and fantastic—at once.

The Groad existed underneath Boston. Everyone knew that the
Groad was a part of Hell. No one was really certain, however, what
Boston's new landmark was, except that there were VERY strange
things in it; strange monsters, strange places, strange people . . .
some with superpowers even.

Humans stayed out of the Abstracta. At least at first.

The Abstracta had one benefit over its nightmare-realm
predecessor: it was a contained realm—it maintained a fixed size. If
it showed no sign of shrinking and being gone from Beantown, it
also showed absolutely no sign of growing any larger, remaining
firmly within its Cambridge, Beacon, and Embankment route limits
(not even extending onto their sidewalks). Indeed, scientific tests on
the Abstracta tended to show that it couldn't grow any smaller or

larger. Externally at least, it was a static realm, one held to constant dimensions by an intricate web of balanced internal forces and energy stresses.

This information made Bostonians heave a collective sigh of relief.

Once it was determined that neither would the Abstracta expand to swallow up the city, nor would it suddenly disgorge an army of monsters into Boston, most people forgot about it and went about their daily business.

There were bills to pay, and love and hatred to pursue.

But human nature being what it was, after a while people began moving to live inside the Abstracta: innocents, thrill seekers . . . criminals. They pushed inward through the Soft Wall to find something new.

(Others—PI's like Malone—entered the Abstracta on 'find and retrieve' missions.)

And, in the reverse case, a few of the Abstracta's own creatures overcame their initial reticence to leave it, exited the Soft Wall, and entered Boston life themselves. Some with benign motives, others to seek deadly, murderous fun.

In possibly the planet's weirdest city already, this latest version of business as unusual quickly became usual.

CHAPTER 4

Malone

Next Morning. 97 Bedford Street.

Malone stared at Robopol Lt. Steelberg, who stood framed in the bust-up apartment doorway. "What's wrong, Metal Guy?"

"A lot, Malone." Steelberg, a six-foot-tall white robot wearing a crumpled beige suit and hat, stood aside to let Malone through the apartment door, then followed him inside.

Steelberg led the way through to the bedroom. As they walked through the living room, Malone's PI instincts kicked into gear. Driving over here from the Abstracta (after a refreshing night's sleep he'd returned there for his car, thankfully without incident), his mind had been filled with pleasant thoughts of seeing Trudi Carmen again. Now those pleasant thoughts fluttered from the coop of his mind; he became all business.

(Malone did consultancy police work for Robopol on cases that defied the robot police force's cold logic. Steelberg never called him out to a crime scene except there was something completely screwed up about it.)

Inside the bedroom, Steelberg pointed to the bed. "There she is."

Malone took one look at the corpse lying on it and almost threw up. "Who's this, Metal Guy?"

"Jayne Howman, one of our receptionists. She'd not been into the office for two days—she didn't call either—and we couldn't find her in any of the city's hospitals. So I figured to come over and check up on her wellbeing."

Malone didn't reply; his gaze was riveted on the corpse. He'd never seen death like this before. Jayne's body looked eroded, like an arid gray field savaged by torrents of bad irrigation. The body was naked; deep red ditches ran all over it, from her head (where her nose and right eye had been completely melted into her face) down to her feet (her left big toe having been similarly eroded away). The expression on what remained of her face was completely unreadable, largely because she no longer had either an upper lip or any right-side front teeth.

Steelberg broke into his thoughts. "She looks like a pack of rats were surface-mining her."

Nodding, Malone turned his attention from the corpse to glance around the bedroom. The room was cozy and neat, ideal bachelorette quarters. A small picture of the dead woman—a busty blonde with a crew cut—smiled back at him from her dressing table.

He sucked in a breath then looked back at Steelberg. Something already struck him as odd here. "Metal Guy, why isn't she smelling? From the look of things—"

"That's not all that's odd, Malone." Steelberg, its white oval face reflecting lamplight, waved metal fingers at the body on the bed. "She's dead, right? Her body all sliced open. So . . . where's all the blood?"

Malone winced at that additional oddity. The bedclothes around the corpse were as clean as if it were lying on a morgue slab.

"They're all like this," Steelberg added.

Feeling a cold shiver go through him, Malone looked at the robot. "*All?* She's not the only one?"

Steelberg shook its metal head. "Miss Howman here is the seventh so far. All women killed over a two-week period."

"And you're just calling me?"

"We didn't know, Malone. You know how busy we get." Its silicon brain began audibly humming as it retrieved data from its hard drives. "The first victim was a Marie Kinney. Two weeks ago her girlfriend calls in to say she's not come home. That's a normal enough complaint: the pair had had a quarrel and Marie left, said she was going clubbing. She never comes back. Her disappearance is filed down in Missing Persons—"

"And the others? Come on, Metal Guy, you can't have that many missing people and not suspect some sort of foul play."

"You forget that Missing Persons gets less priority than violent crime. Files there process slower. Lots of people cool off after a lover's tiff and return home. And sometimes the complainant forgets to inform us that they're back."

"Okay, go on. So you missed the other bodies?"

The robot nodded. "At first, yeah. The biggest problem was . . ." it indicated Jayne Howman's horribly trenched body again, "or rather *is* . . . the fact that the stiffs don't stink 'cos they don't rot. If they did, cotenants would notice and call us. If Miss Howman hadn't been working with us at Robopol we might never have found her." Steelberg waved a plastic-coated finger in the air. "Once I got inside and saw her—I had to break down the door, it was locked and chained from within—I sent an emergency alert to HQ, asking Missing Persons to dispatch officers to the residence of anyone who'd been reported by their employers as not having checked in for work in the past month. So far, we've six positives, all their doors locked from within. There may be several more victims though."

"That first victim, er, what's her name again?"

"Marie Kinney? What about her?"

"Where'd you find her if she didn't return home?"

"She was pulled out of a dumpster in Chinatown Park an hour ago. Her body's in exactly the same state as this one. Obviously, we haven't informed her girlfriend yet."

Malone stared at the robot blandly, wondering if it was being facetious.

"And one more thing, Malone . . ."

"Yeah?"

"All the victims are lesbians."

"Lesbians?"

"Yeah, whoever's doing this is targeting the gay female community."

With an uneasy feeling, Malone reflected on that a moment, then he stared at Jayne Howman's corpse again and tried to reconcile the horror of its cold abused rigidity with the smiling portrait of the woman that sat across the room.

He turned to Steelberg, imagining the flashing dots of the robot's eyes as traffic 'Stop' signals. "The killer sounds female then. Either that or a misogynistic transvestite. Have you checked the lesbian nightclubs? Easiest places to pick up that many women."

Steelberg nodded. "Yeah. We've got three positive IDs. Three of the victims were seen leaving clubs with a slim dark woman."

"CCTV footage?"

"Yeah, but it's useless."

"How so?"

Steelberg creaked a metallic sigh. "Two of the CCTV recordings are of excellent quality, good frontal shots; but in both only the victim's face shows, not the killer's."

Malone looked incredulously at Steelberg. "Are you serious?"

"There's a computer in the living room. Come with me and I'll show you."

They walked out of the bedroom. A pink tablet PC lay on Jayne's coffee table. They powered it up, then Steelberg streamed a wireless feed across to the device from its memory banks.

Malone sat and watched the two CCTV videos. What the police robot said was true: In both cases, two women had been captured on camera whilst exiting a nightclub. It was clearly seduction, not abduction—both victims were laughing and holding hands with the other woman, and both seemed quite drunk. But in both cases, their companion's entire head and face were missing; all the video showed above her black dress was a spiral swirl like milk being stirred into coffee.

Malone winced. He didn't like this one bit. He had Steelberg replay the video. Afterwards he liked his conclusion even worse: The locked doors, the blood-drained bodies, the inability of the cameras to record the murderess's face, all pointed to just one thing.

But this was Boston, USA, not Transylvania.

One more test to make though, he decided.

He stood up. "Turn it off, Metal Guy, but email me a copy." He pointed through the bedroom door. "In this case I doubt fingerprints would be any good either."

"How'd you know that, Malone? There's no matching prints from any of the murder scenes."

"I need to examine the body."

They returned to the bedroom. Malone knelt by Jayne Howman's corpse and examined her neck. Her gray skin was clammy to the touch, and there was something nauseatingly unnatural about its non-decayed state. Additionally, there was the sheer revolting nature of her demise to deal with: Her left breast, for instance, had been sliced in two by a deep trench; its melted mammary fat had spilled down Jayne's side into another deep meat trench that had itself sliced several of her ribs in two.

Malone fought off his instinctive nausea and kept looking. Behind him, Steelberg stood motionless, a silent sentinel whose digital brain was rerecording the room.

Malone found what he sought: two deep punctures in the corpse's neck, below her right ear. Both piercings were slightly hidden by the flesh erosion, but once he found them, they were unmistakable.

Sighing, he stood up and turned to face Steelberg, who was now busy straightening the creases out of its eternally-crumpled hat. "Metal Guy, call HQ and ask them to check each of the six other bodies they've got for two neck punctures . . . spaced about two inches apart."

"Punctures?"

Malone grimaced down at Jayne Howman's body, then added, "Yeah. I think we're looking for a lady vampire."

CHAPTER 5

Malone / Adrienne

Leaving Steelberg, Malone drove over to see Adrienne Lake for their noon appointment. She lived over at Millennium Place, a condo not too far from Jayne Howman's building.

As he drove, Malone pondered the murders. On close reflection, he revised his profile of the murderess. This was quite the puzzle: Steelberg's enquiry to HQ had confirmed that each of the other six murdered women also had fang punctures on their necks. However, Malone realized that taken alone, the vampire explanation didn't match the facts. True, the corpses were all drained of blood, but vampire bites didn't dissolve away flesh. Such damage would be more likely the product of an enzyme of some kind—of venom. So what kind of creature was the murderess? A vampire or a snake-morph? Snakes had fangs too.

***

Malone took the elevator to Adrienne Lake's fourth floor apartment and buzzed.

Adrienne let him in, stifling a yawn as he walked past her. She was a pretty brunette in her mid-twenties, with gray eyes seemingly jaded from living too fast. She was barefoot, her feet bone-white in contrast to the brown rug. She wore a red wrap sashed tight about her waist.

"Please sit," she said, gesturing around her expensively furnished living room, then added, "Would you care for coffee? I was just about having a cup myself."

He nodded; he could use a pick-me-up now. She vanished into the kitchen; he heard her pouring. She reappeared in the doorway. "Cream? Sugar?"

Malone nodded. "Both."

Adrienne retreated again, then reappeared bearing two steaming cups. She handed one to Malone, then sat opposite him.

Malone took a sip of his coffee. "Tastes great, thanks." He handed her the black ring. "You'll need to confirm it's the right one."

She examined it, squinting inside the black circlet, then slipped it on her right middle finger. "It is." A relieved smile curled her lips. She leaned back and crossed her legs. Her wrap dangled open, showing Malone a lot of shapely thigh.

"How much did it cost to get it back?" Her question was disinterested, asked for facts rather than any actual concern over the money spent.

"Nothing." Malone pulled five wads of notes from his jacket and threw them onto the coffee table. "Here's the cash."

Adrienne's eyes widened in surprise. "Nothing?" Her gaze dipped once to the money, then lifted to hold his captive.

He nodded, then, knowing she was going to ask him to anyway, he told her what had transpired, explaining in some detail about both Jackson and his girlfriend's deaths, then about Fuzzy Joe and the berserkers.

Adrienne listened mostly in silence, sipping her coffee and nodding occasionally. She shuddered as he described the fight with the berserkers. "Blood everywhere?" she gasped, her breathing growing faster (a common reaction Malone had noticed in women when he told them of his scrapes with death), then looked strangely jealous when he mentioned Trudi Carmen. Malone recognized that reaction too, as well as the smoldering 'interested' look now slowly filling Adrienne's eyes like someone was topping her up with arousal.

"I'd really like to know what makes this ring of yours so valuable," he finished. "I know that to you it's merely of sentimental value, but the berserkers aren't any sort of a sentimental lot. And that woman, Trudi? What did she mean—?"

"How about we discuss this over sex?" Adrienne interrupted, putting down her cup and walking quickly over to sit in his lap.

Malone decided to go with the flow; he'd be lying to himself if he said he didn't find Adrienne attractive. And it had been a while since he'd been with a woman.

Adrienne stood up again, pulled Malone to his feet. "Come into the bedroom," she said. "I've a lot of me to show you."

***

Malone was currently single again. His last girlfriend, Josephine 'Slave' Bailey, had been a 'lifestyle submissive.' He'd adapted to her BDSM leanings as best he could, but then, claiming she needed some space—time apart or whatever—Slave had suddenly packed up and moved west to San Francisco. The last time Malone had spoken to her on the phone was three months ago, before she'd apparently met and fallen in love with one Miguel Fernandinho Lopez. Next thing he'd heard, the two were planning marriage. Letting her go had been painful, but . . . romance went on.

***

Adrienne led Malone into her bedroom. In contrast to Jayne Howman's sensible bachelorette pad, this bedroom was sybaritic. The evidence of serious money was everywhere, from the seemingly hundreds of pairs of dresses and shoes in the walk-in closet, to the rack of designer perfume bottles on the light blue wall, to the queen-sized bed that looked like it could easily sleep ten people.

Malone had scant time to really reflect on the décor, however. Now they'd settled the intervening formality of agreeing they were going to have sex, Adrienne Lake was wasting no time in getting what she wanted from him. She'd shed her crimson wrap the moment she was through the bedroom door; now she hastily helped Malone get his pants off. Then, while he unbuttoned his shirt, she sat on the edge of the bed and took his penis into her mouth.

Already half-erect, on its release Malone's manhood leap out of his pants like a cougar. He gasped as her lips engulfed its swollen head and she began sucking him. While the distracting pleasure of fellatio flooded his crotch, he discarded his upper clothes.

Adrienne got up then pushed him down to a sitting position on the bed. Her mouth slurped off his penis. "Get your shoes off quick," she gasped, then knelt between his legs took him between her lips again.

Malone got his shoes off quick. Then he pulled her up off his member and pulled her down onto the bed also. He'd stopped Adrienne just in time; a few more bobs of her head on him and he'd have exploded in her mouth. It had been ages; he'd not even masturbated for the past month.

She grabbed him again, stroked insistently. He pushed her hands away.

"Relax and let me do you," he groaned, then spread her legs and knelt between them.

Adrienne was already very wet, her upper thighs smeared with her drippings. He spread her small inner lips and slipped a finger inside her, twisting it slowly in the thick white sexual secretion. She shuddered and let out a soft catlike purr. He slipped in another finger beside the first, then dropped his tongue to her clitoris and licked. With his free hand, he slid back her clitoral hood then sucked her engorged sexual bud. She stiffened, then relaxed, then stiffened again. Malone began sliding his fingers in and out of Adrienne, sucking her clitoris, then licking it, then sliding his tongue down through the wet groove of her sex and swirling it around his thrusting fingers. Adrienne simply gasped and moaned. Once she ran her fingers through his hair, then she let him go and began making thrusting motions with her hips. He lifted his eyes from her sex for a moment; her eyes were closed and she was squeezing her breasts from the sides, squashing them hard together.

He resumed licking her clitoris and fingering her.

It didn't take long after that. Adrienne let out a series of loud gasps then went limp, breathing heavily.

Malone licked her all the way through her orgasm, then quickly inserted himself into her dripping sex. His penis felt like a stone now. His testicles weren't flesh, but twin aches swinging between his thighs. No way was he going to last long after his extended abstinence. (Immediately Adrienne had come onto him, he'd realized that cunnilingus was the only way he could satisfy her before himself. And far be it from Bud Malone to leave any woman wanting in bed.)

Malone made ten thrusts into Adrienne and exploded, his orgasm almost painful in its intensity. His orgasm trigged a second climax in Adrienne. Her eyes wide, she grabbed his buttocks hard and pulled his penis further inside her, dampening her screams by biting deep into his left shoulder. He was aware that she'd drawn blood from his flesh, but the other delicious agony—the pleasure of his orgasm—was more than sufficient anesthesia. He did, however, keep sufficient mental alertness to realize that she wasn't sucking blood from the wound.

Adrienne did however bite him again, though not as deeply.

He collapsed on her. They kissed. She tasted her sex on his tongue; he tasted his blood on hers.

"That was great," Adrienne told Malone. "You're really good with your tongue."

He laughed. "Some days it works better than on others. I'm glad you enjoyed it."

She cuddled close. "Oh, I did. We've definitely got to do this again, and soon too."

***

Sitting up, their backs pillowed softly against the immense headboard, they spoke in depth. Sated with sex and feeling at peace for the first time today, Malone asked Adrienne where the black ring had originally come from.

"Daddy gave me the ring for my last birthday," Adrienne explained, her expression even more satisfied than Malone's. "He would never tell me where he got it and after a while I quit asking."

Malone knew 'Daddy' was Vancouver industrialist Rudolf Lake; Adrienne was his sole heir. "I'm just perplexed as to why people think it's so valuable. I mean, the berserkers—who aren't the smartest chips off any block—were willing to kill for it. It looks ridiculously ordinary."

"Ordinary?" Laughing, Adrienne held her right hand up and waved it about. "Oh no, baby, it's definitely not ordinary." She grinned at his enquiring gaze. "Okay, hold on, I'll show you."

She leapt out of bed, walked over to the wide window with its expansive view of southern Boston and, out to the east, the Golden Dragon Casino. Watching her move, Malone felt conflicted. Adrienne was definitely good-looking and shapely, and this brief encounter had indisputably proved their sexual chemistry. He tried visualizing them in a relationship, but found it hard. It wasn't her wealth: no, she wasn't more spoiled than any of the other rich women he'd met. (He understood that, it wasn't a turnoff: beyond the possession of a certain amount of money you expected respect from others, expected the less privileged of the world to pander to your whims; after all you could afford to pay to be groveled to.) He suspected his relative indifference to Adrienne's charms had to do with his recent encounter with Trudi Carmen.

Adrienne pulled the drapes shut, shrouding the room in semidarkness. She climbed back into bed beside Malone.

Once again she held up her right hand before their faces. "Now watch."

Malone watched. At first there was no change, the black ring was merely a point dividing Adrienne's pale finger in two. Then . . .

What the . . . ? Malone felt sudden unease as the ring altered to a bright golden color. The primary cause of his bother (lots of compounds—both natural and synthetic—had photoreactive properties; *that* he'd have been able to accept as normal) was the circle of black writing now seemingly carved into the gold ring's almost transparent substance. Try as he might, he could make no sense of the lettering.

"It's weird, isn't it?" Adrienne asked in a subdued voice. "Creepy too, if you ask me."

Malone wrapped a protective arm around her. "Yeah, it is creepy. The black words look like they're floating inside the ring, like it's liquid."

"Like a 3D graphic."

"Do you understand the writing?"

"Are you kidding? It looks even weirder than Chinese."

"Does the ring do anything else?"

"Nothing that I've seen." She turned her hand left and right. "It's real pretty now though, and a great conversation piece at parties."

They stared at the transformed ring awhile longer, then Adrienne got out of bed and parted the drapes again, on which the glittering ring instantly resumed its previous dull black color.

As Adrienne turned back towards the bed, Malone pointed to a framed portrait on the wall by the bathroom door. A plump blonde with a thin hawkish face and hard blue eyes. "Who's that?"

Adrienne turned to the picture and scowled. "My ex-wife Kate Shaw. She's the one I suspected of stealing the ring in the first place. She denied it, of course."

Malone nodded. Adrienne walked back to the bed and stood by it staring at him. Her expression was now a little worried; she'd given too much information about herself away to someone she wanted to impress. "You don't mind me being Bi, do you?"

He shook his head. "I can deal with it."

Adrienne grinned demurely. "It's okay, Malone; if we become an item I won't screw around on you with girls."

"It's okay," he said. "I just thought she was a relative; there's a slight resemblance around the eyes. He smiled. "She's pretty."

"Looks aren't everything." Adrienne's face twisted up all ugly. "All Katie ever did was leech me and waste my money. She wanted all of everything. She kept spending and spending; it was like she was trying to bankrupt me or something. Then, when I wouldn't let her have any more money, she began selling my things. My jewelry started disappearing. That's how the ring went missing in the first place."

Then Adrienne grinned impishly. "Katie *was* a good lay though."

"You think *she* might have been Jackson's girlfriend who wanted to sell the ring?"

Adrienne smirked. "I wouldn't put it past her." Her humor dulled, her expression turned less angry, became sober. "In fact, I'm almost positive it was Katie. You say the rat thought dead bits of her were in the room too? She-it, man, but that's a really horrible way to die. God rest her greedy soul."

She crawled to the foot of the bed and retrieved her wrap from the floor.

Malone watched her slip into the red garment; Adrienne had a nice figure.

Adrienne noticed his eyes on her. "You like me. Will you call me?"

"Most definitely." He got out of bed and began dressing too.

CHAPTER 6

Malone

At her front door, Adrienne Lake kissed Malone softly on the lips. "Call me," she whispered, then vanished back into her lair of luxury.

Driving away from there, Malone felt on a high note. Yes, he'd definitely call Adrienne; maybe they'd even fall into a dating routine. Rich girl or not, she wasn't a bad type; she had empathy. Her being bisexual didn't bother him; sexuality was just one of those things. But . . .

He felt his shoulder. *Ouch! She's a biter, and her teeth are damn sharp.*

Grinning, he swung his BMW onto Arch Street. In the oncoming lane, a woman was driving a blue antigrav Ford. She smiled at him as they passed one another. She had nice eyes. Malone wondered what she would be like in bed: Would she bite too, or would she simply lie back and gasp, overwhelmed by her sweet sensations? Or was she a screamer? He laughed, there was no way of telling; every woman behaved differently in her passion. Sometimes the beautiful ones enjoyed sex much less than the plain or downright bad-looking did; the vagina was, after all, a separate organ from the face. Maybe God gave ugly woman more sexual pleasure as compensation.

His thoughts turned to the strange characteristics of Adrienne's ring. The black ring was clearly something special, but what was it exactly? He figured the lovely Trudi Carmen knew the ring's secrets: she had, after all, asked him to keep it safe. But safe from whom or from what? And where was Trudi? And *who* was she anyway?

Malone decided that for the moment at least, the black ring was safe enough with its owner. At least he knew where it was.

Besides, right now Adrienne's ring was only a peripheral concern. His real problem was catching the vampire.

His mind calculating various investigative angles, Malone drove up through the city. He'd already decided that the best place to start his search was at a library; read up a bit on the ancient Nosferatu, see if there was anything Hollywood had overlooked in their repackaging of the legends. (He was headed homeward, the Boston Library Consortium was at 10 Milk Street, just down the road from his house.)

His shoulder twinged again. He grimaced, wondering if the real reason Kate Shaw had divorced Adrienne was because she kept biting her during lovemaking.

A thought struck him. He fished out his cellphone from a pocket, connected its wireless headset, then dialed Lt. Steelberg.

The robot cop picked up on the second buzz. "Hey, Malone, you got something already?"

"Not yet, Metal Guy, just starting on it. Say, at the moment I'm out in traffic and haven't yet reviewed those CCTV vids I asked you to email me. Can you fill me in on something?"

"Yeah, sure, what do you want to know?"

"Does either recording get the make or numbers of the cars the women left in?"

"Hold on a minute." There was the humming sound of increased brain activity as Steelberg mentally replayed the footage, then it said, "Yeah, they did, but it's three different vehicles."

"Three?"

"Another vid just came in, this one from XX, a ladies' club on Essex Street. Nothing new—it's same as the others, the murderess's face is all blurred out."

Malone had now reached the Milk Street intersection; the Boston Library Consortium lay directly across the road. "Okay, send it to me too. Back to the car numbers: any leads there?"

He imagined he heard synthesized disgust in Steelberg's metallic voice. "Nada. Two of the vehicles belonged to the victims driving them; the third—a white AG jaguar—belonged to Marie Kinney, the first victim."

Parking outside the library building, Malone nodded. "Okay, our bloodsucker's smart then, she realizes we might trace her vehicle. Still, two can play that game, Metal Guy. Have Robopol check for any of the victims' cars that are still missing. There's the slight chance that, seeing as she doesn't know we're onto her yet, she might keep up with the same MO."

"Will do, Malone. That all?"

"For the moment, yeah."

Lt. Steelberg hung up. Malone got out of the car, looked around the street, then strode up the library steps.

CHAPTER 7

Adrienne

Nighttime in the Golden Dragon Casino was the best time of all for Adrienne Lake.

Though not a gambler herself, Adrienne was addicted to the glitter and glitterati, to the sense of destinies being forged and destroyed at the card tables, at the roulette wheels, at the many other games of fate contrived with the sole aim of separating people from their money, with the primary payback for the players being a thrill of losing oftentimes even greater than that of winning.

Women and men broke their backs here on Lady Luck's capricious altars.

Delighting in the press of people, Adrienne mingled, beautiful in a long black evening dress and with her hair up. She strode from table to table watching the magic; watched wheels end their spin and decide someone's fate; watched the dice roll and bounce; walked past the card players with their poker faces, the superior bluff everything to them.

But they're bluffing themselves too, aren't they? Adrienne knew they were; she knew the single unalterable law of gambling was that the house always wins. The players played, some better than others. Some amassed fortunes in a night; others, on that same night, stuck guns in their mouths and pulled the trigger.

Through it all though, the game went on forever. It was thrilling to be wrapped in that excitement, to vicariously feel along with the players, to sniff in the atmosphere of decadence (like inhaling the expensive cigar smoke that invariably trailed it), for what could possibly be more decadent than a complete disregard for money, the most precious substance in existence?

Adrienne, well known in the Golden Dragon though she never played, accepted a sherry from a smiling hostess and continued enjoying the frenetic blended atmosphere of success and failure.

A loud scream of excitement from a roulette table announced that Dallas Washington—the Texan Billionairess—had either just won or lost half a million dollars. Adrienne giggled. To Dallas's kind of money, it made scant difference if the roulette ball ended on black or red. All that mattered was the momentary thrill of uncertainty while the wheel spun its course. Still laughing, Dallas kissed her girlfriend TLC—Tamara Lorraine Carter—who looked coked up to the nines again. Adrienne sipped her sherry and shrugged. Nothing new there. There were bets on amongst the jet set as to how long it'd be before TLC's nasal septum fell out.

Casino owner Sookie Ling (who was at Dallas's gambling table) was laughing too. Adrienne figured Sookie had good cause to laugh: Dallas Washington lost at least thirty million dollars to the Golden Dragon each year.

Beyond Dallas and TLC, a black man grinned broadly and punched the air as he won at something, then kissed his female companion. Adrienne watched the croupier slide a tall stack of chips towards him.

Catalyzed by the laughing happy people everywhere, Adrienne's thoughts turned inward. Gripped by a sudden sobriety—a reflective need to be away from the party for a while and alone with herself—she made her brisk way out of the gambling hall. Out, away from the rising and falling piles of gambling chips, their levels fluctuating as rapidly as the frequency display bars in a digital equalizer.

Out onto a west-facing balcony.

It was cold out here; chill breeze ruffled her hair. Gripping the bannister, she stared out at the world. (Above the rooftops and treetops, Boston's in-city mountain, the Abstracta, stared back at Adrienne like a monster's eye, its unrelenting off-white color despite the night making it seem as though it fed on the darkness.)

I really need to get my life together, Adrienne thought. *Okay, I'm young and rich—daddy's got way more money than I could ever spend—and I'm beautiful and I'm definitely having fun, but . . .* Her gaze dropped to the ring on her right hand, the black stone circlet a stark contrast to her white fingers on the railing. Her thoughts turned to Malone. She'd heard lots about his character, was impressed that he'd returned her money unspent, even when there was no chance of her ever knowing if he'd kept back part or even all of it. He was a definite contrast to her ex-wife Kate. *And, oh yes, we definitely clicked in bed!* She grew warm between the legs remembering how expertly he'd licked her sex.

It was complicated though. Adrienne really liked Malone, but she was certain he had women all over the place. Lots and lots of them. He was too good-looking and classy to be single. And Adrienne wanted commitment, she didn't want to be just a second-string booty call. It was of course great having Malone as *her* booty call, a private dick to fill her up between the legs at 2 or 3 a.m. But it would be much nicer if they could have a relationship, go steady. And yes, she'd meant what she'd told him: she'd play it straight with him, wouldn't cheat on him with any girls. So he was fortyish; so what? His manhood hadn't felt fortyish when he'd been sliding it inside her.

But . . . the specters of all Malone's unseen 'other women' haunted Adrienne. It was so frustrating to meet a great guy and find he was already taken.

"Hi there," a bright female voice broke into her thoughts.

Startled, Adrienne looked around. "Hi," she said back.

"I'm Lily," the woman said. "Do you mind if I join you out here?"

"Not at all," Adrienne replied. The newcomer was beautiful, with long black hair, flawless white skin and full red lips. Lily seemed to be Adrienne's age—mid-twentyish. Like Adrienne, she too wore a long black dress, her feet bare white against red strappy heels.

Largely due to her perceived romantic roadblocks with Malone, seeing Lily filled Adrienne with a rush of genital warmth.

Lily had an air of dirty sexuality to her; Adrienne (who'd slept with her fair share of women) could tell. She'd likely be great in bed but unreliable as hell out of it. A one night stand? Hell yes! A relationship? Hell no!

But there was a problem: *Is she gay?* With men, it was easy to tell what they wanted (sometimes all you had to do was sneak a peek at their crotches). With women, less so. Except in designated lezzie meeting places and clubs, one always needed to tread lightly, lest the other rich bitches labeled you a dyke and avoided you socially. Then she laughed softly to herself. *Who the heck am I fooling? I am a dyke! Everyone knows I am—I've been out of the closet since seventh grade. Hell, I've just gotten divorced from another woman!*

Nothing to lose then. Adrienne smiled strawberry-sweet at Lily. "Are you here alone?"

Lily nodded. "Yes, just like you. I noticed you haven't placed a bet all evening."

"You've been watching me for a while?" Her tone was mocking but playful.

Lily placed a delicate hand on Adrienne's shoulder. "I'm not stalking you, believe me."

"What then?"

"I've been trying to determine if we're right for each other."

Adrienne giggled. "So what do you think? Are we right for each other?" She gestured out towards the Abstracta's white bulk. "Or are we birds flying to different roosts tonight?"

Lily put her face close to Adrienne's; so close that Adrienne could smell her breath. Mints. "You got a boyfriend?"

Adrienne looked deep into the other woman's beautiful eyes. "Regretfully no at the moment. There this one guy I really like, but I'm still working on him. You know how these things take time." Then she thought, *What the hell?* and kissed Lily, pulling the other woman towards her so their bodies crushed together.

It was a long, drawn out kiss. Adrienne felt herself heating up down below, her sex growing increasing wet. (Behind them in the gambling hall, the odds of fate reigned supreme, the fickle goddess of fortune rewarding or beheading her worshippers on a whim.)

Panting, they finally separated.

"Your place or mine?" Adrienne gasped.

"How close is yours? Or should we just get a room here for the night?"

"No, let's go to my place. I want to cook you breakfast in the morning."

Adrienne dragging Lily after her, the pair practically fled the casino, aroused antelopes chased by roaring lions of lust.

***

They lay naked together in Adrienne's bed. Outside the moon was a sickle reaping the heavens.

Adrienne squirmed as Lily ate her. *Yes! Yes!* As Lily's tongue roved back and forth over her clitoris, delighted thoughts exploded like bombs in her brain, pulping her mind. Groaning, she spread herself wider, then gasped in rapture when Lily, accepting the invitation of the gaping vagina, wet two fingers and slid them inside it down to their last knuckles. She began a smooth in/out rhythm with her fingers, one that quickly had Adrienne humping her crotch up off the bed to meet them, working to help them venture deeper into her willing wet sex.

Lily repositioned herself so her crotch hung over Adrienne's face. Adrienne smiled up at it—the lovely white thighs and buttocks, the little-lipped lake of womanhood in its forest of black fur—then, remembering to not be selfish (so hard considering the pleasure she was currently in!), she spread the extensive labia and stuck two fingers deep inside Lily. She was surprised: Lily's wet spot was quite dry, strange considering how her lover's arousal seemed, if anything, greater than hers.

On being reciprocally penetrated, Lily jerked like she'd been stabbed, then, her entire body trembling, she gasped, "No, no, darling! I'll get mine later!"

Adrienne ignored the reproof. Holding the squirming woman's buttocks firmly in place above her head, she continued working her fingers in and out of the spread vagina, raising her mouth from the pillow to suck on the clitoris.

It was hard work, as Lily's cunnilingus had her on the brink of coming, but then, unexpectedly, Lily herself reached orgasm. Her body went taut and she lifted her mouth from Adrienne's sex and mewled like a cat in pain.

Then, her fingers also vacating Adrienne's aching sex, Lily wrenched her body from Adrienne's grasp, spun round, and lay beside her. She kissed Adrienne passionately, her fingers snaking down again to bury themselves in the sopping crotch. Their lips pressed tightly together, she resumed rubbing, leaning up over Adrienne till she half lay on her.

Lips still on lips, Adrienne came, feeling like a shaken then uncorked bottle of champagne. The orgasm was everything she'd expected it to be when Lily had picked her up. As the sensations thrilled Adrienne, Lily kept her fingers working down between her legs. The feeling peaked; Adrienne forgot herself. Wrenching her lips away from their kiss, she grabbed Lily tight and bit her deeply on the shoulder, sinking her teeth in till the blood flowed. She was aware of the red liquid filling her mouth and flowing back down into her throat, but she didn't care (she was in way too much ecstasy). Neither apparently, did Lily mind: despite having Adrienne's teeth deep in her flesh, she kept sliding her fingers in and out of her, till Adrienne's pleasure exhausted itself and her body went slack.

Adrienne lay there, breathing hard and fast and staring at the ceiling, her lips smeared with blood. She kept her eyes on the ceiling—she was very embarrassed over her biting Lily. What on earth would Lily think of her now?

Finally, she dared look at her lover.

"I'm sorry for biting you," she gasped sheepishly. "But you had me coming so good that I couldn't help myself." (Had she turned Lily off? Oh, and she'd bitten Malone too, but thankfully, he'd not seemed to mind. Another plus for him!)

To Adrienne's surprise, Lily was looking back at her in clear amusement. "That's okay, darling," she said. "I'm about to do some biting of my own."

Then, despite how good she felt—and she felt utterly honeyed— Adrienne was suddenly equally filled with horror.

Lily's face and body were changing: Like black magic, her flawless white skin turned brown and hairy. All her gorgeous hair vanished. Her face became almost pig-like, swollen and huge with long yellow fangs and doglike ears. She also grew huge leathery bat wings. Saliva dripped between her teeth. Dark obscene hunger burnt in her now-crimson eyes.

The bat monster that had been Lily lifted off the bed. It hovered in the air over Adrienne, its slowly beating wings fanning her sweaty body with cool breeze. The vagina that Adrienne had just so ardently fingered and licked was a lipless black slit between its legs.

Terrified, all memories of their just-concluded luscious copulation drained from her, Adrienne raised a hand towards the monster and flapped her wrist as if to shoo it away. "Y-y-y-you . . . y-y-you . . . Nooooo—!"

The bat monster fell on Adrienne and sank its teeth deep into her neck. Her budding scream cut off.

Adrienne knew she was dying. First, it hurt hell of a lot and she feebly (and vainly) fought to free herself. (The teeth in her neck felt like they were dug in all the way back to her spine!) She felt the monster's lustful delight as it drained her life out of her, an infernal joy that had to come from Hell itself. It slithered over her like a snake, the sensation of its hairy brown body on hers filling her with a horrible disgust that she no longer recognized as nausea.

And then, abruptly, the pain vanished and dying like this didn't really feel so bad after all. (*Better this way than a car crash any day!*) Adrienne now just felt like a bottle being emptied, her useful liquid content all being drained from her.

And then finally—for some reason expiring this way had taken way longer than she'd thought it would—it was over. The horrible brown winged monster that she'd previously made love to withdrew its teeth from her neck and lifted up into the air, where it flapped its wings and looked at her.

The last thing Adrienne saw before her mind fogged over was her killer's terrible sated smile. And . . . the beast looked utterly repulsive, disgusting beyond belief.

"Oh, fuck, Lily," she gasped. "You mean I *really* slept with your ugly ass?"

The hovering monster frowned at the insult. Adrienne Lake died.

CHAPTER 8

Malone

Malone was sitting up in bed reading 'Mythos Transylvania' by Karla Albrecht when the air over the foot of his bed split open.

The hole in the air—an oval window about two feet high—showed a street under an afternoon sky. Malone realized he was staring into the Abstracta.

Someone was peeking out of the hole. He grabbed the gun he always kept beside him in bed and trained it on the split.

Then, recognizing who it was that was looking into his bedroom, he relaxed.

"Trudi? What in—?"

"Shh!!" Trudi Carmen hissed in a strained voice. Her pretty face was taut with stress, her emerald eyes worried, her ruby hair all mussed up, her clothes dirty. "I've no time to talk now—I'm in some serious shit."

He nodded.

"Hold on to this for me," she said, flinging something through the hole at him.

The object landed on the bed by his hip. He picked it up. It was a white ring. He stared at her in surprise. "What's going on?"

"Bring this ring and the other one to me in the Abstracta." The hole in the air was already shrinking, his view of Trudi Carmen now halved. "I'll wait for you tomorrow at Graveyard—it's a club on Cemetery Road in Witchland. I'll tell Christine—she's the owner—that I'm expecting you." Malone now thought he heard shouting behind Trudi, an impression reinforced when she winced, then added (through an aperture now so small that her face looked like a reflection in a mirror), "Okay, Malone, I need to run for my life now." She frowned. "Hey! Be there tomorrow with the rings. Don't

44

let me down, man; this is life-and-death important. I'm counting on you."

The hole in the air closed up.

For a while, Malone sat staring at where the hole had been. It wasn't just the unexpectedness of its appearance: once again, he was unable to get over Trudi Carmen. Then he began worrying about what sort of danger she was in and whether he should rush over to the Abstracta to save her. *But I can't! I don't even know where she is!*

Finally, he got a hold of himself again and returned his attention to the ring she'd thrown him. It was white and featureless and seemed made of stone, just like . . . just like . . . just like . . .

Struck by a sudden worry that had nothing to do with Trudi's current straits, Malone leapt out of bed and turned off his bedroom lights.

Heart racing with expectation, he waited.

It happened. Like someone had filled its white stone with orange juice, the ring altered to an almost transparent gold. And in that gold floated words that seemed cut through the stone; words in a script Malone had only ever seen once before.

He sat on the edge of the bed, staring at the transformed ring. *They're a pair!* he realized.

But a pair of what?

He turned the lights back on, then sat back down in bed, thinking hard. Okay, Trudi had asked him to bring *both* rings to Graveyard. Adrienne had the second ring. He looked at the time—it was 2 a.m., too late to call her, she'd likely be asleep by now. But first thing in the morning he'd go see her. He doubted Adrienne would say no to letting him borrow her black ring; definitely not once she saw its white twin. She'd most likely ask to go along with him to find out what the pair of rings did. That was fine; they'd go together then.

Having resolved that as best he could for the moment, Malone placed the white stone ring on his nightstand and resumed his reading about Transylvania. So far he was having no luck with turning up anything new; almost all the vampire lore he'd so far read (he'd also borrowed 'What's at Stake—A History of Bloodsuckers,' and 'Mothers of Darkness and Death: Vampire Women through The Ages') ingeminated the same traditional belief: vampires only sucked blood from their victims, they didn't also poison them with acidic venom.

Undeterred by this, Malone read doggedly on, the horrible specter of Jayne Howman's horribly abused body etched in his mind. There had to be pertinent information somewhere concerning this case.

The monster killing Boston's womenfolk had to be stopped. And Malone would find and destroy the infernal creature even if the job killed him.

CHAPTER 9

Adrienne

Adrienne Lake resurrected. Opening her eyes, she realized she'd not just woken up from sleep. *No, I was actually dead, deader than a doorknob.* The fact of her demise was incontrovertible; for a brief instant she'd been a resident of Hell. And what she'd seen down there? Adrienne resolved to be a better person from now on, to even attend church occasionally.

But then, something cold and unholy—something even more frightening than the wages of sin—had yanked her scared spirit away from the terrors of the unrepentant dead and pulled her back upward on a silver thread. For one moment she'd caught a glimpse of her rescuer's skeletal face—fleshless bone and long fangs wrapped in a musty gray cowl that shed clouds of bats—as it reeled her in like a fish.

She'd imagined that she would be this obscene monster's dinner; but no, it had just returned her to her body. And now . . .

She felt impossibly weak. She gazed at her shut window drapes. It was morning, the light hurt her eyes. Slowly, her memory of last night's events returned. *No, I dreamed all that, didn't I? I picked up a hot number at the Golden Dragon who fucked the shit out of me and then turned into a giant bat and bit me to death? But . . .*

But she hadn't been doing any drugs, so she couldn't have hallucinated it, could she? Not unless someone had slipped something into that last sherry she'd drunk. Which, though unlikely, was possible; it had happened before. (It was why she never accepted drinks from people she didn't know at parties; easiest way to wake up as the unwilling bologna in a three-person sandwich. That too had happened before.)

Her mouth felt odd. She hadn't yet worked out why.

Separated by time, the razor-sharp horror of her awakening dimmed. She smiled, wondering how dumb she could be to imagine she'd actually died last night. Yes, someone *had* spiked her drink. It had to be; that would explain her vivid nightmare, the burning people in the lake of fire, the skull-face reeling her up.

With the drapes shut, the bedroom felt natural. Too natural. Its crypt-like comfort scared Adrienne, made her feel like maybe she really had met Lily and had that horrible experience.

She staggered to the window to let the sunlight in.

Even as Adrienne reached the drapes and pulled them apart, she had the clear sense that she was doing the wrong thing, that she'd not simply hallucinated everything, that she'd not just dreamed that she'd visited Hell and afterwards been resurrected.

And right at that moment, she finally worked out what felt odd about her mouth. Her teeth! Two of the top front ones were now long and pointy! Her mind flared up with shock of realization: *Shit, I didn't dream it up! I'm now a—!*

But by then it was already too late. She'd gotten the drapes wide open and the bright morning sunlight poured in on her.

Adrienne instantly discovered her terrible mistake: this routine daylight entering her bedroom felt as hot as if she was standing on the surface of the planet Mercury, or inside a furnace.

She screamed when she caught fire and began burning fiercely, the incinerated flesh flaking off her face and torso to pile as ash on the carpeting.

A short while later, Adrienne's corpse—now just black skeleton from the waist up—collapsed to the floor. Above her charred body, burning window drapes spewed smoke out into the morning.

This time Adrienne Lake experienced no resurrection. She remained dead for good.

CHAPTER 10

Malone

Malone called Adrienne's phone twice without getting a reply. Before he could redial again, a call came in from Robopol's Lt. Steelberg.

"What's up, Metal Guy?"

Malone listened to what Steelberg had to say, then horrified, he leapt out of bed and hurriedly began dressing. Almost as an afterthought, he remembered the white ring Trudi had thrown at him in the night and put it in his pocket.

Then he rushed out of his apartment.

***

Malone stood with Steelberg beside Adrienne Lake's bedroom window, both of them staring down at her corpse. Her half-burnt body lay on its back, blackened eye sockets regarding the ceiling from within the charred skull.

The bedroom itself had somehow escaped a ravaging by fire. The window was completely gutted—the frame was destroyed, and both drapes, along with several feet of wall either side of the window, were burnt—but that was all the damage.

Malone instantly noticed the skull's extra-long upper canine teeth. He looked at Steelberg, almost too surprised for words. "Sh-sh-she . . . *Adrienne* was the vampire?"

The robot cop made a show of adjusting its crumpled hat on its head. "I don't think so, Malone; at least not the one we're after. Hey, you know her?"

Malone nodded. "Yeah, she was my most recent client." He walked over to the bed and sat on it. A taste of incredible bitterness filled his mouth on remembering how they'd kissed and loved each other in this room and on this same bed just yesterday; how the seeds of a relationship had been sown, and now . . . He regarded her body and grimaced; except for her wrists and hands, everything above her waist was charred skeleton sprinkled with ash. But no, he realized— Adrienne couldn't be the vampire. Yesterday, when they'd been testing the black ring, she'd gotten out of bed to close the drapes— had twice stood in the bright glare of the midday sun—and nothing had happened to her. So she'd not been a vampire yesterday.

He looked at Steelberg. "No, I don't think she's the one we're looking for either," he said in a cold voice. "What happened? I mean, how much do you know about what happened?"

The robot tapped the charred window frame. "A neighbor noticed the smoke and called the fire department. They broke down the door and found her like this. They called us. I got here, saw her teeth and called you." It raised a hand to forestall Malone's next question, then continued, "While waiting for you to arrive, I had our guys track Miss Lake's movements last night. She spent the evening at Sookie Ling's place, the Golden Dragon Casino. She didn't gamble, just drank a bit. Then she was seen kissing a dark woman in a black dress and red shoes."

Malone winced. "Poor Adrienne."

"The pair left together in Miss Lake's car. The suspect left her own car in the Casino lot. It was registered to a Ms. Cathleen Bachara."

"Who's that?"

"A new corpse." Steelberg regarded Malone, its eyes flashing crimson dots in the egg-like white face. "The body count's rising, Malone—we're up to nine stiffs now. We don't wrap this up quick; someone will soon turn it into a homosexual political issue. You know how they wank to this stuff at City Hall."

Malone nodded distractedly, his mind hard at work trying to piece together what had happened in here last night. The very sight of Adrienne now—the remains of this person he'd liked—distressed him intensely: the shapely white buttocks and legs, the dark brown pubic hair, the dainty feet (their toes tipped with chipped pink paint) were utterly at variance with the stark sprouting of pitted bone projecting from her black-cauterized waist as though her lower half was a flower pot growing a skeleton tree.

How did this . . . how did Adrienne become a vampire herself instead of . . . ?

Steelberg was saying: "You know how good the casino's security cams are, right? Well, we've got our sharpest videos of the suspect yet . . ."

"And?" Malone interposed on oral autopilot.

". . . Still no dice. Her face is a complete muddle on the vids, both those recorded inside and outside the buildings."

"Any helpful descriptions of what she looked like? Identikit maybe?"

"No one remembers; no one really took notice. 'Pale skin, red lips, long black hair' is the best we've got so far, which could be anyone. The Identikit robots are still trying to piece together a composite image."

"I've got it," Malone said.

"Got what? A clear picture of the suspect?"

"I know why Adrienne turned instead of dying like the others."

"She's still dead, Malone."

Malone got to his feet, strode from the bedside to squat by Adrienne's corpse. He stroked the fangs in its gaping mouth. "Yes, but her death was accidental, I think. She didn't realize she'd . . . Look, Adrienne here had a tendency to bite during . . ." he caught himself just in time (his left shoulder twinging with memory), "during romantic encounters."

"How'd *you* know that?"

"The bedroom walls just told me. Look, Metal Guy, let me finish explaining this, okay?"

"Sure, go on."

"Okay. To help us with this case, I'm currently studying several books on vampirism and the occult, and one recurrent theme—or belief if you like—is that drinking vampire blood will turn you into a vampire yourself." He straightened up again, shrugged at the robot policeman. "You connect the dots."

Steelberg peered out the window at downtown Boston. "Hmmm. So Miss Lake drank the suspect's blood during their er . . . romantic encounter, and then . . ." It smoothed down its rumpled beige suit. "Okay, Malone, I'll buy that. Another one for the morgue then, and now we're completely back to square one. Our murderess has to be laughing at us. Hey, Malone . . . Malone, are you paying attention?"

Malone wasn't paying attention. Now that they'd sort-of resolved the mystery of Adrienne's horrible death, he'd remembered what he'd originally wanted to see her about.

The black ring.

Being protected from the entering daylight by the drapes they'd been parting, both of Adrienne Lake's hands had survived her incineration. Both hands now looked like gloves her skeleton was wearing. Malone's quick examination of Adrienne's right hand, however, showed no sign of the black ring he'd retrieved from the Abstracta for her, and which she'd slipped on her finger yesterday.

While his robot companion watched him in a pose that spoke of bemusement, Malone walked quickly to Adrienne's dresser and searched its top and drawers for the ring. Then he checked Adrienne's handbags. Then he searched both nightstands.

The black stone ring was nowhere to be found.

Oops, Malone thought, his PI intuition assuring him that matters had just gotten a whole world more complicated.

And . . . Trudi Carmen. *Oh boy, is she going to be pissed off by this, or what?*

"What you looking for, Malone?" Steelberg asked after a while.

Malone waved the question off. "I'm just checking to ensure she's not been robbed too." He pointed to the fifty thousand dollars he'd returned to Adrienne yesterday, which was neatly stacked by her designer perfumes. "But her money's still here, so this clearly wasn't a robbery."

The robot groaned. "Malone, we already know that. Stick to the case, wilya? What else did you learn from those books of yours?"

Malone discussed the case some more with Steelberg, but his mind was elsewhere. Why had the vampire murderess taken the black ring? Remembering the arcane letters that had flashed inside it when the room was dark, Malone doubted she'd taken it off Adrienne's finger for purely fashion considerations.

But the trail wasn't cold just yet. He still had his midday appointment in the Abstracta with Trudi Carmen. She just might be able to shed some light on this case.

Malone kept this to himself. He had no proof that the missing black ring was actually pertinent to this case. Despite his strong suspicions to the contrary, the vampire woman might simply have taken it because she thought it was pretty.

And besides, robots couldn't enter the Abstracta anyway—the soft wall barrier scrambled their electronics. (There *were* robots inside the Abstracta, but those were native to the realm.) It was one reason why criminals loved hiding out in there—Robopol couldn't get to them.

Any investigating within the Abstracta was up to Malone to do.

Breaking off midway though an explanation to Steelberg, Malone grimaced down at Adrienne's corpse again. And, oh yes, he definitely intended seeing this case through to the end.

With Adrienne Lake's horrid death, business had just become personal.

PART 2:
WITCHLAND

CHAPTER 11

Malone

Seated in his parked BMW at the corner of Beacon and Walnut streets, Malone was pensive. He had the white ring in his pocket, some money, his gun, and sufficient anger over Adrienne's passing to goad him through this investigation. The green expanse of the Boston Common lay on his right—through untrimmed grass he could see several mongrel dogs playing beside the frog pond—and on his left stood a quartz-like mountain.

The sheer imposing white mass of the Abstracta gave Malone cause for concern; created an anxiety in his soul. This was the general feeling most people had once confronted with this mountain that was actually a hollow container.

Certainly, measured from the outside, the Abstracta had its physical limitations (Beacon and Cambridge streets and Embankment Road), but once one penetrated the Soft Wall to the Abstracta's interior, it seemed a limitless realm.

Malone was pondering how many types of 'pocket universes' existed. There were those ones accessed through the OD's (the otherworld doors). Then there was The Groad, a corrupted part of Hell situated directly under Boston. *And now*—he raised his eyes up the Soft Wall's dirty-white stone—*we've got this . . . with all the odd insanity that lies behind it.*

He stared at the Abstracta's pale surface for a few moments longer, then down the road he was on. Then he realized that he was simply procrastinating. *I've a job to do, and anxieties or not, I intend doing it.*

He checked his watch: 11:45 a.m. Almost time for his appointment with Trudi Carmen at Graveyard. His heart quickened at the thought of seeing her again; yes, he was looking forward to this meeting . . . except the part where he had to explain that the black ring had been pilfered.

Sighing at that last bit, he turned the key in the ignition and drove the car around the street corner and straight into the white bulk on his left.

***

Driving through the Soft Wall was like driving through a cloud. Here, the barrier seemed to be between six and ten feet wide—at one point the entire car was completely enclosed in the fluffy substance—but that might just have been an illusion: Malone suspected the Soft Wall expanded to the thickness of whatever object was fed into it. (Maybe to adjust the non-native matter to its home realm?) This belief was borne out by personal experience: each time Malone walked through the Soft Wall the trip lasted only two steps.

His BMW exited the barrier's other side. He was immediately reminded that he was no longer anywhere close to home. For all intents and purposes, Boston, Massachusetts might now be located back in Soviet Russia in the Stalinist age.

Here and now, Malone drove through an avenue of large golden flowers, each of them six times a man's height. The road itself seemed made of quartz—it sparkled in the sunlight. The sun was normal here. In certain parts of the Abstracta, one got a blue or green or white sun in an azure or black sky. Malone had never been to any of those places, and felt no pull to visit them. The oddity out here in the 'normal abnormality' had yet to jade his investigative curiosity.

He concentrated on the road. The initial floral aisle had now given way to a kind of suburb, though the houses on either side of the road didn't match one another for time period: 13th century Ottoman architecture rose on his left, 18th century Quaker homes (complete with horses and carriages) dominated his right. Malone wondered whether the residents fought religious battles over whose God was the real one.

He reached a road sign for Giant Lane and turned left. On this new road all the house doors were twice as high as normal. Malone figured the residents each had to be about ten feet tall for those entrances to make sense.

He drove on, made two more turns, then reached Witchland. Alright, Cemetery Road was around here somewhere.

Witchland was delineated by a huge gray wall split by a thirty-foot-high carved crystal arch that spanned the road between its two divisions. At the top of the arch sat a massive black keystone carved in the form of a skull and crossbones, only this skull had vampire teeth.

Malone frowned; was this a premonition of trouble to come? *Yeah, I'm forewarned of danger and death alright.*

He braked and looked about. He needed directions. Then a moving shadow fell over the car. Malone looked out and grinned. It was a sentinel. Sentinels were humanoid—ten feet tall 'men' covered with shiny green scales. This one was naked but appeared sexless, lacking genitalia of any sort.

"Hey!" he hailed it, leaning out of the window as it walked past.

The sentinel paused. Placing a massive green three-fingered hand on the car window frame, it bent low to peer into the BMW. "Can I help you, friend?"

The sentinel blinked its yellow froglike eyes and waited for Malone's reply.

Malone nodded. "How do I find Cemetery Road? I'm looking for Graveyard; it's a club there."

The sentinel nodded its scaly head, its green lips creasing in a smile. "Keep driving, friend. Third turn to the right. You can't miss it."

"Thanks." Malone drove in beneath the crystal arch with the vampiric black keystone, feeling his ears tingle oddly as he entered Witchland.

***

Malone drove. This part of Witchland was sparsely housed; grassy expanses separated its few buildings. Trees were equally few and far between, and without exception all looked sickly, like backwoods folk barely eking out a living from the soil.

Malone drove with caution, ever conscious of danger.

The sky was overcast and dotted with gray and black birds, several of which seemed to have more legs than usual. There were lots of crows and vultures in evidence.

He turned onto the third side street on the right. All at once, he was driving through an extensive cemetery. It was weird how the burial grounds had just crept up on him, like the tombstones were somehow ambushing him with their new unexpected profusion. Now headstones lay everywhere on both sides of the car, marked with inscriptions like they were the newspapers of the dead. Old and new, plain and covered with dust, many with the words of farewell long ago etched into their stone erased by time's unforgiving passage.

Malone kept going; up ahead he'd spotted houses.

Further in from the road stood isolated mausoleums, those concrete supervisors of the dearly departed that ensured no ghost went astray. And now, here amidst the graves, there were many more trees growing, like the plants had unionized to shade the tombs from the hidden sun. Unlike the miserable specimens Malone had encountered shortly after passing through the crystal gate, these plants flourished; all sported thick brown trunks and vibrant green foliage that dappled the tombstones with shadows.

Malone winced at the healthy trees; corpses sure made great fertilizer.

Combined with the sunless sky and the vultures, Malone felt cold. He was wary of this extensive graveyard. This was the Abstracta. Here, it was the work of a minute and a spell uttered in anger to raise the dead as hungry brain-eating zombies.

He'd now reached the houses. Everything was really one sprawling village unit—a series of chalets surrounding an old stone mansion with the legend *Graveyard* glowing in massive green neon above its front double doors. Several cars were parked around the mansion, and people (most of whom thankfully looked normal) stood around chatting. Other people were entering and leaving the auxiliary buildings.

What disturbed Malone now was how the entire club—both its main building and the outlying ones—was situated *inside* the graveyard. Tombstones lay between the individual buildings, in some cases running up to the walls. Other headstones lay scattered haphazardly around, clearly uprooted and discarded here for want of elsewhere to put them.

Which meant . . . occupied graves still lay beneath the houses. Oops.

Halting his car at the foot of Graveyard's driveway, Malone was less than pleased. Situating a building on a burial site was always a bad idea. (Every cemetery man he'd ever met had had scary tales to tell about what went on there at night.) Building directly over the graves was an even worse idea. You got the dead *that* pissed-off and there was no telling what they'd do given half a chance at retribution.

And, worst of all . . . the building nearest to him seemed to actually be a converted sepulcher. And was that 'Ladies Toilet 6' inscribed on it? Hell no! They were pooping and peeing on the dead here?

Malone groaned; it got yet worse: the short drive to the main building was paved with tombstones. Tombstones as flagstones? How irreverent could you get?

He gunned up the car, then drove up the morbid driveway to Graveyard, through lush grounds where headstones sprouted like mushrooms, past tall trees from the branches of which swung slumbering bats, all the while acknowledging that never before in his life had he visited anywhere more appropriately named.

A parking attendant told Malone that the only vacant lot space was around the rear of the mansion. Malone thanked the man, but declined his offer to help park the car.

He drove round the building himself. He wanted to study this morbid place some more before entering it. A glance at his watch informed him he was fifteen minutes late for his appointment with Trudi Carmen. He shrugged; it wasn't like him to be tardy, but in this case five minutes more wouldn't kill anyone.

He parked, got out, locked the car. And yes, like he'd suspected, the lot was paved with tombstones too.

Viewed from the rear, Graveyard itself looked like an immense sepulcher. To Malone's mind, the mansion's gray stone pulsed with a sickly ambience. It seemed specifically built to affront the dead. No, it didn't itself look built from salvaged grave material, but there was no telling what lay inside its walls.

He stood there, alone at midday with grim troubled thoughts, staring out over an expanse of graves that stretched to the limit of his vision. A green field of death, with the headstones its concrete tree stumps. The air was dead out here, as though those buried underground had killed it. An eerie feeling settled over Malone, intuitive knowledge that it wasn't just human corpses planted in this fertile earth, that anyone unwise enough to till its sod would unearth creatures better left sleeping.

Chilled, he knelt and began reading the memorial inscriptions carved into the lot's ghoulish flooring.

Mary Steward; 21.09.1936 – 14.03.1971. Honey, me and the kids love and miss you . . .

Dale Harvey; 03.5.1700 – 11.10.1706. Ye young lamp quenched tae soon . . .

Edward 'Gameboy' Cole; 31.02.1970 – 09.11.2001 A loving husband and father, snatched away by terrorist monsters . . .

Malone quit; it made for depressing reading. He straightened up, then spent a few minutes longer staring out over the endless cemetery. With the gravestone inscriptions so fresh in his mind, this proved even more depressing. How many people were buried out there, how many bodies squirreled away? He couldn't help this morbid mental image: with the irreverent use the owners of Graveyard had already put part of the cemetery to, it was hard to not view the rest of it as simply storage space where the dead were cached away for future use. Or to view the dead as tenants shortly to be evicted from their homes.

Okay, I'm properly downcast now, he decided. He patted the ring in his pocket. *Time to go meet Trudi; seeing her is certain to cheer me up.*

As he turned around a gust of wind hit him and a shadow covered him.

Malone looked up.

A giant gray bat was descending fast toward him. Buffeted by the wind from its wings, he noticed it was both larger than a man and hairy as an ape, with fan-like ears, glowing red eyes, and a massive pig-snout. Its open screeching mouth revealed a large pink tongue and long yellow fangs.

Malone realized that the huge bat was attacking him. He leapt out of its way, ducking down between his car and the one beside it. Once safe, he pulled his gun from its hip holster.

The monster bat soared past overhead, its foot claws digging the air for Malone. Crouched between the cars, he watched it make a sharp right turn and vanish between several trees on the west side of the yard.

Heart pounding, he stood up and looked warily around. He couldn't see the bat anywhere. He doubted the huge creature had left though; he'd not offered any defense to make it think he wouldn't be easy pickings. While scanning the levels of overhead foliage, Malone's mind worked fast: *Okay, the books all say vampires transform primarily into bats. But is this bat a vampire after me, or just a normal oversized Abstracta animal out hunting lunch? But . . . he gazed at the moody sky in confusion, bats are nocturnal, why would this one be hunting in daylight? Or maybe . . . just maybe, it was roosting in the trees and I startled it?*

He waited a minute more. The giant bat didn't show. Malone decided he couldn't stay out back here anticipating its return; the lovely Trudi Carmen awaited him inside Graveyard.

But . . . Malone wasn't about being dumb here. He decided to make a run for the rear of the mansion. Once there and with his back to the wall, he'd make a much more difficult target for the bat should it attack.

The moment he stepped out from between the cars, the bat reappeared. This time there was no announcing noise of beating wings; instead, the animal held them out stiff from its sides and glided in at Malone.

Alerted by its shadow (the one thing it hadn't considered) Malone flung himself down onto the flagstones, his cheek pressing against the cold inscription *Heather Louise Bowen: 31.08.2043 – 01.09.3026*, and a picture of an ancient blue-haired lady in a shatterproof frame.

The bat zipped low overhead, its claws ripping Malone's jacket. For a moment he was enveloped in the animal's odor—it smelt ancient, perfumed with mausoleum stink.

Malone stayed on the ground, rolling onto his back. He'd decided to play possum. *So the bat wants to play cat-and-mouse games, eh? I'll let it think it's hurt me. Then it'll have to come get me.*

Dropping his gun, he began writhing in make-believe pain. While jerking and twitching, Malone ensured that his right hand fingers remained near the gun's grip. One snatch and he'd blow the creature a new hole.

So where the hell was it then?

The bat had meanwhile banked sharply. This time, instead of re-entering the trees, it hovered in space over the lot, its red eyes staring at the prone twitching man.

It flew in closer. Malone tensed, his fingers at the ready. He wanted the animal to be almost on top of him before he shot it. It couldn't land—it would never be able to get aloft again—so it had to snatch him up into the air. And he'd better not miss; the bat *was* big enough to carry him off.

But what happened instead was . . .

The bat suddenly dropped out of the air to the ground.

What the . . . ?

The gray monster landed in front of Malone and transformed into a man.

Malone blinked; the change had occurred incredibly fast.

The man was of average height and dressed in a black suit and cloak. He had a very white face, long black hair, red eyes, and long upper canines.

A fresh chill settled over Malone on seeing the man's teeth. If he'd not believed in the vampire legend before, here was living proof. Or maybe, *undead* proof. Malone was now worried; all the books mentioned crosses, holy water, and stakes as being the only truly effective offense against bloodsuckers. And here he was with just his pistol; and not even one silver bullet in sight.

And how come broad daylight wasn't burning up this vampire?

The vampire man scowled down at Malone and reached out a hand. "Give me the dead ring you have on you—I saw the redhead throw it to you through the hole in the air she opened up."

Not moving from his supine position and keeping the expression of pain on his face, Malone replied weakly, "You know, except you're in drag, I was actually expecting a lady." He winced. "She has my other ring. I want it back. Where the hell is she?"

Rather than replying, the vampire reached down to grab Malone. Seeing the man's teeth were spread wide to bite him, Malone grabbed his gun off the floor and stuck it in the vampire's mouth.

The vampire's eyes widened in shocked realization that he'd been fooled.

Malone pulled the trigger.

The vampire's brains exploded out through the back of his head. Bright red blood squirting from the fresh holes in his skull, he crumpled lifeless on top of Malone.

Malone shoved the twitching corpse away and stood up. He stared down at the vampire's body. He was both relieved that his gun had killed it, and confused by what was now happening to its body: the vampire's corpse was dissolving, its clothes and flesh breaking down into a mess of worms and mud that cloaked a bare human skeleton.

Then this mess too was all gone, and Malone was staring at the bare tombstone-floored parking lot. *Okay, so now I know everything's connected. They know I've got the ring, and they're vampires, and they're not affected by daylight. And oops . . . there's more than one of them.*

Alerted by a noise behind him, Malone spun around, gun poised to fire.

It was the parking attendant. Malone relaxed.

The man froze on seeing Malone's gun. "I heard a shot," he said, hands raised in a pacifying gesture.

Malone nodded. "Yeah. I had some trouble with your local wildlife."

The attendant's eyes widened in worry. "Oh no. Have the wolves been digging up the graves again?" He looked nervously out across the field of headstones, then stared back at Malone. "But I can't see any animals, sir."

"Don't worry about it." Malone slipped his gun back into its holster, then checked his watch. "I'd better get my ass inside," he said. "I'm thirty minutes late for a hot date."

CHAPTER 12

Malone / Trudi

Malone entered Graveyard.

The gothic mansion's interior was as gloomy as its morbid exterior suggested. To Malone, walking through its lobby was disconcerting. The room's combination of black walls draped with purple velvet curtains, excessively dim lighting, and dark furniture—ebony/mahogany wood with black leather upholstery—did nothing to lighten his mood. Hidden speakers played creepy organ music at low volume. The room smelt like withered flowers or a hag's deathbed. The receptionist reminded him of the man/bat who'd attacked him outside—long black hair, seemingly whitewashed face, and long teeth which Malone hoped were fake. Gory horror film posters hung behind her ornately carved desk. The most prominent of these showed a tall man—clearly Dracula—with his teeth sunk deep in a busty blonde maiden's throat.

Several people sat in the lobby chairs, most of them obscured by shadows.

Malone was relieved to see that the floor in here wasn't also paved with the deceased. Its dark burnished marble was gloomy enough. His recent skirmish outside with the vampire had him far too jumpy for these sort of surroundings. His unease showed on his face.

"You don't like it much in here, I can tell," a pleasant female voice said on his left. "But what else did you expect from a place named 'Graveyard?' We're a vampire-themed club."

"Huh?" Malone turned to see the speaker. A woman was staring coolly at him. She had short dark hair and dark eyes in a morgue-pale face. Her mouth was painted a deep scarlet. She wore a floor-length black robe trimmed with red, below the hem of which peeked pointy black shoes. The robe's high flaring collar reached up to her ears. Her perfume was morbid; it smelt ethereal, like beauty with death blended into it.

With a smile he found creepy, she extended her hand. "I'm Christine; I run this place."

He shook her hand. "Bud Malone. I'm here to see—"

"Trudi Carmen," she finished for him, then realized he was staring at her extra-long upper canines. "Implants, I assure you, Mr. Malone. There are no real vampires here inside Graveyard; everything is completely make-believe."

She laughed. "Come." She took his arm and guided him towards the reception desk, then past it and the spooky receptionist, who bared her teeth menacingly at Malone.

"How can you tell there aren't any real vampires in here?" Malone asked at the door to the club interior, while they waited for a woman splattered in 'blood' to exit into the lobby. "You all look so convincing."

"Because I don't let them in," Christine replied, her voice completely matter-of-fact. A gentle pressure of her body on his urged him towards a black spiral stairway.

"But you do know they exist, right?"

"Of course they do; why else would *you* be here?" She paused with a foot on the bottom step. "Don't worry about it—there are ways of keeping the undead out."

"Garlic and crosses?"

"Herbs are useless here in the Abstracta. Christian symbols work much better. And there are other, more specialized protections; but I won't bore you with details of those."

Malone was about mentioning his fight with the vampire outside and asking why bullets had killed the creature, then he changed his mind. Instead he smiled at Christine and gestured to the stairs.

She led the way up the spiral stairway, which was decorated with wooden gothic crucifixes. Seeing the arrayed holy symbols somewhat relaxed Malone.

They ascended two flights, then proceeded along a gray stone passageway off which other long corridors branched. Their footfalls echoed back and forth in this long space.

Two Graveyard maids bearing trays walked past, giving Christine respectful bows. Both women wore uniforms from 18th

Century Europe—velvet and lace with frilly bonnets. Both had whited faces and long teeth.

"You're very authentic," Malone said with some admiration.

Christine flicked stray strands of brown hair off her face then replied, "We take pride in being so." She paused before a dark mahogany door. "Here we are."

She knocked.

The door split a crack. A third of Trudi Carmen's face peered out.

Christine gestured back over her shoulder. "Malone's here to see you."

Trudi opened the door fully. She wore a pink T-shirt tied off over her navel and faded jeans cutoffs.

Christine stepped aside to let Malone by.

"Hi," Malone said.

"You're late, you know," Trudi said. Her eyes, though, were amused, not mad.

He indicated his ripped-up jacket. "You'd never believe why."

She raised an eyebrow, her face forming an enquiry. Malone walked past her into the room and sat down. Trudi stepped out into the corridor and began whispering with Christine.

Malone looked around the room. It was medium-sized, with a double bed, several chairs, and a bookcase and closet. Its dark red wall paint could easily be mistaken for blood, which he guessed was the idea. The walls were embossed with large crosses. The room had fluorescent lights shaped like red candles and black curtains decorated with white bats. By the bed's carved headboard, wide open windows revealed the endless deathscape topography out back.

Several questions instantly formed in Malone's mind. He got to his feet and walked over to stare out of the window. Had Trudi witnessed his fight with the vampire?

"I just opened them," she said, stepping up to his side. "It was growing stuffy in here."

He turned to look at her, quickly deciding that she had an 'eager' face. Her shining green eyes, her full pink lips—her entire expression had an expectancy to it. *She likes excitement,* he realized, *that's why she's out here. For her, it isn't about the money or whatever cause she'll profess. She just likes to play.*

His eyes dropped to consider the rest of her. She was a few inches taller than his shoulders, and damn, that hourglass figure again, everything just perfect down to her bare feet! Halfway back up to her eyes his gaze snagged on her chest. Why on earth wasn't she wearing a bra for what was clearly a business appointment? Her breasts were huge!

"You want to tell me what delayed you?" she asked. "Or are you too distracted at the moment?"

He lifted his gaze to her face again, feeling a sudden surge of passion flood him, a torrential desire for Trudi Carmen that bore off all his other concerns in its raging emotional waters. Her lips! *Oh God, I could kiss her right now. But no, we're here for business.*

He grinned back at her. "Well, you must admit the view in here is quite distracting."

She laughed. "A great line, Malone, but for the moment I'll take a rain check on being your eye candy."

He forced his eyes off her, his initial question taking center stage in his mind again. "Trudi, I parked out back; that's my car down there. What I'm trying figure out is: when I was walking along the corridor outside with Christine just now, we passed several side passages that were all much longer than this room's width, and they in turn led to other rooms—I saw their doors—which is obviously impossible if your room looks out directly onto the lot. Is this place actually a—?"

"A Node? Yeah it is. In different versions, Graveyard exists all through the Puzzleverse."

"Puzzleverse?"

Trudi Carmen left the window and walked over to sit in a chair. She crossed her legs, stared at Malone. "Like in 'jigsaw puzzle.' It's just another name for the multiverse. You know how it is—no one's yet figured out how everything fits together yet, so 'Puzzleverse.'"

He nodded (one learnt new terminology everyday) then went to sit opposite her, across a coffee table. His gaze instantly returned to her generous chest.

Trudi rolled her eyes then stretched out a hand. "The rings please."

He dropped the white ring in her palm. "There's a bit of a problem with the black one."

She gasped, her breasts bouncing with her shock. "You don't have it? I asked you to look after it." Glaring accusingly at Malone, she slipped the white stone circlet onto her left middle finger.

Malone sighed. He wished she'd put a shirt on. But he knew many women (usually the hot, stacked ones like Trudi here) enjoyed torturing men with their great bodies, considered it their human right to do so. Genetic teases, that was all they were.

Steeling his manhood against Trudi Carmen's distracting chest, Malone explained about Adrienne Lake and Boston's 'Dead Lesbians' vampire case. Beginning with how he'd initially located the ring through Fuzzy Joe the rat fence, he told her everything. He disliked the way Trudi's eyes kept widening with each revealed detail; it meant they were in greater trouble than he'd thought. He rounded up his narration with an account of the vampire attack outside. (Her one comment during this last part of his tale—"Oh, that was you?"—explained why no one other than the parking attendant had bothered to investigate the gunshot at the rear of the building: Like Trudi, everyone had seemingly assumed the attendant was chasing away wolves come to dig up the graves and eat the dead.)

By now, Trudi was slumped in her chair like someone had staked her. Unfortunately this pose—with her legs split and draped over both arms of her chair—revealed to Malone that she wasn't wearing any panties under her cutoffs. The sight of her vagina, its left lip large and flat against her red pubic hair, gave him a painful erection. He wondered how she could be so unaware of the effect she was having on him, all spread out the way she was.

But she clearly was. She lay back in her chair, left arm flung across her eyes, groaning, "Crap! Crap! Crap! And I went to all that trouble to get this one! Now I have to do it all over again!"

Malone switched chairs so he was looking across Trudi's thighs instead of between them, then said gently, "Trudi, what exactly is all this about?"

After thirty seconds of further self-recrimination (Malone was VERY pleased that she wasn't angry with *him*), Trudi Carmen calmed down, unhooked her legs from the chair's arms, sat up, and explained:

"Everything's connected, Malone. The rings and your vampire case—they're all part of the same problem."

"The vampire that attacked me asked me for the other 'dead ring.' That's what he called it."

"That's their name—the dead rings. One white, one black, they're a power pair, each useless without the other. Like the Chinese Ying-Yang dualism." She gestured out the window at the graves everywhere. "You already noticed that they both turn gold when there's no light."

"Trudi, what else do they do besides look pretty?"

"They're the keys to unlock the Dead Sky. You wear one on each middle finger and then make this familiar gesture at the heavens . . ." She leaned forward, made two one-finger-salutes at Malone. "Then the sky opens up like a door and intense darkness pours through, and we have permanent night in daytime."

Malone wasn't liking this at all. It was obvious why the vampires would want the rings; or was it? Those here didn't seem affected by daylight. "How much darkness are we talking about?"

"A limitless amount. Lilith wants to—"

"Who?"

Trudi scowled. "Yeah, I'd better backtrack a bit. Lilith Nightfall is the nightmare who's been killing Boston's lesbians. She's an abstractive vampire . . ." She noticed the look on Malone's face. "You're not familiar with them?"

He shook his head. "Only with the regular kind. There's too much weirdness everywhere now to keep track of it all. Up until thirty minutes ago I had no idea that there were vampires here in the Abstracta; I thought maybe an OD linking to Romania's Carpathian Mountains had opened up somewhere in the city. So, abstractive vampires it is then. What's different about this lot? I already know they're not harmed by daylight and that their bite dissolves flesh. How does *that* happen?"

Before replying, Trudi got up, walked to her closet, and slipped on a wool pullover. Even though she'd clearly covered herself up because of the suddenly chilly atmosphere in the room and not from any consideration for his state of arousal, Malone was nonetheless both relieved and grateful for the let-off: Trudi's body was too perfect to be left unwrapped—he felt her figure should bear a 'Government Health Warning.'

She pulled on pajama bottoms and bobby sox then shut the windows. Bum perched on the windowsill, she said, "An enzyme in the abstractive vampires' saliva dissolves flesh. They don't inject venom, their saliva just gets into the bite and digests away the victim's body tissue." She shrugged. "Well, you saw the results. As for other things, you've already discovered their immunity to Abstracta daylight and how they can be killed by routine weapons . . . in here at least. In addition, they can't stand crosses and other religious objects, and holy water dissolves them like acid, so you can imagine that they utterly despise priests. Taking a page out of old Vlad's murder cookbook, they tend to impale every holy man they catch."

Malone winced. "Okay, if not exactly harmless, they sound manageable with the right weapons. But . . . why does Lilith Nightfall want the rings?" His face took on an angry cast. "And more importantly, why is she killing innocent women? Adrienne for one was a close friend of mine."

Trudi sighed. "Lilith Nightfall is a lust-driven monster. She murdered all those women simply for food." Trudi's own face now reflected Malone's anger. "Most likely after screwing them first. You know, sex before dinner to work up an appetite, or just because she's horny? She and her gang need no other reason to take human life than the sheer fun of doing so. They're vampires; to them we're merely cattle, nothing more than lunch or dinner. Forget all those sparkly teenage movie bloodsuckers—you'll never meet a vampire with a decent bone in their body." She hissed prettily. "Vampire romance my ass!"

Malone looked uneasily about the room. With all this talk of vampires, the surrounding blood-red walls now really seemed like the real thing. Also, the room's stone ceiling felt like it floated overhead, like it could at any moment drop to spatter their blood. And in addition, now that he'd discovered the monster he sought, he felt like a fly about to be entangled in a hungry spider's web. The memory of Adrienne's half-corpse both disgusted and motivated him. And Adrienne had gotten off lightly, hadn't had her life burnt away like someone had injected concentrated acid into her veins.

Trudi was saying:

"I'm not sure how Lilith came on Adrienne and her ring. She may have been keeping tabs on you, I don't know. Most likely, it was just dumb luck."

Malone pointed at her left hand. "How'd you get this white ring anyway? More dumb luck?"

She scowled. "I stole it from the damn abstractives, Malone. Look, don't sidetrack me."

He nodded, smitten by how pretty she looked when angry. "Okay, let me see if I've got our problem right: Lilith Nightfall . . . is she the vampire queen or what?"

Trudi nodded. "Lilith isn't really their queen, but she's the undisputed leader of the abstractives, utterly the most ruthless, most bloodthirsty, most lust-driven of them. Make no mistake about it: Lilith Nightfall is absolute evil incarnate. Total obscene malevolence. There's not a single shred of good in her. She lacks both compassion and conscience, and she's completely dedicated to her objective of unlocking the Dead Sky."

"Yes, I get that," Malone said impatiently. "But assuming you're right about her intent, what does Lilith Nightfall get out of flooding the Abstracta with darkness? It's pointless, isn't it? In here, darkness and light are one and the same to the vampires."

Trudi shook her head, swirling red hair everywhere. "No, they're not. At night—almost like they're drawing energy from the darkness—the vamps are much stronger." She grimaced. "You're wrong about something else also, Malone."

He waited.

"Lilith isn't trying to flood just the Abstracta with darkness. She's got way bigger ambitions than that. Using Boston as a conduit, she intends covering the entire USA with permanent night. And then the vampires can really come out to play."

Malone gulped and gaped at her. "Can she *really* do that?"

Trudi Carmen's face assumed an intensely pained expression. "She gets her hands on both dead rings, and as surely as my last period ended yesterday and I've two breasts, it's done."

And then, like she wanted to emphasize that last point, Trudi moaned, "Oh, it's so hot in here all of a sudden," and pulled her pullover up over her head.

Poking stiffly out from her T-shirt like they'd been frozen by her previous chill, Trudi's nipples were suddenly staring Malone in the face again. He was almost grateful for the problem threatening the United States of America when she stripped off her pajama bottoms too and flung both them and the sweater across the room onto the bed.

He nodded sagely as she settled back into her chair. *Okay, I've no way of confirming that her period actually ended yesterday; I guess I'll just take her word for it. Which means we're in a truck-load of trouble.*

Trudi stretched then stared intently at Malone, her eyes glittering like wet gems. "We need a plan," she said, holding the finger with the white ring up like an accusation.

"Yeah," he agreed, "we really do. Okay, tell me everything you know about the abstractive vampires."

***

Malone was surprised by the first bit of info that Trudi shared with him. "What? There's only *three* of them?"

"Yeah. There were four, but since you just killed one . . ." She laughed bitterly. "They could make more of themselves by feeding normal people their blood, but . . . top-of-the-food-chain logic, you know. There's a limited number of humans in here to bleed to death, so they have to be careful not to use us all up. If Lilith gets her wish, though . . ."

Malone nodded, his eyes cold. "Yes, I follow you. With the entire US as their hunting grounds, the vampires will have no need to keep their numbers down."

"And remember, these aren't the normal vampires everyone's used to. Out in the real world and under permanent night, their powers will be greatly enhanced—they'll be like superman-vampires." She shuddered. "Humanity will have no kryptonite."

CHAPTER 13

Kenya

Kenya Jordan was just finishing her stripping routine in Queen's Harem when she noticed the woman. Naked, her dusky thighs parted wide either side of the silver pole that barely obscured her vagina from the women dancing below her platform, her eyes locked on the dark figure sitting at the table almost directly opposite her.

Sweaty female hands roved over her buttocks and down her thighs, others shoved dollar bills up into the crack of her ass. Kenya had large buttocks, money hardly ever dropped out of her crack. She gave the tippers her professional smile—eyes wide like she was high, her lips slightly parted—then gripped the pole, shoved her breasts forward, and flung her head back like she couldn't control her body any longer, like the loud eurobeat music was caressing her lady parts.

Usually when she danced for the girls, Kenya did feel like the music was making love to her.

Not tonight though. Tonight, she just went through the motions. The woman opposite—bone-white face, red lips, black hair, black silk top and trousers; looking like an erotic gargoyle beneath the club lighting—held her full attention.

Kenya knew she'd seen her before. And remembered where.

Kenya normally danced at XX. She was here tonight because her roommate Jackie O had period pain which Midol hadn't helped, and seeing as it was her night off anyway, she'd offered to fill in for Jackie. It didn't hurt that Queen's Harem, located on Melrose, was a much classier joint than XX, which meant better tips: there were several hundred dollar bills around her feet already and two business cards with lipstick kisses on them. (One expensively dressed middle-aged lady had even swiped her credit card between Kenya's buttocks; then when Kenya had turned to see who it was, had kissed the card and winked, a lustful promise in her blue eyes.)

Kenya gyrated and ground her black body, making love to the pole like it was one of the hotter women feeling up and kissing their girlfriends under the strobe lighting. It was hot. Sweat ran off her head between her short braids, it dripped down her face and down over her dusky breasts and belly, it dripped off her heavy mocha thighs onto the money around her feet in their six-inch heels.

But if Kenya's body was dancing, her mind wasn't. She was waiting for the song to end so she could rush offstage and call the cops before the raven-haired woman across the room left the club. And she was worried and scared; as well as very angry.

Two nights ago in XX, Kenya had been watching Jayne Howman while stripping. Kenya liked Jayne and was trying get to know her better, on a romantic level, so she tended to watch her a lot. She and Jayne had made lots of eye contact, had even flirted a bit, but nothing more naughty had happened between them. Then, two nights ago when Kenya had come out to dance, Jayne had been conversing with the woman now seated across the room. Angered after seeing the pair kiss, Kenya had kept her eyes on them all through her routine, even tripping and flubbing her dance steps when they'd departed hand-in-hand, obviously hurrying off to go find a bed and enjoy each other's bodies. She'd left the stage completely depressed.

That was bad enough. But then, yesterday morning, Robopol had called at the club. Jayne Howman was dead, murdered, the big white robot cop had announced, and did anyone know who she'd left with last night? Kenya knew and had told, but apparently the CCTV vids were messed up—Cindy must have been masturbating to the strippers again—and didn't catch the woman's face. So that was that.

Until now, that was. Here the murderess was in Queen's Harem, sitting and looking all innocent and sexy. And most likely looking to pick up someone else.

Kenya was thrilled to be able avenge Jayne's death. Somehow she made it through her song, made a desultory show of gathering up her underwear and tips, then, money clasped to her breasts, she blew a kiss into the room and fled.

Outside, she rushed up to her dressing room, her heels hampering her progress.

"Frigging hot dance, Kenya!"

She waved to the woman complimenting her and streaked past.

"Gotta empty my ass!" she gasped at the cleaner who advised caution on such high shoes lest she break her neck.

Up the stairs, down the corridor, almost twisting her ankles and clattering over, and then she was inside the dressing room. She locked the door, flung her load on one chair, sat in another, grabbed her purse and began rummaging through it for her phone.

"Now where the hell are you?" she gasped. "Aw, shit, don't tell me I left ya at home. I gotta call the fuzz!"

"Are you looking for this?"

Kenya spun around. Her heart sank. It was the woman from downstairs. An evil smile on her bone-white face, she was holding Kenya's Blackberry up in her slim, pale fingers.

"G-g-gimme b-b-back my damn p-phone!" Kenya stuttered. "I-I-I gotta make an emergency call!" Her eyes weren't on either her phone or her intruder, however, but were rather fixed behind the woman, on the dressing room door, which was still locked. *How on earth she get in here? And so quick? I just left the damn stage!*

"My phone . . ." Kenya repeated, now scared. "Give it back now!"

"No, I don't think so." And with that, the woman clenched her hand tight around the Blackberry.

Kenya gasped as her phone shattered between the woman's fingers, the streamlined black device crumbling to a mess of plastic and metal fragments as easily as if the white digits were squeezing through pastry.

Kenya had never seen such a demonstration of strength before in her life. Now she was really terrified.

Looking deep into Kenya's eyes, the woman flung the destroyed phone away. Then she smiled. "Now that we've gotten your stupid police report out of the way, it's time we were properly introduced." She extended her hand towards Kenya, "I'm Lily."

Kenya's first instinct was to shrink back from Lily, but the latter's eyes were still staring into hers, and now, Kenya felt a paralysis of the mind overcome her. Suddenly, she saw nothing wrong in shaking Lily's hand.

She took the slim white fingers in her ebony ones and shook them, feeling hers tingle as she did so. Then, not understanding why she did so, she lifted Lily's fingers to her lips and kissed them.

"That's better," Lily said. "We're friends now, almost lovers." She looked around the room then back at Kenya. "Get dressed, honey. We're going cruising."

"Sure thing, baby," Kenya obediently replied, then began putting her clothes on.

***

Chatting about nothing in particular, they left the club. Despite her knowledge that her companion had most likely killed Jayne Howman, Kenya now saw nothing wrong with being in her company. Each time she tried reasoning otherwise, something paralyzed her mind afresh, making her feel once again well-disposed towards Lily.

They took Lily's car, a black Ford convertible with the top down. Kenya couldn't tell the specific model, but that wasn't in any way important; what was was the sudden raging heat between her legs that demanded satisfaction.

Lily smiled at Kenya. She moved her hand from the gearshift to stroke the black woman's thighs. "I'm going to enjoy this," she said. "You are too."

Kenya nodded mutely. She'd been silent since entering the car, not paying much attention to their route, content to simply drift as erotic flotsam in Lily's sexual current, but now she realized they were heading towards the Boston Common. She looked down at her body, between her breasts in their pink halter to her denim-skirted crotch, which now felt almost painful in the intensity of her sexual arousal.

A short way up Tremont Street, Lily swung the car off the road and into the park. They bumped through grass, rolling between the Boston Common Baseball Pitch and the Parkman Bandstand, till Kenya saw the Abstracta's white bulk peeking through the maples now blocking their path.

It glows like a chunk of moon rock fallen to earth, she thought.

Lily parked by the Frog Pond.

"Why come here?" Kenya enquired. "My place is nearby."

Lily laughed. "So's mine, honey." She leaned over and kissed Kenya. Kenya felt another burst of incredible heat in her crotch. Now her juices really began to flow. She kissed Lily back passionately for awhile, then Lily broke away. Kenya reached for her again; but Lily shook her head.

"Uh, uh. I want to watch you fuck the gearshift."

Kenya's eyes widened at the statement. "Oh no, I ain't doin' *that*."

Lily grabbed Kenya by her braids and pulled her face close till their lips were again inches apart. "You're my bitch tonight," she snarled through grit teeth. "You'll do whatever I tell you to. Now get your fat stripper ass between these seats, sit on the damn gearshift and fuck it."

Scared and thrilled at the same time, Kenya did as she was bid. Lily moved her body close to the driver's side door to allow Kenya sufficient room. Kenya positioned herself so she had one leg in each front foot well, then after bracing herself against Lily's right shoulder with one hand, and pulling her panties aside and parting her labia with the other, she squatted down over the gearshift and let it slide up into her sex.

She was shocked. Oh, the metal/plastic rod felt so good inside her! So big!

"Now move," Lily commanded. "Fuck this car like it's a man."

Kenya obeyed. She began sliding her sex up and down the gear knob.

"Shit!" she growled, an orgasm hitting her almost immediately, her love juices flowing down and wetting the shaft.

Dusky body shuddering, she sat down hard on the knob, shifting it from 'Park' back into 'Drive.' *Oh shit! I hope she's got the handbrake engaged!*

Back pressed against the car door, Lily watched with gleaming eyes. While Kenya used the car as a sex toy, she assisted the negress's pleasure, stroking her breasts and thighs. As the black woman rode up and down on the now messy gear lever, Lily rubbed her swollen clitoris, helping her to another orgasm.

Finally, Kenya's legs gave out and she dropped all the way down onto the gearshift again, sheathing it completely in her sex. Her vagina contracted around the sweet plastic, more of her liquid drenched it. This had been an incredible one-of-a-kind experience.

Her body running with perspiration, Kenya pulled Lily to her and kissed her hard. "I wanna do you now, baby," she gasped.

Lily nodded. "Yes, but in the back seat. First I want you to fist me, and then I've a surprise for you."

Kenya quickly slid her vagina up off the gearshift. The stick was coated with white cream. She and Lily relocated to the back seat. Her body still tingled; she desperately wanted that 'more' that Lily had promised her.

Throughout her pleasure, Kenya's mind had been ticking with a warning—*Girl, you need to get your sorry ass out of here, you damn fool; there's something you're fuckin' forgetting!*—but there seemed no substance to her worries. Just this lovely, utterly beautiful chick with the bony face and hot slim body that Kenya wanted to dive into.

Run away, Kenya, you're gonna fuckin' die! that portion of her mind shrieked at her. But it was a very faint admonition—like water dimly glimpsed as reflected sunlight at the bottom of a deep well—and each time Kenya sought to dig deeper into her fears, that strange mental cloud blocked off her thoughts and assured her that everything was going to work out just fine and that there was no danger whatsoever; and that the police robots had simply made a mistake: that they'd found Jayne Howman, who'd been playing a belated All Fool's Day prank, and even if that wasn't so, Jayne's death hadn't been . . . no that wasn't strong enough . . . 'couldn't have been' was the appropriate expression . . . the fault of Kenya's current gorgeous pale lover, this beautiful source of new erotic sensations from the car gearshift and with more such unbelievable pleasure soon to follow.

And so, knowing she was in absolutely no danger at all, Kenya Jordan helped Lily get her slacks and soiled panties off. Then she helped Lily arrange herself in the convertible's rear—left foot up on the front passenger seat headrest, right leg up over the back seat.

Finally, she considered Lily's vagina. Lily was sopping wet between the legs, her thighs slick with her spilled cream. Kenya saw no need for additional lube; she just spit on her fingertips to wet them, made a 'duck bill' with her hand, and pushed her thick fingers between the thin sexual lips. The hand entered the vagina to scant resistance.

"Oh boy!" Lily moaned as she was penetrated and stretched. "That feels *soooo* good."

Kenya grinned, glad to be able to give her pleasure. "Yeah, mama, I can see you've done this before."

She began fisting Lily with long smooth strokes, while Lily groaned and gasped and came. Watching her lover orgasm, Kenya felt thrills of power ripple through her. "Who's whose bitch, now huh, bitch!" Grinning with pleasure, she sped up the strokes of her fist in Lily's vaginal barrel, twisting her hand this way and that, while Lily writhed and trembled on the end of her impaling arm like a dragonfly being pinned by a bug collector.

The car shook a bit. Night breezes cooled them. Amphibian and insect noises were the ambience of darkness.

Lily, her eyes spreading wide in the final throes of her orgasm, gave a sudden violent wrench of her hips.

At that twist of Lily's body, Kenya instantly felt a blindingly sharp pain at the end of her right arm. She screamed. Then she gaped at her arm in disbelief. Her entire right hand beyond the wrist had been ripped off by that last wrench of Lily's crotch. Horror spreading over her face like storm clouds over Alabama skies, Kenya stared first at her severed hand which still jutted from Lily's crotch—at the red mess of tendons, bone, and torn flesh protruding from the white-smeared vagina—and then at her wrist, from which blood now spurted in crimson jets over Lily's body.

She gaped at Lily. "W-wha-wha—?"

Lily gave a horrid gurgling laugh. "I promised you a surprise, honey, didn't I?"

And now something else happened. Lily's face altered to an animal's—a vampire bat's—atop her delicate sexy body. Then her entire body made the same change, so that instead of lovely female flesh, Kenya was now trapped in the back seat with a giant bat.

Then this terrifying hairy monster reached out and grabbed Kenya's bleeding wrist stump and stuck it deep into its mouth, so deep into its mouth that the severed end jammed into its neck (almost paralyzing Kenya with additional agony), so that her spurting blood flowed directly down its throat.

Next, two long and thick fangs anchored themselves in the already burning forearm flesh. Kenya felt 'Lily' sucking the blood from her arm, drinking her in like red wine. As it fed, the monster's eyes burned a hot crimson in their sunken sockets.

The bat drained her for a good long while. Kenya's pain now knew no bounds. Fear and horror warred for dominance of her soul. She first screamed to the surrounding trees for help, then stopped abruptly when yet another agony—one even more terrible than the combination of severed arm and biting fangs—slowly flooded her.

God, no!!!

Her arm felt like it was burning up. She stared at it, not understanding what she saw. It looked (and felt) like bits of her right arm were being scooped out, or like something was sucking its flesh and skin away from the inside. Beginning at the bat-monster's mouth, several deep red trenches had appeared in her arm, and, accompanied by the burning feeling, were shooting up toward her shoulder. She could see her bones exposed in the holes. The pain was almost impossible to bear. She began fighting to free her forearm from the bat's black-lipped mouth, beating at its head with her undamaged left hand. But it clawed her cheek so she fell back.

The burning trenches of missing flesh had now reached her right shoulder. Kenya knew if she had an axe, she'd have lopped her arm off.

She knew she was dying here in the back seat of this car; she already felt faded, like she was becoming her own shadow.

The bat—Lily—was sucking extra hard now. Once the trenches reached Kenya's shoulder, they seemed to develop fresh energy: their spread accelerated—she watched them streak like darts beneath her top, down her torso to her legs, felt the torment of a thousand invisible rats burrowing through her internal organs.

And her heart . . . her heart felt like wax melting to a puddle. Oh, the agony! She clawed at her chest, ripping her top open, digging her nails into her left breast, all in an effort to halt this horrible pain that felt like a pack of rabid dogs feeding on her core.

There was no bleeding, just deep red lines of raw evacuated flesh. And, impossibly, at the bottom of some of those meat trenches Kenya saw crimson rivulets flowing up towards her ravaged heart.

It was unbelievable.

Then, as Kenya's blood loss won out over her pain and her consciousness plummeted towards its nadir, she noticed the most unbelievable thing of all: While drinking her to death, the vampire bat was at the same time rhythmically clenching its thighs tight against the severed hand in its vagina, masturbating with it.

That did it for Kenya Jordan: she gave up what remained of her will to live, and died.

After her death, satisfied that the negress had been completely emptied, the vampire bat flung her ruined corpse off its hairy form. Kenya ended up draped over the rear door, her head and shoulders outside the car, her buttocks and legs inside it.

Next, grunting with bestial pleasure, the bat rose up into the night sky. Its powerful body trembled with contractions of ecstasy as Kenya's severed hand fell out of its sex.

Once the huge vampire bat was high above the trees, it flew off towards the Abstracta, and shortly afterward vanished through the white monolith's Soft Wall.

CHAPTER 14

Malone / Trudi / Christine

"I've never seen so many graves before in my life," Malone said. "It's baffling that there can be so many in the same place. Where do you find enough corpses? Or are they mostly empty?"

He, Trudi Carmen, and Christine were having dinner up on Graveyard's roof, on a raised terrace between chimneys which afforded them a panoramic view of Witchland.

As Malone had just remarked, the cemetery was the entire landscape about them—headstones, massive stone crosses and obelisks, sepulchers, ancient burial mounds—graves that seemed innumerable. His short drive here hadn't even given him an inkling of how expansive it was.

"Lots of these graves aren't actually on this plane of existence," Trudi remarked, forking fish between her lips. (Thankfully, from Malone's point of view, she now wore a white dress that hid most of her.)

Malone made an 'interested' face. "More OD magic?"

"Uh huh."

Christine took a sip from her glass of red wine. (For dinner, she'd exchanged her robe for a black silk blouse and red pants, while retaining the same pointy shoes.) Then she smiled at Malone. "I imagine Trudi's already told you that this building, Graveyard, is a Node, a point where the worlds collide."

He nodded. "I noticed how the corridors lead off into emptiness beyond the house."

She continued: "So what you're viewing now are the graveyards of a million worlds combined. And rest assured that if you were a grave robber, most of the corpses you'd unearth wouldn't be human; not even close to human. You already know space and time fold over each other, so . . ." She speared some fish on her fork, lifted it to her mouth.

Malone watched her eat. He was amused by how her canine implants interfered with normal feeding; she had to carefully steer the fork between the long fangs.

"Are you certain vampires didn't start drinking blood 'cos it was too much trouble to use a fork and knife?" he joked.

Christine peered blankly at him for a moment, then got the joke and laughed. "You may be right. It is a pain—even after all this while I keep banging cutlery on my teeth." Her eyes turned serious. "With this case you're on, though, you might be able to ask one in person."

He nodded. "Yes, there is that."

Then Malone's phone rang. He got it out. It was Steelberg, which couldn't be good. Making a motion to his dinner companions to keep quiet, he said, "Hey, what's up, Metal Guy?"

"How you doing, Malone? Any breakthrough yet?"

"I'm working on it. I know who we're looking for—a lady called Lilith Nightfall. She's in here though, out of you guys' reach. I'm even surprised you can phone, what with the Soft Wall's interference."

"I've been trying your number since sunup, Malone."

Malone sensed the robot was stressed. "What're you calling for tho? Something's happened?" (Of course, something must have happened.)

"Another corpse. Last night. This one a black stripper named Kenya Jordan. Same tunneled-over corpse."

Malone checked his watch. "I saw you this morning, but you only mentioned Adrienne . . ." Then he winced. "Damn, I get it: the frigging time lapse. How long have I been gone outside there?"

"Counting from last time I saw you, a day? Why?"

"In here it's only been six hours."

"Okay," Steelberg said, "I just wanted to touch base with you. If six hours where you are now is a day out here, just keep in mind that you don't have time for romance or partying or whatever in there. This Kenya . . . she was one of the girls that ID'ed the perp, okay? So I think our vampire lady is hunting down the witnesses. And, Malone . . . hey, can you hear me, Malone?"

"Yeah, Metal Guy, I'm still here."

"Goddamned interference just picked again. Okay, this last kill was real sadistic. She ripped the woman's hand off first and drank the blood out of it . . . splattered the back seat. Malone, . . . hey, Malone . . ."

Steelberg's synthetic voice blitted away into static. Suddenly without any further appetite for food, Malone dropped the phone by his plate of fileted fish. Steelberg's admonition sat in his head. Time normally did flow at different speeds on opposite sides of the Soft Wall. The difference, however, generally wasn't this drastic: most times the speedup/slowdown varied from just a few minutes to an hour. An eighteen hour differential between both sides really was a lot to compensate for.

Malone hated having the knowledge that except he wrapped this up quickly, outside in Boston a new woman could be murdered every six hours.

His two female dinner companions regarded his troubled face.

"Okay," he said, his brown eyes troubled. "Time I got off my butt here. As things stand now, it's a stalemate—the vampires have one ring, we have the other."

Trudi nodded. "So it's either we go to them, or they come to us."

"Better we go to them," Malone said. "No use waiting around for them to attack. There's nothing else for it: we'll have to pay the bloodsuckers a visit and retrieve the black ring." He focused his gaze on Trudi. "The question is: *Where are* the damn vampires?"

She shrugged. "Don't look at me, man. I told you downstairs— I've been trying to find them forever. The way they fly about, they can roost anywhere."

He winced. Yes, she had told him; this had been a rhetorical question. "Not really," he replied slowly. "They must have a hangout somewhere. Knowing our enemy, but not their location, is a pain."

And now, looking at Trudi, an earlier talk of theirs reinserted itself into his mind. This one was a unwelcome distraction; at least at the moment:

***

Downstairs in Trudi's room. They'd been hard at work thinking. Once they'd begun planning, he'd felt the familiar rush of blood to

86

the head, that thrill of promised action which was one reason he still took on PI jobs when he was wealthy enough to retire. Looking at Trudi Carmen, he could tell she felt the same way. Maybe the anticipation of blood, death, and conflict even had her aroused.

A guess instantly confirmed by her next statement:

"Hey, Malone," she said, licking her lips, "if I agree to sleep with you, will you stop staring at my breasts like they're burgers you wanna eat?"

He'd frozen for a moment, stupefied by her directness, by what he'd just heard. He'd decided she was joking. "Lady, you could just wear a bra."

"My breasts need freedom. Bras are a male creation to keep female assets bound in slavery." She'd gazed sternly at him. "So, do we have deal?"

He'd realized she was serious about sleeping with him. "Oh, yes, we most definitely do."

"Okay, later then. Now, let's concentrate on work."

"You're taking this very personal, aren't you?"

"Aren't *you*? This morning's corpse, Adrienne Lake, were you sleeping with her?"

He winced. "Once."

She'd shrugged. "Once is usually more than enough—pussy's more addictive than heroin." She'd swirled to grip her buttocks and part them at him. "It's called *crack* for a reason, you know."

***

Malone forced his head back into the present. He realized that Trudi was looking at him like she could read his mind, her lips curled in that mocking smile she had.

He grunted. "Until we know where the vampires are, we're stuck; the Abstracta is too large and varied for guesswork."

Trudi nodded sagely. "Yeah. Likening such a search to a needle-in-a-haystack find-a-thon doesn't even come close."

Malone said, "But is there a way we can locate the vampires' hideout? There has to be one."

Christine, who up till now had been silently stroking her right fang, nodded. "We'll ask Crystal."

"Who?"

"Crystal Baller—she's an alternate version of me." Seeing the blank look on Malone's face, she added, "Remember this place, Graveyard, is actually a Node, a pan-dimensional nexus?"

Malone nodded. Trudi looked perplexed around a mouthful of fish.

Christine continued: "So, from your reputation, Malone, I expect you're familiar with how space-time works. There are many versions of me, possibly an infinite number. We're not all named Chris, and not all human either. I'm simply one of an eternal sequence of groundskeepers, if you will." She leaned forward over the table. "And to answer your question as to the abstractive vampires' current location, you'll need to visit Crystal Baller."

Malone nodded. "Where do we find her?" He looked at Trudi, who also nodded, her brow creased up in thought.

Christine finished her glass of wine, then got up. "Stand up, both of you."

Malone and Trudi did so.

Christine waved her left hand at them. "Okay, go. I'll be seeing you two later."

"Go where?" Trudi asked. But the world around them had already altered. No longer were they on Graveyard's rooftop with the cemetery everywhere; now they both stood on the bare pink floor of a basketball court, with nothingness all around it. Malone quickly worked out that the distant lights twinkling all about them were stars.

"We're standing on a basketball court floating in the middle of outer space?" Trudi asked in utter confusion. "Malone, that's a planet over there!"

Malone didn't reply. They weren't alone on the basketball court. A giant black woman in a green tracksuit stood by the hoop on their left. She gestured to them.

"*She* must be Crystal Baller," Trudi said.

They walked towards the giantess.

By Malone's estimation Crystal Baller had to be at least nine feet tall: her head brushed the underside of the basketball net, and he knew hoops were set ten feet high. She was bald, had a large chin that elongated her face, and looked to be in her mid-thirties, though her sunken eyes spoke of an eternity of wisdom.

She was bouncing a transparent basketball that contained water in which a lot of round white objects bobbed. Malone's curiosity over what the bobbing objects were was cut short when Trudi began yanking on his sleeve.

They were almost by the black giantess now. Malone looked right at Trudi, saw she was trembling in fear.

He was shocked: badass Trudi Carmen was scared? "Trudi, what's the matter?"

"Look closely at the backboard behind her." Her teeth were chattering.

Malone looked closely and was himself chilled. The backboard was made of stretched human skin, with a bearded face positioned over the basket; and odder still, everything was supported on a huge human leg complete with foot and toes.

Then Malone made one more connection. The floor of this court on which they stood was skin . . . human skin. If there was a human that large.

He looked up at Crystal Baller. The dusky giantess grinned back, revealing massive white teeth, then said, "Welcome, Bud Malone; and you too, Trudi Carmen. My sister Christine told me to expect you."

While speaking, she kept bouncing her transparent basketball, its strange contents sloshing up and down. Malone figured her immense Nike sneakers had to be at least Size 20's.

"We need your help," Malone said, completely disconcerted. His career as a shamus had taken him to some really weird places, but being on a basketball court in the middle of nowhere and surround by stars topped them all.

Crystal Baller nodded. "I know; but . . . first play a game of basketball with me. I hardly ever have competition." She smiled at Trudi. "Sit and watch us."

Trudi, who was still shaking, shook her head. "Uh uh, ma'am, not on your creepy floor."

Laughing loudly, Crystal snapped her fingers. A set of red, white, and blue bleachers instantly sprouted at the side of the court. Simultaneously, a digital scoreboard blinked into existence beside it, announcing 'First Period,' and beneath that, 'Malone/Crystal.'

Crystal Baller peered down at Malone. "Ready now?"

Malone realized he had no choice but to play against her. One thing he'd discovered about deities in general was that one couldn't rush them, and in the case of goddesses in particular, that one humored them as far as one could. "Er, this is unfair," he protested regardless, "you're so much taller than me."

"Not anymore." And suddenly Crystal Baller was exactly Malone's height. "Okay, man, no more excuses, right? Let's frigging play."

He rolled up his sleeves. They moved out beyond the three-point line and she flung the water-filled orb to him. "Your ball."

Malone caught the ball, then almost dropped it. What floated inside the transparent basketball were eyes. Twenty or thirty of them. In disbelief he looked sideways at Trudi, who, once she realized what the ball contained, gave a little gasp of fear then hid her eyes with her hands.

"Hey, Malone! I'm waiting!"

Malone bounced the ball. He'd played a bit in college, but that was twenty-odd years ago. The eye-filled basketball itself was as hard as a marble, but bounced nonetheless. Or was it was the court bouncing the ball? Feeling the skin surface yield beneath his feet, Malone found the possibility creepy.

He focused on the game. While he'd been staring at Trudi, Crystal had lost her tracksuit. Now she wore a sleeveless yellow vest and baggy knee-length green shorts.

They squared off against each other, she a dark female obstruction between he and his objective the basket, her body poised in a half-crouch with her arms outstretched either side of her. Malone drove to her right, she blocked him off; he swerved left, she was there too. He feinted like he was about to go left again, then once he had her off balance, bounced the ball between her legs and ducked right to get around her. Realizing she'd been fooled, she spun around, grabbing for the ball. Malone pushed it beyond her reach, bounced, leapt, and shot for the basket.

Crystal dashed past him, leapt up and snapped the ball out of midair. She landed under the basket, took a step outward and jumped to dunk; but Malone had read her intent. He leapt up with her, and pulled both she and the ball down before she could jam it over the rim of the hoop.

They stood there wrestling for the ball, sweat and a smile on Crystal's brown face. The eyes in the transparent ball rolled about, seeming to watch them.

"We'd better start again," Malone said. "No way am I letting go of this ball."

"Okay, start again," she agreed.

They retreated outside the three-point line again. Malone handed Crystal the ball. "Let's go."

Crystal bounced the ball. Malone glanced sideways at Trudi. She seemed over her terrors, was staring intently at them. Then he realized his mistake: taking advantage of his distraction, Crystal was past him in a flash. He flung himself after her. She had the ball up, had taken two steps, was setting up for a shot. She got the shot up over his block, but he'd thrown off her aim: the ball hit the front of the hoop then flipped sideways onto the skin backboard. They both leapt up for the rebound . . .

And then the bearded face in the backboard opened its mouth wide as a tunnel and ate the ball. It regarded the court with twinkling eyes and a smug smile.

Malone and Crystal landed hard, indenting the flesh floor. Trudi began laughing her head off. Malone stared at her in surprise. She was slapping her thighs, almost toppling off the bleachers in her mirth. He figured that was better than her being scared, but still . . . Behind Trudi, the heavens stretched out endlessly. If she fell into the void . . .

"Hey, you!" Crystal bellowed up at the backboard face. "Give me back my frigging ball, wilya!?"

With a surly look, the face spat out the see-thru basketball.

"That happens sometimes," Crystal informed Malone. She wiped the ball clean of saliva with her vest then handed it to him. "Okay, another dead ball. We start again."

"Hey," Malone whispered as they walked out of the free throw lane, pointing to Trudi, who was still laughing her head off, "I'm worried about her. She can't fall off those seats into space, can she?"

Crystal chortled. "Don't worry, I got my eye on her."

They resumed playing. This time it was slower. Malone didn't think Crystal was tiring, but he was. So he slowed the game down, dribbling back and forth towards the end of the court, keeping just outside the paint, trying to get a shot off; then, when she foiled his moves, dribbling back toward the half-court line to start again. Crystal remained with him all the way, moving with him as he feinted left and right. Malone was impressed: Crystal's black face wore the most intense expression ever. The sweat dripping off her bald head was clearly the moisture of concentration.

Then, like he'd hoped she would, she grew impatient and began lunging at him, swiping her hands to get the ball. He began teasing her, bouncing the ball towards her, then back away again when she moved for it, all the while looking for that one opening.

It came. He pretended to glance at Trudi again. Crystal took the bait and lunged low for the ball. Malone flipped the ball over her head, leapt past her, and dashed for the basket.

Behind him, Crystal fell flat on her face. She sat up, and with no chance at all of catching him, stared moodily after Malone, who was already at the basket and well up into the air, his right arm extended to dunk. Off to Crystal's right, Trudi was watching with her fingers in her mouth. It wasn't everyday one saw a goddess get beat at basketball.

But Malone was tired out now and he hadn't leapt high enough to get the ball over the rim of the hoop. While the face in the backboard watched (licking its lips expectantly and hoping the ball would flip its way again), the ball slammed dead against the side of the hoop.

Cursing his luck, Malone fell down on his back on the skin court. A soft landing, but one that still winded him.

A moment later the transparent ball almost crashed into his head. It stopped falling three inches above his face, where it hung suspended. Its cargo of eyes all settled in its bottom looking down at him.

It was creepy looking up at the eyes, so Malone instead looked towards the center circle. Still seated on the floor there, Crystal Baller was laughing and pointing at him. Trudi was too. Sighing, he looked at the scoreboard. They'd been playing for ten minutes.

Okay, that was enough. He slid out from under the basketball and got up. The ball dropped to the floor and rolled past him towards Crystal Baller. Sweating profusely, his shirt plastered to his back, he trudged after it.

Crystal was laughing so hard she had tears in her eyes.

Malone reached down a hand and pulled the goddess to her feet.

She finally managed to rein in her hilarity. "Alright, Malone, you got game. Old-school game, but you still good."

Trudi leapt down from the bleachers. She jogged over to Malone. She too had tears of mirth in her eyes.

"Oh, wow!" she gasped. "You just need to have seen the way you fell. Man, I've never seen such a bad slam dunk in my life!"

Malone tried not to look too chagrined.

Crystal meanwhile had resumed her giantess appearance. Now once again dressed in her green tracksuit, she gestured to the bleachers and with a gentle smile said, "Come, you two, let's sit and talk."

CHAPTER 15

Malone / Trudi / Crystal Baller

"Okay," Crystal Baller said once they were all seated, "it's time to peek into my magic basketball."

She spun the transparent ball on her left index finger. Though the orb rotated, its ocular contents didn't: the thirty-odd eyes inside it remained fixed in place, staring out at the three of them. Placing a finger to her lips to stop the others speaking, Crystal stared back at the eyes, her gaze intent.

She spun the ball again, stared some more, then stopped it turning. She let it drop into her huge palm, held it out in front of them.

"The abstractive vampires are in Genesis," she said.

Malone and Trudi both looked at her. "Genesis?"

The giant negress nodded. "It's a city on Abstracta's sixth level, a place of many parts." She frowned at them both. "You two are going to the unpleasant part."

"How unpleasant?" Malone asked.

"Rest assured you won't like it. That part of Genesis is a haunt of the darkest evil. It's why the vampires love it: they're under no threat there."

"And yet it's not enough," Trudi said. "They have their cake but want more."

"It's everyone's nature to want more," Crystal Baller said. "In a way, the desire to acquire is proof of life. The day you're satisfied—with who you are, with where you are, with what you have—you've begun dying."

Malone said, "It makes sense that the vampires would hide in an evil place. So, okay, in my line of work, danger is taken for granted;

what we need to know is the nature of the danger. For instance, are there berserkers in Genesis?"

"No. The bigfoot folk dislike the place. It's too boring for them. Most of the people they could kill there are already dead."

"So there aren't any of them there working for the vamps?"

Crystal Baller shook her head, ran a thumb along the angle of her jutting chin. "No."

Behind the bleachers they sat on—all around the skin-covered basketball court—outer space loomed, the dark of ultimate void, pinpricked by suns too inadequate to brighten it up. Malone felt its cold like fingers on his skin. He felt goosepimply. Beside him Trudi shuddered. He took her hand in his. Her hand was cold.

"But," Trudi said as though his touch had energized her, "the bigfoots attacked Malone at the rat's pawn shop. Weren't they working for the vampires then?"

Malone nodded at her question. He'd been wondering the same. (He'd asked Trudi about it. She'd replied that she didn't know herself; she'd just heard a rumor that Fuzzy Joe was about handling a deal for a dead ring, so she staked out his shop from across the street till Malone showed up. As Malone had deduced, Trudi Carmen was, for all intents and purposes, an unrepentant adventuress—she craved excitement like a junkie did their fix, bucketloads of it.)

"No," Crystal replied Trudi's query. "The berserkers wanted the ring for themselves, so they could sell it to Lilith Nightfall. They had no money to pay Jackson, who was selling it, though, so once he'd given it to them, they killed him and his girlfriend Kate. Only thing was, Jackson too had already planned on double-crossing the berserkers. He had a fake ring made and gave that to them, intending to do a clean deal with Fuzzy Joe afterwards."

Trudi nodded. "Okay, I get it now: So the bigfoots went home with the fake ring, then the rat showed up minutes afterwards and found the real ring on Jackson's severed hand and left with it. Then the bigfoots discovered that the ring they'd killed Jackson over was a fake one anyway, and realized that the rat must have the genuine one . . ."

"And so they show up at the pawn shop just after I do and blow Fuzzy Joe to bits and then we start shooting at each other," Malone finished for her. "And then you showed your lovely face."

Trudi swelled at the compliment, preened herself, and said, "Damn, that plot makes my head hurt with its twists."

Crystal regarded Malone and Trudi with amusement. "What's that human saying again? No honor among thieves?"

"Yeah. Though we're lucky that Jackson did double cross the berserkers, else Lilith would have the black ring now." He frowned. "Crystal, you were about filling us in on the dangers of Genesis. Sure we'll go—we've no choice—but I'd like to know what we're walking into."

She nodded. "Your main worry is that Genesis is both a place of creation, and like here . . ." she gestured around her basketball court, "it's also a Node connecting to diverse places." Her eyes fixed suddenly on Malone's. "You're going to encounter a very strange OD in there, man."

She paused, looking away from him into the blackness opposite them. Malone, familiar with the behavior of goddesses, didn't press her for more details about his future appointment with a space-time portal.

"Okay, where was I?" Crystal finally continued. "Yes . . . Genesis is a Node. Which means that aside from those horrors it generates of its own accord, if need be Lilith Nightfall and the abstractive vampires can bring in fresh evil from other planes to take you on."

Trudi made a pretty face. "You mean that we just know we're going in there to kick ass; we've no idea whose ass we'll be kicking? I mean other than Lilith and company?"

"Yeah, something like that." Crystal tapped her magic basketball with a finger, the contact making the water slosh around inside it and the eyes to bob about. "I'm sorry I can't tell you more. There *is* danger, but . . . places like Genesis—Nodes—are hard to read. At such places there are many intersecting futures, too many to sift through." She gazed fondly but sadly at Malone, "I assure you though that you've got your work cut out for you."

She clapped her hands, leaving the ball hanging in the middle of the air. "Okay, darlings, time to leave. Death and danger impatiently await you."

"We'll need to get our stuff from Graveyard."

Crystal Baller's dusky face split in a white grin. "No need. It's all here. What you need anyway."

On her words, they found themselves holding their guns. Malone also felt a spare ammo clip appear in his left trouser pocket.

Malone leapt down from the grandstand, then extended a hand up to Trudi, who climbed down too, though her expression seemed to question the wisdom of doing so. They stood facing the seated goddess, who was as tall sitting down as they were standing.

Trudi raised her left hand so Crystal could see the white ring on her finger. "It's rather dangerous taking the ring into Genesis, isn't it? If Lilith gets it away from us . . . Look, can I just leave it here with you and come back for it once we get the black one?"

She made to slip the ring off her finger but Crystal shook her head. "No, it's not permitted."

"Not permitted by who?"

"Rules of the game, girl. You can't leave it with me and that's final. Just keep it somewhere safe, where—"

"Somewhere safe?" And before Malone or Crystal could stop her, Trudi slipped the ring off her finger and into her mouth. A gulp and a swallow and then she beamed at them. "It's safe now."

Crystal nodded. "But I was about telling both of you that one reason why you need this ring is that it'll help you locate the other one."

Malone gaped at Trudi, who in turn gaped down at her belly. Then Trudi looked meekly up at Crystal. "Help me get it out? Please?"

Crystal laughed and stood up. Towering over them both like an anthracite statue, she said, "No need to. It'll work just the same. You'll be able to sense when either a vampire or the other ring is close by." She winked down at Trudi. "You know you'll have to keep checking your poop now each time you go, right?"

Trudi winced and tugged at her red hair. "Crap! I didn't think of that!"

"Heat of the moment," Malone excused. He looked along the basketball court, from the basket in the half where they'd played their game (and where the bearded head on the backboard now seemed to be asleep), to the opposite basket (which had a similar stretched-skin backboard, only this one had a female face on it, with blonde hair, and the leg on which the whole assemblage stood was female too with blue toenails). "Where exactly in Genesis are we going?" he asked Crystal.

"Vampire Castle. It's an ugly building on top of a hill. Easy as hell to find." She raised a finger to stop him commenting. "But you two aren't going there yet. First you make a detour." She looked at Trudi. "Say, you remember Elton Jones?"

Trudi, who'd been looking embarrassed since impulsively swallowing the ring and being informed she'd have to keep checking her excrement for it, nodded. "Yes, he's an adventurer friend of mine." She peered questioningly at Crystal. "Our paths haven't crossed in ages though. Is he in Genesis?"

Crystal nodded, then said, "Okay, both of you, stand back." She waited till they'd moved slightly behind her, then flung her magic basketball towards the farther basketball hoop. Six feet later, the transparent ball froze like it had struck an invisible wall, then exploded against the air. Its water and glass spread out into a shimmering rectangle around the borders of which its many eyes floated.

Next, the rectangle's liquid interior faded away to reveal the view of a street.

"Behold Genesis," Crystal said. "The really creepy part of it."

Malone didn't think the revealed street looked odder than most odd places he'd visited. The note of seriousness in the goddess's voice, though, gave him cause for concern. He looked through the portal at the murky sky laced with thick gray clouds, like sunset at midday.

"Where do we find Elton Jones?" Trudi asked. (She'd grabbed Malone's hand again. He suspected it was more their current location than their destination making her edgy. But she'd already gotten over her previous bout of shivers, so what . . . ? Or, was it that, now that the time for action was at hand, she was growing aroused? He checked out her nipples; they didn't look swollen.) "And . . ." Trudi's expression became perplexed, "What's Elton doing here anyway?"

"He's in St. Peter's Cathedral on Cherry Street," Crystal replied, gesturing down the street in the door. "Follow this road till you reach the Cherry Street intersection, then go left. Why Elton's here? He's got a score to settle with the vampires: Lilith and her crew ran amok in Edenfield, a village Elton was hired to protect, killing everyone and burning the church. The priest was Elton's younger brother

David." She made a face. "That reminds me, you'll need a priest too."

Malone asked, "What does a priest have to do with any of this?" He was about to say more, but then noticed a long spiky tentacle flail out over the roof of a building down the street and snare something four-legged and winged out of the sky. (*Damn, was that a flying pig?*) Okay, now he got what Crystal meant: Genesis really wasn't as innocuous as it looked.

Trudi, however, hadn't noticed anything odd. Her hand still tightly gripping his, she replied, "Vampires, particularly abstractive ones, hate everything holy. And there's no clearer representation of God than priests. Buddhist priests, Hindu priests, Christian . . . Moslem . . . doesn't matter your faith, denomination, or sect; so long as they're holy women or men, they're a vampire target. They've likely murdered all those they can find in Genesis." Her green eyes flashed angrily at Crystal. "Am I right?"

The giant black goddess nodded solemnly. "Yes. Priests are a major danger to vampires, so they purge them wherever they can." Then she smiled. "But you'll find a priest when you really need one."

Malone asked, "Does this guy—Elton Jones—have a priest with him?"

Scowling, Crystal pointed to the rectangle with its frame of eyes. "Enough of the damn interrogation. If I keep answering your questions, next thing I know you'll be trying to convince me to enter Genesis with you to rid the world of Lilith Nightfall. Alright, now get in there and kick some asshole vampire ass." She laughed at their surprised expression. "Trust me, I hate those three even more than you do. I could stomach the other two, but Lilith wants too much."

"I thought you approved of the human desire to acquire more?" Malone said.

"She's not human, and she's driven by the most intense lust I've ever seen. Allowed to have her greedy way, Lilith Nightfall would suck the entire universe to death. And we can't have that happening—I like the universe. Besides, it's offensive, not to mention grossly disrespectful, to us gods when you mortal creatures refuse to get the point." Then, maybe realizing she'd said too much, the giant goddess wiped a hand over her bald head and frowned down at Malone and Trudi Carmen. "See, what I mean? You've got me rambling again. Alright, enough of school. You two get your butts through that door and into Genesis before I close it off and send you back to Christine."

"We're leaving," Malone said quickly. The look on Crystal's face said she was dead serious about not helping them if they persisted in questioning her.

Trudi already had one foot through the OD and in Genesis. She suddenly seemed desperate to be away from the skin-covered basketball court. Once fully out on the street she walked off a distance from the opening.

"Thanks for all your help," Malone told Crystal and made to step through after Trudi, who gun in hand, was now waiting impatiently for him and gesturing at him to hurry.

"Hey, Malone."

Malone turned back to face Crystal Baller.

"Come over here. I just remembered something I need to tell you."

He pointed outside, at Trudi. Crystal shook her head. "Nah, just you, man. C'mon get your ass over here."

Malone walked back over to Crystal again. "What's the matter?"

With a wide grin, the goddess nodded towards Trudi, who, alone in a new realm, was looking nervously about, gun poised to shoot. "Rear entry, Malone. That's what works best for her."

He gaped at her. "Huh?"

"She likes it doggy-style."

He gaped wider. "Oh."

"Oh, yes. Get her down on her hands and knees and get behind her. And she doesn't really enjoy cunnilingus, so just your fingers first."

He nodded. "Ah." Then seeing Crystal Baller wasn't about saying any more, he grinned embarrassedly, waved at her, and turned and shambled off towards Trudi.

Distracted by Crystal's instructions, he grabbed the edges of the otherworld door while going through it. Those eyes he touched squirmed unpleasantly beneath his fingers.

Malone quickly pulled his hand off of them and stepped through into Genesis.

Behind him, he heard, "And, Malone, you owe me one more game."

He spun around to reply Crystal, but the door in the middle of the street had vanished.

Flicking the safety off his gun, he hurried over to join Trudi.

PART 3:
GENESIS

CHAPTER 16

Malone / Trudi

At first glance Genesis looked normal enough—just another modern urban center beneath an overcast midafternoon sky. They'd seemingly emerged in a business area—stores on both sides were interspersed with apartment brownstones surviving from before the district became commercialized. There were lots of fire escapes, flapping curtains, and open windows everywhere.

The only thing missing was people. There was no one in sight.

Then, about fifty yards down the street, Trudi and Malone began noticing human remains—stripped skeletons in doorways, rotted and swollen corpses in the gutters, half-eaten bodies hanging from windows. They passed a front door blocked from shutting by a mess like melted pink wax with fingers and a nose jutting from its front half.

"Yeah, this is the bad part of town alright," Trudi said.

They walked much faster.

***

Now that they'd left Crystal, Trudi Carmen felt much better. She was embarrassed at how scared she'd felt in the black goddess's presence. Something about that place—the endless nothingness of space all around it, the creepy skin court and backboards, the giant woman herself—had completely freaked her out. She'd hid her fear as best she could, but she knew Malone had noticed. When he wasn't staring at her breasts, that was. She grimaced: *What is it with guys and boobs anyway? We show T and A and they turn to jelly!* Not that Trudi disliked the attention, but business was business. (In her short

105

white dress and sneakers, she didn't exactly feel dressed to fight; she felt she was better attired for tennis!)

Out here, even with the grisly remains everywhere, Trudi felt more sure of herself. Death was familiar to her. This abundant carnage was however definite cause for concern. She glanced sideways at Malone. His face was stony; clearly he felt the same as she about their morbid surroundings.

She felt a buzz in her belly, like a weak electric shock. *Oops, that's the dead ring.*

Trudi's swallowing the ring had been one of those 'I have to make some kind of statement now though I'll regret it later' moments she sometimes had. She figured everyone had them, maybe just not at such inconvenient times.

Trudi now found herself once again considering a vampire trait that always perplexed her. *It's damn strange, how once people become vamps they instantly lose all human empathy, completely forget their human origins and start viewing themselves as part of the overlord master race—the Undead Bloodsucker's Reich or whatever.*

Yeah, that was damn strange, she thought.

***

Malone studied the rooftops ahead of them, trying to pinpoint which one had launched the spiky tentacle that had snared the flying pig out of the air.

Trudi pulled his arm. "Wait."

They froze. A moment later he saw what she had: On the other side of the street, two houses ahead of them and four stories up, a giant spider was crawling down a brownstone's frontage. The monster arachnid was supported by a thick wet cord that emerged from its spinnerets and was anchored to the roof.

"It must be at least six feet long," Trudi whispered as they stepped into shadows to hide from it.

Malone nodded. He'd also noticed that the sidewalk beside that particular building was dotted with bleached bones. And . . . by the brownstone's front door were piled several long dirty-gray cocoons that thankfully weren't moving. Alarmed by the sight of them, however, he looked up to ensure the spider had no companions on this side of the street. A rotted face hanging out of a window stared back down at him.

Shuddering, Malone returned his attentions to the street.

He and Trudi watched the spider pull its bristly black bulk through a window, then they dashed past it.

After crossing the next intersection, Malone figured they'd now passed the roof with the pig-snaring tentacle. Also, here the skeletons and corpses had abruptly reduced in number. So maybe the huge spider only prowled those blocks behind them.

He relaxed a bit. "The Cherry Street corner can't be too far off now," he told Trudi. "And it should be a safer walk."

Trudi said, "I don't think so, man. My belly's been buzzing non-stop for the past minute."

Malone stared at her. Her beautiful green eyes were wide with dread, her scarlet hair plastered to her forehead and neck by fear-sweat. "That means the vampires are close by."

Trudi nodded. "Yeah. But where?"

They both looked up and around.

"I don't see anything," Malone said.

"Me neither," Trudi agreed. She was now grasping her belly like it hurt. "Damn, this was a frigging bad idea, Malone. It really feels like I need to poop. You know, the moment we're through with this insane caper, I'm taking the most powerful laxative I can find, and—"

"Shush!" He steered her off the sidewalk and into the lobby of the nearest building, the smashed neon sign of which announced it as the Hotel Bizarre.

The hotel was trashed and empty. They stood staring out of the ajar lobby doors.

"Did you see something?" Trudi asked. "Tell me!"

"A shadow down the street seemed to be moving. I didn't see what made it though; it might have been a bird or something else. Earlier, I saw a—"

Now it was Trudi's turn to shush Malone by placing her palm over his mouth. They both froze in place and watched the street. A massive winged shadow floated over the intersection, hovered in place for several seconds, then was gone.

Malone looked at Trudi. "Wait here."

She glared at him. "Where the hell are you going?"

He waved his pistol at the street. "That bat might still be around. I want to see if I can kill it."

She shrugged. "Don't waste your time. The buzzing's lessened—it's gone. Besides, it wasn't Lilith Nightfall."

"How can you be sure?"

"Crystal said the rings sense each other. Lilith must know that too and she has the other ring. So if the bat was her, she'd have realized we were in here and not just flown off." She spat. "That one was another abstractive asshole looking for someone to bite or a priest to fuck up. Killing it will just alert Lilith that we're here in Genesis."

Malone conceded the wisdom of her argument. "She'll sense the ring sooner or later."

Trudi shook her head. "Not unless she's close by. So we've still got an advantage."

Malone reached for the lobby door. "Okay, time to get—"

Trudi screamed.

Malone spun around. A tiger was charging at them. The beast was huge, a Bengal with hunger in its golden eyes. Its striped body rippled with power as it approached.

Claws out, it leapt for the kill.

Malone got over his confusion as to where the tiger had appeared from long enough to shoot it.

The tiger collapsed dead. Malone looked to see if Trudi was alright. She seemed unhurt but was shaking. He held her close. "You okay?"

She nodded. "It just suddenly appeared in the middle of the lobby." She giggled self-depreciatingly. "Wow! Some adventurer I'm turning out to be, eh, Malone? Turning to jelly at every opportunity?"

He grinned. "Trust me, I've been in situations myself where the option wasn't whether or not to crap my pants, but simply how many times to do so." He gestured at the dead tiger. "We'd better get out of here in case there's more of them around."

Trudi winced. "I hate this place. Spiders and bats outside, tigers inside. Oh, frigging hell, what now?"

They'd both turned to exit into the street, only now the door wasn't there anymore, just a blank blue wall hung with a large poster of Audrey Hepburn as Holly Golightly in *Breakfast at Tiffany's.*

They swung back around, in time to watch the dead tiger transform—they actually saw its body thinning flat—into a tiger-skin rug lying at the foot of a four-poster bed.

And the entire Hotel Bizarre lobby had now become a luxurious 60's-themed bedroom. Plush blue carpeting, two orange leather sofas, a glass coffee table, an expensive clothes cabinet, a vanity mirror, a stocked bar, a fridge . . . No windows.

Malone checked out the bedroom's single door. It led to a bathroom equipped with a sunken marble tub with gold fittings.

He turned back to Trudi, who was checking out the fridge.

"We're trapped," he announced.

Trudi pulled a plate of roast chicken out of the fridge. "Um um, that sucks. We won't starve though." She waved a drumstick at Malone. "You didn't really eat your dinner; you want some of this?"

He was amazed at how casually she was taking their abrupt confinement. Barely a minute ago she'd been scared stiff, now she seemed to have blithely discarded the experience. He prodded the tiger-skin rug with a foot, almost expecting it to revive and attack them again.

She shrugged at his perplexed expression. "Lighten up, Malone. We both know we're not getting out of here till the room lets us leave. Knowing that, we might as well enjoy ourselves in the interim." She took a bite of the drumstick, then waved it him again. "This is really good, are you sure you won't have some?" She gestured into the fridge, "There's Pepsi and beer here too," then over at the bar, "Wine, brandy, what have you . . ."

"Yeah, I think I will. I suddenly feel ravenous—has to be all that exercise playing b-ball."

Trudi found an empty plate and piled it high with food. "And once we're done eating," she whispered over her shoulder at him, "we can have a bath and get to know each other better."

Her words gave Malone an instant erection.

CHAPTER 17

Malone / Trudi

After eating, they did get to know each other a lot better.

Soaking in a warm bath amidst sweet rose fragrance and bubbles and relaxed in the comfortable crook of Malone arm, Trudi told him a little bit about herself. It was largely as he'd suspected:

"I'm originally from Chicago. My parents are stupendously rich. I had the option of either getting married to additional money and becoming a royally frustrated rich bitch, or of spending their wealth hopping into dangerous situations and trying not to get killed." She giggled. "I obviously chose the latter. Besides, a woman does happen to meet all the hunks out in the field anyway. Mom and Dad definitely don't approve of my doings, but they never balk at sponsoring my adventures either." She made a face. "You know, I never really considered it like this before, but maybe . . . maybe they're actually hoping I'll get eaten by a monster and stop embarrassing them amongst their friends."

Laughing, Malone slid his fingers between her submerged thighs.

She giggled. "What's that you're doing down there, Mr. Malone?"

"Get up and turn around," he said in a hoarse voice. "Kneel over the edge of the tub. Imagine you're that unlucky guy in prison who just dropped the soap. Me, I just want to make certain you washed your behind properly."

Trudi assumed the position with speed.

Crystal was right, Malone realized, *this lady really does appreciate rear-entry.* Hard penis throbbing in his crotch, he got behind Trudi. He kissed her buttocks in turn, at the same time rubbing his hand back and forth between her legs. His hand motion whipped up a lather of soap in her crotch through which her sex peeked.

She began trembling; he slipped two fingers into her body. The vagina split happily in two, gladly welcoming his questing digits. He moved them in and out.

"Put yourself in me!" she gasped back at him after a while. "Put yourself in me!"

He put himself in, holding her bent over the edge of the tub with one hand, while the other fed his swollen manhood into her wet womanhood. She was very slippery.

He began moving with her, getting a nice rhythm going between their bodies. They rocked back and forth together. His crotch smacked her buttocks; the bath water slapped both their thighs like waves breaking on seaside cliffs. Trudi knelt gasping with her breasts and right cheek flat on the wet bathroom floor tiles. Her left hand fingers were in her mouth, her arms folded tightly against her ribs. Her red hair was a dripping scattered mess.

"Oh, oh, oh!" she gasped as Malone slid in and out of her. "Oh, oh, oh!"

Malone rode Trudi's hips like he was a cowboy at a rodeo. Her sex felt fantastic around his. Her body was a massive turn-on, the white hourglass of her figure viewed at its best like this, with her big breasts flattened at her sides and the twin globes of her buttocks spread wide. The line of her spine wiggled between neck and anus like a snake as she twisted left and right to better accommodate his recurring penetrations. At a critical point, morbid images of Adrienne Lake flashed through his mind and he almost lost his erection, but right at that moment, Trudi began coming and the excitement of her satisfaction drove the threatened ED far from Malone.

"Oh my!" Eyes squeezed tightly shut, Trudi was biting her fingers in delirium as her internal storm broke and sweet orgasmic rain drenched her. She felt filled, filled and fulfilled, and Malone felt wonderfully deep inside her. Each thrust of his penis seemed to reach her throat, pushing fresh gasps of satisfaction from her lips. Her body felt liquid, like it was the bathwater sloshing over her sex. *Oh, oh, oh! Wow, what a climax!*

Feeling his own orgasm close at hand now, Malone squeezed Trudi's buttocks hard and pumped faster, squashing her against the edge of the sunken tub. Their bodies smacking together loudly and splashing bathwater out of the tub, he exploded into her. Oh God, it felt heavenly. He kept thrusting as the semen poured from him into her hungry clenching receptacle (Trudi reaching back with both hands and grabbing his buttocks, digging her nails in deep). Then, drained and weakened, he collapsed on top of her, his heart beating fast and furious.

"God, you're something," he groaned in her ear while she purred contentedly beneath him.

After a while, when Malone's racing pulse had normalized again, they got out of the now tepid water, dried themselves off with the luxurious towels provided, and returned to the bedroom.

"No doors yet," Malone noted drily. "We're still prisoners of the bedroom."

Trudi nodded, then yawned and stretched, her big breasts rising high up on her chest. She was standing on the tiger-skin rug, her feet making imprints in the thick striped fur. "We might as well get some sleep then." She kissed Malone. "Don't know 'bout you, baby, but you've relaxed me so much I could sleep for a week."

Malone watched her pretty feet on the striped rug. The tiger's mouth was open as if to protest being trampled. He nodded. "Me too. The one thing missing from this room is a TV to help us keep awake."

He followed her to the bed where they lay in each other's arms.

Trudi fell asleep almost instantly. Her head pillowed on his shoulder, Malone lay on his back thinking.

The grim part of his mind considered the flow of time outside the Abstracta: he hoped their delay in this room wasn't costing lives back in Boston. He glanced around the blue walls, wondering when an exit other than into the bathroom would open up.

The optimistic part of his consciousness, however, was pleased with their progress. Over the course of a mere eight hours (normal USA time) he'd both discovered who the murder culprits were and was on his way to taking them down. (Malone doubted the vampires would come quietly. And after what they'd done to Adrienne, he didn't want them to.)

And . . . he grinned broadly . . . he and Trudi Carmen were now an item.

Yes!!!

Malone was utterly delighted that Trudi was his, more over the moon than the fairytale cow. He gazed down lovingly at his sleeping beauty and stroked her red hair, controlling his temptation to waken her with a kiss.

Oh, baby, he thought, *you've no idea of the kind of loving you're in for. Oh, am I so going to love and cherish you!!!*

Pleasant thoughts of their new romance in his heart, Bud Malone fell asleep.

CHAPTER 18

Lilith / Le Bleach

From the arched stone window of her bedroom on the top floor of Vampire Castle, Diana Le Bleach watched the afternoon sky darken over western Genesis.

"I miss Zander," Le Bleach said. A tall thin blonde, she was currently wrapped in a floor-length yellow silk robe. "Unlike gloomy Vermyn, he was fun."

Lilith Nightfall, just returned from Boston and lounging naked on the bed behind Le Bleach, laughed at her comment. "You think too much of enjoyment, Diana. Sex isn't everything."

Le Bleach turned to face her. "Look who's talking. Do you, who fly off to Boston on the slightest pretext, want to reprimand me over the little pleasure I have?"

Lilith lifted a hand from stroking her breasts and waved it at her companion. "Oh, Diana. I've asked you to come to Boston with me. You flatly refused."

"Not until you have both dead rings and their world is ours."

"The feeding is great there, well worth the risk."

Le Bleach frowned. "Is it? Every interaction with the humans threatens us with disaster."

"Disaster? They're nothing but our cattle. We drain them like they drain their cows. And soon, we'll have a whole continent under our thumb to feed from." Lilith's expression turned hungry. "Imagine that, Diana: a whole continent of human cattle to bleed." She laughed. "It's odd, you know, how food is simply destined to be food. Consider mankind's millions of cows, for instance. One would have thought that with all the slaughter they've endured through the ages, the cows would all have long ago emigrated to India, where they're held sacred and protected, but no, they hang around everywhere else to be eaten, to fulfil their destiny as human sustenance."

Le Bleach grimaced, and then, like she was cold, she pulled her robe tighter around her body. She left the window and strode to sit on the bed, where she took Lilith Nightfall's hands in hers. (Across from both women, a silver mirror showed just an empty bed with the impression of bodies in it.) When Le Bleach spoke now, her voice was reverential. "You're our leader, Lilith, and we all bow to your will. You led us out of the Outer Darkness to this wonderfully foul place, and my faith in you is absolute. I support you totally in your plan to unlock the Dead Sky. But still, I think your mingling with the humans before the right time will only bring us trouble."

Lilith made no reply, so Le Bleach went on: "We've two good examples: First, Vermyn, who had his pocket picked by a human girl when he went to ask the rat pawn dealer if he knew anything of the black dead ring."

"True, but that was unforeseeable. He had to have the ring with him to show to the rat." Lilith stretched her nude form. "Besides, you're forgetting that I came across the black ring while on a feeding trip in Boston. So it equals out."

"And Zander, who was murdered by that human?"

Lilith winced. "Ah, Zander again. Was he that good in bed?"

Le Bleach's face hardened. "Don't make fun of me, Lilith!"

Lilith giggled coldly. "It's hard not to, Diana, you worry over the most ridiculous trifles. The facts of this case are plain and simple, and I wish you would accept them like Vermyn does: We abstractive vampires are superior to the human race. Like it or not, we are their evolution. They defeating us is as impossible as the Earth's cows revolting and defeating them. They lack the intelligence, and what's more, *the strength* to take us on. And once we fill their premier nation's skies with permanent darkness . . ."

"Lilith, a human killed Zander."

She waved it off. "Mere luck. Please stop belaboring that fluke."

"Vermyn didn't think so. Lilith, there's only three of us left now."

Lilith Nightfall yawned at her fellow vampire. "Okay, Diana, the next time you see a handsome man, we won't kill him—unless he's a priest of course. We'll turn him so you'll have another boyfriend." For a moment Lilith wondered what had happened to Adrienne, who she'd taken the black ring from. Adrienne had turned that night. She shrugged; the woman had likely burnt to ash first thing next morning. Too bad—such deaths couldn't be helped. Then she giggled at the insulted look that had come over Le Bleach's face during her musing. "Diana, I assure you, there's no danger at all. Good things come to those who wait."

"Bad things come to those who are complacent."

Lilith's face hardened. "Have faith in me, will you," she said coldly. "I'm not stupid. We have one ring. Soon I'll find the other one, and then . . ." Her expression turned dreamy. "You really need to feel what it's like to soar the skies outside the Abstracta."

Le Bleach was intrigued. "Is it that fantastic?"

"It's the most incredible feeling ever felt. Even in my normal body I feel all-powerful, like a goddess, like I could crush those puny humans in my hands, tear their bodies to shreds and let their blood fill the gutters of their cities." She sighed. "And I will, too, but not before the time is right." She tapped the black ring on her right middle finger. "And it soon will be. Once I find the man who has the white ring, I . . . you . . . all of us . . . we'll be all-powerful. We'll rule not just their United States of America, but their entire world." She sighed again. "But until then, we all make do with scraps—I with the women of Boston, Massachusetts, and you and Vermyn with the occasional priest you pick up."

Le Bleach brightened from her glumness. "I found a priest. I've got the bastard down in the basement. I was—"

"We'll visit him later," Lilith said, reaching up her pale fingers to Le Bleach. "Now, come! Make love to me! I want to feel your hot tongue deep inside my body!"

Her expression as grim as if she was about to be whipped (sex with Lilith was often painful), Diana Le Bleach removed her yellow robe, revealing her slim frame. She climbed into bed beside her leader, who enveloped her in a cold embrace and instantly pressed their lips together.

Their tongues moved slowly in each other's mouths, their hands roved, touched, teased. There was no rush; this world was theirs. Here in Genesis, time was theirs, safety was theirs. Except for the rare human idiot with a death wish, no one dared visit this place of the Shadow of Death. (Vermyn was out there right now. Since his younger brother's murder he'd been flying restlessly over Genesis [over their part of the city anyway] seeking someone, anyone, *anything* he could vent his rage on.)

Le Bleach moved down Lilith's body, her tongue sliding from neck to nipple to navel to clitoris.

"Your hole tastes of blood," Le Bleach said. "Is it your period?" she asked hopefully.

"No, just the remains of the last human cow I fucked."

"Was she any good?"

"Very. Stop talking and eat me. I'm so aroused."

"You're always aroused, Lilith."

"It's my nature. And besides, so are you, Diana, though you pretend otherwise."

Le Bleach spread Lilith's vaginal lips and dug her tongue deep into the reddened hole. While licking out Kenya Jordan's blood, she wondered what the dead woman had tasted like freshly bled. Delicious, she was certain, not like all the old withered priests she had to make do with, the stupid old farts, their blood thinned to almost watery consistency by their endless fasts.

Sensing Le Bleach's distraction and displeased by it, Lilith yanked on her blonde hair.

"Ouch!"

"Turn around. Bring your pussy up to my mouth, let me taste you too."

They made love in the sixty-nine position for a while, licking and fingering each other, then Lilith smacked Le Bleach's buttocks. "Get the strap-on and fuck me."

The green strap-on phallus was short but very thick. Lilith licked her lips as the other woman strapped it on. Her eyes rose from the plastic penis to Le Bleach's breasts, which were little but had big nipples. She crooked a finger at her lover. "Come! Give it to me!"

Le Bleach approached the bed. Lilith Nightfall folded her legs up to her shoulders and gripped the back of her thighs. Her black eyes were pits of lust for Le Bleach to fall into. "See how I've spread myself in readiness? Fuck me hard."

She gasped, her eyes widening with delight as Le Bleach filled her with the dildo. Le Bleach thrust mercilessly into Lilith, steadying herself by gripping Lilith's bone-white calves. The green phallus tormented Lilith's sex, stretching her hole, rippling its walls with pleasure.

Lilith Nightfall began coming. It was a dark and horrible orgasm, throughout which she fantasized of herself wading through rivers of human blood, bathing in lakes of it, drinking so much of it that she died of blood-intoxication.

Her dark orgasm ended. She lay gasping, arms out at her sides, while Le Bleach continued to pound her sex with the dildo. Finally, she reached up and grabbed the other vampire's hair and dragged her face down to hers. Their kiss was long and bloody, each savaging the other's lips and savoring the mingled crimson dribble.

Then Lilith strapped the dildo on.

"Down, on your hands and knees!" she ordered the other woman. "Present your anus to me!"

Le Bleach quailed. "Please use the other one, Lilith. This one's too thick for my ass. It hurts me!"

An evil sated smile on her face, Lilith ran her cold fingers along Le Bleach's cheek. "Oh, but I want to hurt you, Diana darling. Right now, I'm in the mood to cause you pain. I'm going to rip up your little anus so good it'll widen down into your vagina. Then you can shit and piss through the same hole. Just imagine how convenient that'll be for you."

Fear in her eyes, Le Bleach got down on all fours.

After smearing the green dildo with secretion from Le Bleach's dripping vagina, Lilith forced it between her buttocks. It was an incredibly tight fit and Le Bleach instantly began yelping in pain. Ignoring her squealing, Lilith gripped Le Bleach's waist firmly and rammed the strap-on deep into the woman's rectum. She left it in there awhile, laughing while Le Bleach groaned and squirmed in agony, then slid it out again. The top of the dildo now had a thin line of blood (just like a vein) on it. Lilith collected the blood with a finger and licked it.

"You taste good," she told Le Bleach, then added musingly, "You know, I once fucked Cunt Dracula's ass. She bled literally everywhere, the silly old slut. Maybe, Diana, I'll make you bleed everywhere too."

Le Bleach had tears in her eyes from the huge anal intrusion. "Oh no, Lilith, C'mon, get it over with, please."

"But this is for your benefit, not mine." Sighing with pleasure, Lilith Nightfall began thrusting in and out of her lover's backside. She worked her left hand between Le Bleach's legs and began stroking her clitoris. "Now come for me, you skinny little hypocrite!" she growled. "I'm not doing all this hard work in your ass for nothing. Come for me!"

Diana Le Bleach remained there on all fours as the fat green dildo filled her rectum over and over again. Each time the rubber penis slid out it created a massive suction pressure in her rear like someone was attempting to vacuum her guts out through her backside.

Ouch! Ouch! Ouch!!!! she thought with each additional anal invasion, her cheeks wet with her tears. *It fucking hurts! Lilith is such a horrible callous bitch!*

"Orgasm for me, Diana!" Lilith Nightfall insisted angrily. "Don't pretend you hate this!"

Initially, to surf above her pain, Le Bleach concentrated her attention outside her bedroom, on the perpetually overcast sky of Genesis. (For a moment she imagined she saw Vermyn in flight out there, a monster bat looking for some unfortunate someone to rip into.) But soon, Lilith's skillful fingers on her clitoris worked their magic.

First Le Bleach's sexual noises were yelps of pain, but then they became squeals of pleasure, and then finally, groans and shrieks of the deepest erotic ecstasy. And now Le Bleach's tears were tears of joy.

CHAPTER 19

Malone / Trudi

They awoke within seconds of each other, a cold draft ushering them out of the realm of dreams.

The blue room of their captivity now had another door, this second one opposite the bed at the spot where the Audrey Hepburn film poster had previously hung. The door was shut but had a golden key in its lock.

"Time to dress up and go," Trudi said, rubbing sleep from her eyes with her knuckles.

Malone kissed her, feeling a thrill as her soft lips pressed against his and her eager tongue sought his. Just being near her filled his heart with an unutterable joy.

They broke apart and sat up.

Trudi pointed to the new door. "Think we should peek outside first?"

"Not till we're both dressed and ready to leave. Or else weird shit might happen and we'd still be naked."

That settled, they both quickly got out of bed. Trudi ran into the bathroom to make water. Malone, who'd relieved himself shortly before dawn(?), got to work pulling his clothes on. Time was of the essence: he was conscious that the room might at any instant change its mind and hold them prisoner for longer.

Trudi flushed, exited the bathroom, and joined him in getting dressed.

Both strapped on their guns, looked around to ensure they'd not forgotten anything, then headed for the new exit.

The moment Malone touched the key to unlock the door, the entire bedroom vanished. He and Trudi found themselves once again in the dusty lobby of the Hotel Bizarre.

"It's almost like no time has passed at all," Trudi said once over her surprise at the transition.

Malone nodded. "Good for us. It means there's been no interlude for the vampires to have done more evil."

"Except we somehow spent an entire day and night in that room."

"Baby, I really hope not."

Trudi yawned. "I'm just kidding. It's just really odd to wake up in the morning and it's suddenly evening, you know? And *yesterday* evening at that."

"And it'll soon be night. Best that we've found the cathedral and Elton Jones by then."

"Yeah, it shouldn't be too far off now. Did Crystal say which turning to the left it was?"

"Nope, just that we'd see the street sign."

Guns drawn against the threat of danger, they stepped outside the Hotel Bizarre. The air was cold, the evening well under way.

They'd proceeded only a short distance when Trudi stiffened then looked at Malone worriedly. "The ring . . . it just buzzed again . . . and again."

Instantly alert, Malone pulled her close to the wall of the house they were passing. Then he stood on the edge of the sidewalk looking around for the vampire.

Show yourself, you son-of-a-bitch.

"Look out!" Trudi yelped suddenly, flinging herself at Malone. He was aware of a whistling sound from overhead, then of Trudi hitting him and knocking him off the sidewalk and into the road. They landed together, she on top of him.

Behind them, something hit the ground hard. Gasping, Malone pushed Trudi off him and looked back to see what it was.

It was a huge freezer. Like a blue diamond, the freezer lay stuck into the cracked sidewalk by one of its bottom corners, its cover wrenched off by the force of impact.

They both looked up. Three floors above, another massive freezer was tilting out of a hole in the wall.

"It's the vampires!" Trudi said as the white kitchen appliance fell towards them.

They evaded it, dashing across the street to the safety of an overhang.

"I really hate this damn place, baby," Trudi gasped. "The vampires are so strong and—"

"Shh!" Malone said, pointing up across the street at the hole in the wall from which both freezers had just fallen. "It's not the vampires. Look."

Trudi looked. An immense orange caterpillar-creature was chucking a television out of the hole after the freezers. The television smashed to bits on the sidewalk. The caterpillar retreated back into the hole, then reappeared to throw out a washing machine as well. It looked across the street at Malone and Trudi, then, as though alarmed to see them, vanished for good.

"I guess it doesn't like household appliances," Malone said, stepping out from under the overhang. "Let's go."

Trudi walked out after him. "Baby, I can still sense the vampire around here somewhere; the ring's buzzing like cra—ooof!"

That was the last thing Trudi Carmen ever said. Malone heard a sudden loud 'whoosh' of air behind him like the sound of a jet engine picking up speed. He spun around just in time to see the massive black vampire bat streak past him, and in its wake, Trudi's head separating from her body.

"NOOO!!!!" he screamed as Trudi's head fell one way, her body the other.

The sight paralyzed Malone. He watched helplessly as Trudi's severed head—mouth frozen open in horror, green eyes gaping at nothing—bounced to the edge of the sidewalk and dropped into a hole that may have been a storm drain.

He stared at Trudi's body spurting blood over the sidewalk, her lovely legs still kicking like she was refusing to accept her demise. Then, full of rage, his heart feeling like a stone in his chest, Malone set off running down the street after the monster that had killed her.

The monster bat was already heading back towards him. Despite his rage, he wondered at the size of the thing—its wingspan was such that the bat filled the street. How had it hidden itself from he and Trudi then, or even snuck up on them unnoticed? Malone parked both questions in a dusty mental lot for future retrieval.

Anger in his eyes, he shot at the bristly airborne monster with the glowing crimson gaze. He saw the projectiles hit and punch through its body. The bat froze in midair, its forward progress halted by the unrelenting onslaught of bullets.

Malone fired till his gun clicked empty. The huge bat fell to the ground and lay there with its wings twitching. Dark blood bubbled from its fragmented flesh.

It wasn't dead though.

Keeping a close watch on it, Malone switched clips. Then, weapon held ready, he walked towards the bat, intending to compound its misery. He wanted it to suffer before dying.

He stood by the creature, about to pull the trigger, when suddenly it switched shapes on him. Suddenly there was a fat man in a gray suit grappling with him and trying to sink yellow fangs into his neck.

Anger gave Malone strength. He slammed his gun up under the vampire's chin, saving himself from being bitten. Then he lost his balance and tripped over the curb, falling backwards onto the sidewalk. He just avoided braining himself on a fire hydrant. His gun flew out of his hand.

The vampire, who was extremely ugly—with sunken yellow eyes like circles of rotting cheese, a thin hooked nose, and a massive double chin—stood gloating over Malone.

He pointed back up the street, at Trudi's corpse. "The little bitch got what was coming to her. She should never have picked my pockets and stolen the ring from me. Lilith has been giving me hell ever since."

"You're about to go join Trudi," Malone said coldly. "Believe it."

The vampire laughed. "I, Vermyn?" He reached down and, with seemingly no effort, yanked Malone to his feet; held him upright with a hand wrapped around his neck. "No, human garbage! *You* are going to join your thieving girlfriend in Hell. You'll have no mercy from me—I saw you kill my brother!"

Malone figured Vermyn's brother was the bat he'd shot outside Graveyard. It didn't matter; what did was that this piece-of-shit vampire had killed Trudi Carmen, whom he'd loved, and the son-of-a-bitch was about dying himself, even if Malone had no idea how to dispatch him yet. (Apparently getting shot here in Genesis didn't harm vampires too badly.)

Vermyn said, "Where is the ring? I must have it." The fat man again peered up the street at Trudi's headless body.

Malone laughed grimly. "I don't have it, butterball, and neither does she."

Vermyn tightened his grip around Malone's throat. "Don't lie to me, you scum, or I'll rip your head off just like I did hers."

"Okay, you win," Malone said, a plan forming in his mind. "She did have it, only she was wearing it as a nose ring. It fell down a hole along with her head."

"Where!!?" Vermyn yelled, then, not bothering to wait for Malone's reply, demanded, "Show me the hole!" and dragged him along the street by his neck.

Malone went willingly, and not just because he knew Vermyn could snap his neck like a twig if he chose to. It was imperative that Malone get over beside the freezers that the caterpillar-creature had thrown down from the third floor. He needed something he'd seen there. He knew there was no way the vampire Vermyn would dare kill him now he'd admitted to having the white ring; the fat man gave Malone the impression he was scared of Lilith Nightfall.

They reached Trudi's body. Avoiding looking at her remains, Malone pointed to the hole. "Her head rolled in there. It's up to you to get it out."

Vermyn stared at the hole, his piggish face pinched up in thought. Malone felt the vampire's confusion over what to do now, felt the fingers around his neck loosen their chokehold.

Moving like lightning, he slipped his neck free. Then, employing a judo throw, he flung Vermyn forward into a storefront pillar. At the loud crack of the vampire's head hitting concrete, he turned and ran across the street towards the discarded freezers, praying that the caterpillar-thing wouldn't choose this moment to start discarding more 'junk.'

His luck held. He quickly located what he was after: a bit of loose metal he'd noticed after the first freezer had burst apart. It was long and sharp, and most important, had a thick flat crosspiece three inches from one end. Malone grabbed up the makeshift cross and headed back across the street.

Vermyn (who'd been stunned by his impact with the pillar) was just getting to his feet when Malone reached him.

"You're going to pay for that, you piece of human shit," the fat vampire sputtered. "I'm going to make your days a living hell. I'll—"

"In the name of the Father, the Son, and the Holy Ghost I condemn you to Hell!" Malone growled, slamming the makeshift cross into the vampire's chest. His intense rage gave him the strength he needed to drive the point of the metal between Vermyn's ribs and deep into his heart. Or maybe it was something more, something *divine*: Malone was aware of the cross, immediately it touched the vampire's body, becoming hot in his grasp and of blue fire flaring up at its tip just before it punctured the gray suit.

On being staked, Vermyn's fat face took on an expression of the most intense surprise. "I . . . I . . . I . . ." was all he could stutter, his double chin wobbling like an intelligent creature. Then, gripping the crosspiece of the metal sticking from his heart as if to remove it, he fell forward onto it, ironically driving the cross all the way through his body instead.

Vermyn stopped moving. His body instantly began to rot and decompose, turning to earth and worms. Its job done, the makeshift cross toppled over and slid off the sidewalk, vanishing down the same hole that had previously swallowed Trudi's head.

Malone winced on losing the weapon, then he spat on the disintegrating vampire. "Screw you, asshole. And that goes for the rest of you abstractive monsters too."

He stood there till all that remained of the vampire Vermyn was evaporating ash, then he heaved Trudi's headless body up over his right shoulder and proceeded down the street again.

Behind him, the caterpillar resumed dumping things from its hole.

Malone would have liked to take Trudi's head along too, but it was likely lost somewhere down in the sewers, dinner for Genesis's rats. His destination, St. Peter's, was a church; hopefully he'd be able to bury Trudi Carmen there with some dignity. He felt she deserved that much.

And before that, there was the matter of retrieving the stone ring she had in her belly to attend to.

Bud Malone was weeping profusely as he made his way towards Cherry Street.

CHAPTER 20

Lilith / Le Bleach

With a pleased expression, Le Bleach swung open the dungeon door. "Here he is, Lilith."

The old priest lay on his back on a pallet in the middle of the room. The pallet was splattered with his blood. At the noise of the cell door opening, he looked towards the two entering vampire women. Both women were still naked, both had leering grins on their faces.

Whimpering sounds issued from the priest's lips. He was unable to speak because Diana Le Bleach had sewn his mouth shut with fishing line. Blood covered his swollen lips, lines of it had run down his naked body and congealed in the white hair on his chest.

Le Bleach had fucked the priest up big time. She'd also broken both his arms above the elbows so he couldn't make the sign of the cross at them. Both arms were now queerly bent; it was impossible for the priest to move them at all. Even bending his fingers made him flinch in agony. His ankles she'd cuffed together.

"Good job," Lilith remarked. She sat by the priest on his pallet and stroked his bald head, greatly amused by the dread of her in the man's sky-blue eyes. "I wonder what you were doing in my realm, old man." She turned to Le Bleach. "Did he say anything?"

"I never gave him a chance to. I just knocked him out. Then I stitched his mouth shut so he couldn't curse us."

"Mmm. Where'd you find him?"

"He was standing at the Norton and Cherry Street corner looking around like he was expecting someone."

"Cherry Street? That's where St. Peter's is, right?"

Le Bleach nodded. "One of the last churches in the area that we've not yet desecrated," she said in an angry voice.

Lilith smiled coldly. "You take things too seriously, Diana. Maybe I should fuck your ass again; that should help you loosen up."

Le Bleach quailed at the suggestion. Lilith Nightfall laughed. "I was only joking, darling." Then she turned to the priest. "Or maybe Father Asshole here would like to watch me fuck *your* asshole. Would you, Father?"

The old man, sweat beading on his forehead from the agony of his broken arms and sewn-together lips, nonetheless vehemently shook his head.

Laughing some more, Lilith turned back to Le Bleach. "But seriously, Diana, lighten up; vampire life consists of more than simply blaspheming God."

"Like what?"

Lilith was about retorting, then she saw a funny side to the question. "You're right, there. Where's the Bible you said he had?"

Le Bleach searched through the old man's things, which were piled in a corner. Lips curled in disgust, she held the thick Holy Book up for Lilith to see. "Here."

Lilith looked up from painfully squeezing the priest's withered penis. She looked first at Le Bleach and the Bible, then at the naked old man. "I bet you don't know what we're going to do now?" she asked him.

The priest began shaking his head fervently. "Hmmm!! Hmmm!!" His attempts to speak caused the fishing line to tear up his lips afresh so fresh blood spurted from their punctures.

Lilith smiled. "So you do know, huh?" She got up off the pallet then gestured to her companion. "Alright, Diana, do it."

After handing the Bible to Lilith, Diana Le Bleach walked over to the priest and squatted astride his chest. She winked at his dismayed expression. "Lucky for us both that Lilith just widened up my ass, eh? Now I've no problem shitting on you."

With that statement, she began defecating on the old man, gripping her knees as her anus puckered to pump out jets of dark watery feces that dripped off his sides onto the bed. The priest initially thrashed in resistance, but the effort merely caused his shattered left humerus to rip out through his bicep. The blood flowed freely; the priest ceased his struggling.

"We're vampires," Lilith commented drolly, "living on a completely liquid diet like we do, one must expect our excrement to be watery."

Le Bleach continued pooping on the priest. When she was done his chest was a complete mess. Then, while not taking her gaze from the priest's horrified eyes, she stretched out a hand to Lilith. "Toilet paper please, honey."

Lilith ripped out several Bible pages and handed them to Le Bleach. "These enough, Diana?"

"I'll need more." Leering at the priest, she spread her ass cheeks and wiped her anus with the Bible pages, front-to-back, then discarded them by the old man's head. The priest began weeping, tears of outrage spurting from his eyes.

Le Bleach laughed at his appalled horror, then extended her hand to Lilith. "More toilet paper, please."

"Any particular gospel of crap you'd prefer?"

"John. I've always hated that poop about God loving the world and sending his only Son."

Lilith ripped out half of the Gospel of John and handed it to Le Bleach, who rubbed the pages of God's Word between her buttocks till they were smeared a dark brown. By now the old priest was weeping copiously; the tears were flooding down his face. Le Bleach shook the shit-smeared Bible pages at him. "This is what we think of your fucking God—of all gods! Get it!?"

She dropped the pages into the pile of shit on the priest's chest, then stood up from her crouch. She walked over and kissed Lilith. Then they both stood laughing at the priest, who now, coated with excrement and besmirched Bible pages, and with blood bubbling from his stitched mouth, looked a pathetic, ridiculous sight. And he was still crying.

"You're right, Diana," Lilith Nightfall said. "Blaspheming God is so much fun." She waved the Bible at Le Bleach. "Are you certain your ass is clean enough now?"

Le Bleach pretended to think awhile, then she shook her head and took the Bible from Lilith. "Just one more wipe." She rubbed the entire Bible in her crack, then walked over and dropped it in the pool of her shit.

She smiled back innocently at Lilith. "I'm good now, hon. Nice and cleansed of my sins."

"Ah, you're so much fun," Lilith said. She pointed at the priest. "Let's drink him now. All this pleasure has gotten me thirsty."

Le Bleach mused. "I was thinking of waiting till later, when Vermyn gets back. But you're the boss."

They advanced on the old priest, who, realizing that his life was being threatened, made a valiant attempt to get away from them. All he succeeded in doing, however, was flipping himself over on the pallet so he lay on his belly. And now he began moaning in absolute agony—his attempt at flight had folded his left arm under him at its fracture point. Four inches of red bone stuck out from the wound, dripping blood onto the floor.

"Nice of him to turn over for us," Lilith said. "Now I don't have to look at your poop while eating."

Both vampires regarded the weeping priest for a moment. "You know where I want to bite him?" Lilith asked.

Le Bleach shook her head.

"His withered old ass."

As the priest thrashed in pain, the two vampire women knelt on either side of him and sank their fangs deep into his buttocks. Teeth anchored in his gluteal muscles, they drank long and deep, reveling at the taste of the sweet blood on their tongues, of its silky feel as it swept down their throats, at how delightfully filled they were by even the slightest draught of it. Yes, a priest's blood was so satisfying, so much better than a sinner's, if only because they knew how angry the Almighty was to see one of his workers slain.

The blood stained their lips and chins, ran down their necks onto their naked breasts.

Finally, the vampires sat back on their heels.

"He was really tasty," Le Bleach said.

The priest was now completely emptied of blood and they were both sated, their thirst fully slaked. And now it was simply a joy to watch the old man's corpse fall apart, to view it dissolving as the enzymes in their spittle digested him.

It didn't take long. In a few minutes all that remained of the priest was a pale brown mess with bone fragments floating on it.

"God definitely needs tougher workers," Le Bleach said. "It's hard to tell this one apart from my crap."

Laughing, Lilith Nightfall stood up then pulled Diana Le Bleach to her feet also. "Come," she said, "let's check out Cherry Street and that church again. Maybe there's another cassocked asshole there that we can catch for dinner."

They left the dungeon, changed their form to that of bats, and took to the evening skies over Genesis.

CHAPTER 21

Malone

Almost at St. Peter's, Malone came upon the corpse of a priest who'd been impaled on a spear. The body was right there in the middle of the road.

Malone stopped and stared. Coming right on the heels of Trudi Carmen's death, he was doubly shocked by what he saw.

The dead priest's lips had been sewn together with fishing line, forming a puffy mess in the lower half of his face. In addition, he had no eyes: they'd been plucked out of his face, leaving red pits. He was standing upright: the spear's blunt rear end was fixed in the concrete between his feet; its sharp metal tip was buried somewhere deep inside his body. The lower half of his robe had been cut away to expose his buttocks and genitals. There was a deep gash in the left side of the man's neck, and very little blood on the spear's wooden shaft where it exited his anus.

The body had been treated in some way; it wasn't decaying.

Standing there with Trudi's headless corpse slung over his shoulder (such was his grief over her passing that it seemed like she weighed nothing) Malone coldly regarded this fresh horror. He concluded that the vampires must have first drained out the priest's blood for sustenance before impaling him; the murder had likely occurred over at their castle. Placing the body near a church was simply their warning to others.

Leaving the dead man behind, Malone trudged on with his morbid burden. To Malone, this priest was merely an additional nail in the vampires' coffins. In his mind he'd already decided their fate: no matter what it took, he was ridding the world of the pestilential creatures. Two down, two to go.

Still, he felt uneasy now over having lost the cross he'd staked Vermyn with down the storm drain back there. If he encountered another vampire . . .

He reached St. Peter's Cathedral without incident. He was laughing grimly to himself as he pushed open its wrought iron gate and walked through the withered surrounding hedge.

The score to be settled was rising. The abstractive vampires had now killed *two* of Malone's lovers. Lilith Nightfall had utter hell to pay. And Malone intended collecting on the Devil's behalf.

He crossed the Cathedral's front yard, ascended its front steps, and knocked on the huge wooden entrance doors.

At first there was no response. Then a gruff male voice asked, "Who the hell is that?"

"Bud Malone from Boston. I'm here to see Elton Jones."

CHAPTER 22

Lilith / Le Bleach

Unknown to Bud Malone, Lilith Nightfall and Diana Le Bleach were at that moment watching him from directly across the street. They'd been flying down Main Street when the sweet smell of Trudi's blood had diverted them this way.

Now, perched on the roof of the house opposite St. Peter's, both vampire bats transformed back into human form so they could converse. Both women now wore shiny black leather outfits and red shoes that wouldn't be out of place in a nightclub.

"Shit!" Le Bleach whispered angrily. "We got here too late—he's almost inside the church now." When Lilith didn't reply, she added, "I told you we should have desecrated this stupid church, but no, you said. Now he's safe. We won't catch him before he—"

"Shut up, Diana!" Lilith snapped. "We've bigger problems now than mere food."

Le Bleach looked at her in surprise. "But you said—" Then she saw that Lilith was laughing. "What's funny?"

Lilith held up her right hand. The previously black ring on its middle finger was now flashing an odd zebra-crossing color. She pointed to Malone with his headless female burden. "Don't you get it, Diana? He's the one we're looking for—he's got the other dead ring on him!"

Le Bleach's eyes widened in understanding. "Oh, oh!"

At that moment, Malone was admitted into St. Peter's Cathedral and the doors shut behind him. The sound of their closing echoed across to the vampires.

"Interesting," Lilith said softly, "there's more than one person in the church."

Le Bleach frowned. "What do we do now, Lilith? You know there's no way we can get inside there."

Lilith scowled back. "Don't be so pessimistic, Diana. There's always a way to get what one wants, particularly when one wants it badly enough." She turned away from Le Bleach, fixing her black gaze on St. Peter's. "And at the moment, nothing is more important than our getting the white ring from that man inside the cathedral."

CHAPTER 23

Malone

The first thing Malone noticed once through the cathedral doors was the massive combat helicopter being assembled inside it. All the left side pews were stacked up high by the wall, creating space for the chopper, four aircraft engineers, and their crates of equipment.

"How long have you been working on it?" he asked the squat, heavily-armed man who'd let him into the building. The black helicopter was three-quarters finished now, its roof propellers and guns in place, and Malone could see that the construction crew were currently securing one of its fuel tanks in place.

"Three days," the man replied. Whatever suspicions he'd initially harbored about Malone's sudden appearance at the church doors had vanished once he'd seen the corpse slung over his shoulder. "Please follow me," he added, pointing towards the altar. "Mr. Jones is waiting."

They proceeded down the nave to the front of the church, where Elton Jones stood amidst a group of people dressed in combat gear.

Elton Jones was a muscular man with dark crew cut hair. He and his companions all had guns holstered at their hips.

Elton's companions were a motley bunch. Three women, three men, all unified by the coldness of the gaze with which they regarded Malone. None had guns drawn, but Malone had no illusions that if he made the slightest wrong move in here, he'd be shot dead in an instant.

Elton Jones scowled at Malone. There was no welcome in his eyes. "Who are you, and what do you want here?"

"Hold on a moment; I need to lay my burden down at the Lord's feet." Moving slowly and deliberately, Malone laid out Trudi's body on the foremost right side pew. Because he'd been carrying her with her legs in front of him, it was only now that Elton and his companions realized she'd been decapitated. Several startled female gasps sounded behind Malone. He straightened up to discover one of the women—a tall handsome blonde—staring at him in horror, her fingers over her lips. The others clearly had no idea what to make of him now.

"Who is that?" Elton Jones asked.

"My girlfriend Trudi."

Elton's eyes widened. "Trudi Carmen? What happened to her?"

"Vampires, man." Malone sat down beside the body. "I've had a fucking long day, Elton. Crystal Baller sent me and Trudi to you; only Vermyn jumped us."

Elton's eyes narrowed. In an involuntary reflex, his hand moved to the gun at his waist. "Vermyn? Where is he now?"

Malone shrugged. "Hell, I guess. The fat SOB won't be jumping anyone else from now on."

Everyone's eyes reflected Elton's surprise. "He's dead?"

"He won't be cashing any vampire disability checks, that's for sure."

The gathered women and men gawked at Malone. "Just three more to go now then," the tall blonde said.

"Two," Malone corrected. "I had to dispatch one more back at Graveyard. Vermyn said it was his brother."

"Zander? You killed Zander too?"

Malone shrugged again. "He never told me his name, I didn't ask. But he and Vermyn should be holding their family reunion right about now." He knew he was coming off as too nonchalant, but he didn't care. It wasn't a pose; he really didn't care: too much had been stolen from him at short notice. His initial burning rage had faded now, to be replaced by an emotional vacancy, like his heart was a house without a tenant.

He pointed to Trudi's body. "The vampires deserved what they got."

Elton Jones finally got over his new-found awe of Malone. He said, "Here we are planning to storm Vampire Castle and kill all those monsters and you've gone and done half the work for us."

"Trust me, if I'd know you'd be upset I'd have saved Vermyn for you."

The tall blonde was now regarding Malone with intense interest in her gray eyes. He recognized the look, but having just lost two girlfriends to death, he had no desire to quickly acquire another.

There was a long silence, with everyone just watching Malone. Realizing Elton Jones was currently lost for words, Malone commandeered the situation. In situations like this it was better to be in the driver's seat than to be someone else's passenger.

He made an expansive gesture. "Ladies and gents, please pull your chairs up close, I've quite a strange tale to tell you."

Elton's unit all looked at him, their faces seeking his approval.

He nodded. "Do like the man says."

***

Everyone pulled up crates and boxes to sit on. There were stacks of these on the left of the altar. Some were clearly marked as supplies of food and water; others (the majority) held weapons. One opened crate was chock-full of grenades, another contained a mortar. Malone also noted a stack of rocket launcher cases.

He was impressed. Elton Jones wasn't about taking prisoners. In Malone's estimation, there was sufficient armament and explosive in here to level five cathedrals to rubble.

The tall blonde sat directly opposite him, on a chair brought down from the altar platform. She pointed nervously to Trudi's body. "Can we move her? It's distracting—her lying there like that."

Malone nodded. "Yeah, sure. Where should I put her?" He made to get up.

Elton shook his head at Malone. "Keep your seat, man." He nodded to two of his men. "You guys, put her up in the vestry."

As Trudi's headless corpse was borne off out of sight (to the tall blonde's clear relief), Elton asked Malone, "Why'd you bring her body along anyway?"

Malone had to laugh. "You'll understand once I explain what I'm doing here."

He told his story to his rapt semicircle of listeners.

Behind their huddled group, the engineers continued assembling their assault helicopter.

CHAPTER 24

Lilith / Le Bleach

Lilith and Le Bleach were still watching St. Peter's from across the street. Both sat on the edge of the opposite rooftop, their feet dangling in space.

Le Bleach said, "Should we look for Vermyn and ask him what he thinks?"

"Vermyn is dead, I sensed it while we were flying over here."

"What!? Dead? How?"

"Let's put that aside for the moment; we'll investigate it later." Lilith's brow furrowed. "You see now why it's imperative that we get that ring?"

"I never argued otherwise."

"Your expression often did. But try to get it—until we're all-powerful, we're vulnerable."

"Yes, I understand that now."

"I must have that ring at any cost, Diana, even if it requires destroying this entire city of Genesis."

Le Bleach shuddered at the intense desperation in Lilith's voice. For the first time it occurred to her that there might be such a place as 'too far' in her mistress and lover's quest to attain ultimate power over the human world. *True, unturned humans—just like cows—are a lesser life form than we vampires, but that doesn't mean they don't deserve to live, does it? At the very least, animal rights should apply here. Such wholesale slaughter as Lilith plans is simply wrong!*

But then, she shrugged all such qualms off. Such thoughts—of empathy and compassion—were nothing but pathetic weakness, totally unfitting for the soul of an abstractive vampire. *The universe is for those who take what they want. And Lilith is taking, and I,*

Diana Le Bleach, will stand by her side all the way to Hell and back and take along with her!

She frowned. *What is important now is entering that damned church and pulling out that man. Then taking the white ring from him and drinking his blood. And God help him if he's a priest: I'll pluck out his eyes and shit in their sockets!*

But . . . Lilith didn't raise the topic, and Le Bleach didn't mention it, but Le Bleach was worried. What was the man with the white ring doing here? Could he be hunting them? Was he the same person who'd killed Zander? And if truly Vermyn was also dead now, had this same man murdered him too? And one last thing: She stared at the ring on Lilith's right hand, which still maintained its new zebra pattern. *If we can sense his ring, surely he can sense ours?*

These unshared thoughts considerably dampened Le Bleach's spirits.

They sat there a short while longer, Lilith with delighted anticipation that the ring was within her reach, Le Bleach with her sudden worries over their mortality and vulnerability.

Then suddenly, Lilith smiled into Le Bleach's glum face. "Don't worry, Diana. True, *we* can't get into the church, but I believe we know someone who *can*."

"Who?"

"Duke Norgem of Hedaye owes me many favors."

"The Voodoo Controller?"

"Yes, him. He may be able to help us out of this mess."

Lilith leaned over and kissed Le Bleach, then she got to her feet. "I'm going back to the castle to consult with the Duke. You keep watch here to make sure no one gets away." She stroked Le Bleach's blonde hair. "Most important, darling, ensure that you're not seen."

Lilith transformed into bat form and flapped away into the evening skies.

Feeling slightly better now they had a plan, Diana Le Bleach resumed her vigil.

CHAPTER 25

Malone

Starting right at the beginning, it took Malone quite a while to get to the end of his tale. Frequent questioning from his listeners extended his narration even further.

"Are you sure no one saw you enter here?" the tall blond woman asked afterward. Her name, he now knew, was Clair Stevens, and she was Elton Jones's right hand woman. Judging from the way she kept looking at Malone, she wasn't Elton's girlfriend, just his second-in-command.

"I don't think so," Malone replied. Then, gesturing back toward the team building the helicopter, he asked Elton, "I take it that once the chopper's finished, you'll be ready to move in on the vamps?"

Elton shook his head angrily. "Not unless Father Renato turns up."

"Who's he?"

Elton looked too pissed-off to answer, so Clair Stevens replied for him. "Our priest," she explained to Malone. "He went missing yesterday evening."

One of the men who'd removed Trudi's body to the vestry spat in disgust. "It was that blasted mutt of his. I mean, who the hell ever heard of someone taking a dog on a vampire hunt?"

The other women and men nodded angry agreement. Elton still wasn't saying anything, so Malone looked to Clair to explain further.

She shrugged. "They're right. Father Renato had this mongrel, Poncho, that he took everywhere with him. He utterly loved that dog. We didn't want him to bring it along, but . . ." she gestured at Elton, "even his favorite nephew couldn't stop him."

Malone looked at Elton, who nodded angrily back. "Yes, yes, he's my uncle."

Clair continued: "So he brought Poncho along. It was okay, really; the dog was less trouble than we'd imagined."

"Until yesterday afternoon when it vanished," a muscular brunette added. "It was gone like it had smelt a bitch in heat."

"Yes," Clair agreed softly, flicking hair off her face. "Until yesterday. Poncho went missing and Father Renato went ballistic. The old guy wouldn't listen to reason. Despite the obvious dangers, he insisted he was going out looking for his dog."

"I locked him in the vestry," Elton said, "but next thing I know, he's somehow escaped and left the cathedral to go find Poncho."

"He never came back," Clair finished glumly. "So now, we're in a huge fix. Without a priest, any assault we make on Vampire Castle is as assured of failure as it is of success."

"There's a priest impaled in the middle of the road outside," Malone offered. "You're sure that's not Father Renato?"

"The guy with his mouth sewn up tight?" Clair shook her head. "No, that body was there when we arrived. We left it alone so the vampires wouldn't suspect they had neighbors."

(Malone had mentioned the dead rings, but neither Elton nor Clair thought them a major issue. After Malone explained why he'd brought Trudi's corpse along with him, Clair had said, "I understand how you want justice for your girlfriend and the murdered women, but the rings aren't dangerous until they're combined, right? And since one of them is here with you . . . with us . . . for the moment it's neutral and we can reasonably rule both of them out of the equation." Elton and the others shared Clair's opinion. Malone had grudgingly conceded their point.)

"But . . ." he gestured around at the piled armament, "what's this whole deal about needing a priest to take on Lilith, anyway? I killed two of her vampires in hand-to-hand combat, and there's more of you, and you've lots of weapons. Guys, there's *only two* of them left now."

"It's not that simple, Malone," Elton Jones said. "Le Bleach we can handle—"

"Le Bleach?"

Clair, her face twisted up in disgust, said, "Diana Le Bleach, the other surviving abstractive."

Malone nodded to Elton. "Sorry I interrupted; please go on."

Elton said, "Le Bleach is something of a vampire scatterbrain, small fry. But Lilith Nightfall? She's another pit of snakes altogether. She's stronger and smarter than all the others combined."

Clair said, "And, Malone, we're going to fight them at Vampire Castle. In their stronghold, even stupid Le Bleach will be a huge threat to us." She nodded towards the ongoing helicopter construction, where the engineers were now bolting on the vehicle's rear propellers. "We intended going up by air and blowing Vampire Castle to bits; we planned to completely demolish it. That would have forced the vampires to attack us in bat form in the sky, then we could take them out with our weapons."

"Bullets didn't hurt Vermyn much here in Genesis," Malone pointed out.

Elton winced. "So now you get why we need a holy man or holy woman to bless our weapons and curse the vampires. My uncle was supposed to sanctify everything today, once the chopper was ready. And now he's gone. Shit—the vampires have likely got him."

"He hadn't even blessed the water yet," Clair Stevens said angrily, pointing over at two huge bottles beside the altar. "If we had holy water we could still chance an old-school attack with crosses and stakes, but no, he kept playing with his dog."

"And without holy water we've no way of ensuring Lilith will stay dead," a bearded man said. "We need it to consecrate the castle ruins so she can't come back. She's way too powerful to take chances with. It'll be a complete waste of time to kill her then have her resurrect again once we leave."

"We're just about packing it in here," Elton said. "If my uncle doesn't return, we'll leave the chopper hidden here in the church, head back east, and return with another priest in tow."

"There must be a way to do this without a priest," Malone said.

"Trust me, we've been trying to figure one out all day long," Elton said. "We're not cowards; we'll gladly risk our lives against the vampires with just crosses and stakes." He gestured around at the nodding cold-faced people seated about Malone. "All of us here have lost close family—parents, spouses, and children—to Lilith's foul gang. So we'll fight them to our last breaths, if our death assures their destruction." He exhaled loudly. "But none of us intend dying pointlessly."

"We're open to suggestions," Clair added. The other women and men nodded their grim agreement.

Malone was aware of the eight sets of eyes on him while he pondered this dilemma. It was a strange one. He felt Elton and his unit were being overly superstitious about the need for a priest to bless their weapons, but whether they were or not, they were clearly dead serious about it: they weren't about moving against the vampires without a holy man in tow. *Okay,* he thought, y*es, I killed two vampires, but I didn't kill them inside Vampire Castle, so I really don't know what it's like up there. But . . . Crystal Baller said I'd find a priest to help me when I needed one; but Elton's uncle has gone missing and is likely completely drained of blood by now, so she must have meant someone else . . .*

He decided to say nothing to Elton about the priest Crystal had mentioned. Not until he knew for certain where the man was. The goddess's words at least assured him that there was a priest close by and that he'd show up before matters got out of hand. So now it was a waiting game. Except for one thing:

"You'll have to move soon," he told Elton. "The longer you wait here the more chance there is of the vampires discovering your hideout."

Elton Jones smiled coldly. "There's little danger of them attacking the church; they're terrified of infecting themselves with something holy. We'll wait a day more for Uncle Renato to show up, then pull out."

A loud explosion sounded then, startling everyone. Malone first thought one of the crates of explosives had exploded, but a quick look back over his shoulder revealed otherwise.

Part of the left side of the rear cathedral wall was collapsing inward.

"What in God's name are those things!?" Clair Stevens gasped as huge red monsters stalked into the church.

CHAPTER 26

Malone

Malone gaped at the horrible monsters ripping away the rear portion of St. Peter's Cathedral. He instantly recognized them.

"What are those things?" Clair Stevens asked again.

"They're golems; meat robots," Malone replied drily. "We've got the fight of our lives ahead of us now."

Eight of the golems had so far stepped into the church and more were tearing away stone and metal to make passage for themselves. Each golem was about twelve feet tall and made of rotting meat, the cloying smell of which preceded them. Their bodies seemed cobbled together from whatever carcasses had lain closest to hand during their creation—human, reptile, cow, horse . . . In places their myriad of flesh parts were joined by bolts, at others by stitches. Other parts were connected by thick seams of fat. Most of the golems had no facial features other than yawning tooth-filled maws. All had long claws of fractured bone on hand and foot.

"Think they followed you here?" Clair asked. She and the others had already pulled their guns.

"I don't see how they could have—I'm sure I'd have noticed them walking behind me. They must have been shipped into Genesis by Lilith." He scowled. "Golems are neither holy nor unholy, neither alive nor dead—they're just automata, animated meat with no mind of its own. As such, they can't harmed by Christian ritual or blessed objects."

Those golems already in the church stood looking around as if trying to make up their minds what to do. Most had roughly human shapes, but some looked like animals, and others looked like insects or lobsters. And several of the human-shaped ones had the wrong number of limbs. They made no noise other than the sound of motion.

From their point of entry, Malone figured the golems were coming in from the street. The cathedral's stained-glass windows however prevented clear view of the outside.

Walking with a lumbering 'zombie' gait, a group of the huge golems headed for the helicopter. The construction crew began shooting at them. The meat robots staggered as chunks of flesh were blown off their bodies, but continued forward regardless.

"How do we stop them?" Elton Jones asked.

"Fire's our best bet," Malone replied. "Rockets and grenades would blow them to bits too, but they can repair themselves, and there's also the risk of the rockets bringing the building down on our heads."

"Hell," Elton said, wincing as a golem ripped the head off one of his helicopter engineers. Then his eyes widened in disbelief as the golem shredded the man's corpse, pushing each removed body part into its own horrible mass, making itself bigger. It stuck the dead man's arms into its chest, where they instantly began flexing as if alive.

"Shit!" Clair said, her body trembling against Malone's. "No way am I becoming one of those things when I die."

"Me neither," Elton seconded her. He spun around and began barking orders to his unit: "Andy, Brooke, Davy . . . you guys break out the damn flamethrowers! Tom, Mike, and Lucy—you three come help me unpack the rocket launchers! Clair and Malone, you come along too." He looked over at the chopper again, wincing as another engineer was caught—this one by *two* golems—and pulled apart in midair so his entrails fell out like spilled pie contents. His corpse too was immediately added and assimilated into the bodies of the monsters that had killed him. Elton, his face white with inexpressible dread, yelled, "Go! Go!" and dashed off towards the weapons stocks.

Malone and Clair ran after Elton. Each of them grabbed a rocket launcher. Then, carrying a crate of rockets between them, they hurried back across to the right of the altar, where the rows of church pews had so far prevented the golems from coming forward.

Once back in front of the foremost pews, Malone shouldered his rocket launcher and sighted on the advancing horde, though 'sighted' was a misleading term, as the golems had now filled the rear of the church. They were so packed in there, it would be impossible to miss hitting them. The helicopter was now hidden from view by a twelve foot high fence of meat.

Malone fired simultaneously with two men across the hall. The shells whizzed through the church and slammed into the walking mass of animated meat.

The front row of golems blew apart. Chunks of meat flew everywhere. A dog's rear leg landed on the pew in front of Malone. It kicked once then was still.

"We got 'em," Clair said.

"Watch," Malone cautioned. He'd now realized that she intended sticking beside him. Oddly, he found her presence comforting, a salve to his battered emotions. (He also suspected that the ring in Trudi Carmen's corpse was how the vampires had found them and launched this attack on the church. He grimaced. *And Elton and Clair thought it was unimportant?* He looked back, up beyond the pulpit, toward the vestry. It was utterly imperative that nothing got in there.)

Clair watched like Malone had instructed, and next, astonished, covered her mouth with fingers. "Oh, shit!"

The undamaged golems were picking up the scattered raw flesh of the exploded ones and adding it to their own bodies. One stuck a 'head' into its left forearm; the implanted head's massive jaws immediately began snapping above its new host's wrist. Another golem stuck two blown-off legs into its sides, then fell forward and began walking on them.

And still more of the raw meat monsters were pouring in from outside. Already they filled a third of the church. And now they surged forward.

"Fire, for God's sake!" Elton yelled. "Bring the rear of the building down on them!"

Rockets began streaking up at the cathedral ceiling with its fresco of Creation. Other rockets sped towards the rear support pillars. Large masses of concrete started dropping on the golems and flattening them.

Clair looked worriedly at Malone. "If he does that . . ."

Malone nodded back at her, then turned and yelled to Elton. "Wait till they're all inside!"

"We don't know how many there are!"

"That's the point! At the moment they're only coming in through the rear! Don't open up any more holes!"

Elton angrily called a halt to the bombardment, then yelled over at Malone. "So what do we do now!"

"Try frying them!" Clair yelled back at him. "We'll shoot them first; then Andy, Brooke, and Dave can roast their remains!"

The plan was put into effect, a fresh wave of rockets launched at the golems. All Elton's fighters had strained faces. Women and men, their eyes bugged out with fear. They knew they were fighting for more than just their lives here. Like Elton and Clair had stated unequivocally, being torn up after death and made into parts of a mindless meat robot seemed worse than death itself. The possibility of their suffering that fate had them all scared shitless.

Malone reloaded his rocket launcher and let fly. Beside him, Clair Stevens did the same. The golems blew apart on cue, and then the flamethrowers went into action, drenching the golems in liquid sheets of fire. Smoke filled the church; the stink of burning meat filled everyone's nostrils. The crackle and pop of sizzling golem flesh mingled with their unhuman noises.

Malone dropped his rocket launcher on the front pew.

"I'm going upstairs," he told Clair, pointing up at the cathedral balcony. "I need to see how many of these monsters we're dealing with."

"I'm coming with you," she said, laying down her own weapon.

Malone looked at her closely. Her handsome face was taut with strain; she seemed right on the verge of cracking up. "We'll have to go through the golems," he pointed out.

"I'm coming with you," she repeated.

"Alright," he agreed. "Let's go inform Elton. We'll need backing fire."

They ran across the nave of the church to where Elton's fighters were now barricaded in behind boxes of weaponry. The smoke had cleared a bit; they now saw that their 'bomb and fry' tactic had worked. Wide expanses of sputtering meat—several heaps—covered the left half of the middle of the cathedral. The meat hills were fixed in place by fat that had melted and congealed again. Also a large number of golems had become stuck to the floor by the combination of explosive and fire and were trying vainly to unstick their horrible wet bodies. Behind these, the next rank of meat robots stomped in voiceless frustration.

Elton raised a hand, signaling his fighters to cease their bombardment. "That's held them for the moment," he told Malone with satisfaction. "What now?"

Malone explained what he had in mind. He pointed across the hall, at its right rear corner, where a spiral stairway led up to the balcony. A few golems lurked there, forced out of the general advance by pressure of numbers and unable to work out that if they destroyed the right-side pews they'd have free access to the front of the church. "I need you to clear a path through those ones with rocket fire. Also, do you have any small bombs or IEDs?"

"Yeah, sure, we brought some for the chopper. We were going to drop them on Vampire Castle." He gave Malone a searching look. "What do you intend doing with them?"

"There has to be an OD outside the front door through which the golems are arriving here. It's the only explanation why they're all still coming in that way. If I can block it off, we should be able to cook all these ones in here."

Elton nodded solemnly. "You're a good fighter, Malone. Okay, Clair, get out the bombs for Malone." He turned to his fighters and began issuing instructions.

Clair and Malone got out two bombs, dark green two-foot-long tubes marked USAF and having both a digital timer and a red detonation switch halfway along their length.

Each carrying one, they dashed back across to the right side of the church and began climbing over the pews, heading for the rear of the building, the dispersing smoke affording them partial cover. (Running along beside the right wall would have been easier, but someone had piled hymnbooks and candlesticks at that part of the front of the church.) On their right, the golems had now begun clearing a way forward through the impasse in the most grisly of ways: by ripping apart those of their fellows who'd gotten stuck and making them part of their own bodies.

Shuddering at the sight, Clair said, "I don't see why they don't just move the pews to get around them."

"They're mindless," Malone educated her.

"If they're mindless, who's controlling them?"

"There'll be a voodoo controller somewhere pulling all their strings. If we could locate and kill that person, this attack would instantly end. But trust me, the voodoo controller is likely back wherever the golems originated from."

They were now almost at the rear of the church, taking temporary refuge in a side alley between rows of pews, one closed off from the golem attack by a hill of melded and smoking body parts at its far end. Their destination was directly ahead, but obscured by a press of gory wet bodies with no true rhyme or reason to their obscene construction. (Clair was gagging at the sight of the golems up close.)

Malone and Clair ducked to the ground by the church wall, then Malone waved his hands back at Elton.

A flurry of rockets smashed into the golems by the stairs, filling the air with smoking chunks of their randomly assembled flesh.

"Let's go!" Malone said.

Bombs clasped tight, he and Clair leapt up and dashed along between the end of the pews and the wall, past the scattered bits of raw meat, and up the stairs.

Behind them, the destroyed golems slowly put themselves back together again.

Once upstairs, Malone and Clair ran to the balcony's opposite end, where Malone pushed open a window and looked out.

"It's like I thought," he told the panting Clair. "Look!"

She looked. Just a few feet inside the cathedral gate, golems were emerging from a shimmering distortion of the air and making their way toward the front entrance. The building's walls shook as the new arrivals pulled the entrance apart in their haste to enter the church.

Look across the street," Clair said, pointing. "Up on the roof."

Malone's gaze followed her fingers. Up on the rooftop directly opposite, a thin blonde in black leather clothes and red shoes was waving to them.

"That's Diana Le Bleach," Clair said.

A wide grin clear on her face, Le Bleach turned into a huge brown vampire bat and flew off, speeding away from the cathedral.

"She's likely off to fuck Lilith in celebration of our passing," Clair said bitterly. "Which means Lilith is back at the castle conjuring this shit up." She regarded Malone with desperation in her gray eyes. Her hair was all mussed up, her face smudged with ash and concrete dust. "What do we do now?"

"We throw the bombs into the OD and get our asses back down to the altar."

Clair calculated the distance to the space-time portal. "That's too far for either of us to throw."

"Don't worry. Just prime them, I'll get them close enough." He grimaced. This OD had to be the one Crystal Baller had mentioned.

Clair laid one of the green tubes down on the windowsill and flipped open a panel beside its digital display. "How long should I set it for?"

"A minute. That's enough time to chuck them both out and still get the hell away from here."

"'Hell' is a good choice of word," Clair said while entering the detonation code into the bomb's timer. "Is that where you suppose this lot all come from?"

Malone stared at the golems packed around the church entrance (the wet and rotting heads of the foremost within easy reach of his fingers), as well as those still emerging from the shimmering portal. "Wherever they're from, it's clearly a place of murder and slaughter. Hell's as fitting a name as any."

Clair finished programming both bombs. She handed one to Malone. "Done—one minute each." She checked her watch, then tapped the bomb she'd given him. "Press the red switch and throw. There's no fail-safes if you miss."

Malone clicked the switch and flung the green tube out of the window toward the OD. It arched down, winding up stuck in a golem's chest. The meat robot gave no sign of noticing the metal intrusion in its front; it pressed forward against the others seeking entrance into the church.

"That's good enough," Malone said.

Clair handed him the second bomb; he lobbed that one too out of the window. This one went farther back, landing almost at the space-time portal. The bomb hit a golem on the head, spattering meat, then rolled off the monster's shoulders and down out of sight.

Malone turned to Clair. "Okay, now time to . . ." he began saying, then saw that she was looking away from him, back into the church, her fingers shaking by her mouth.

"Elton's in trouble . . ."

Malone ran past her to peer over the balcony rails. As he went he felt the church wall behind and below them give way, falling like the walls of Jericho to grant the golems free access into the cathedral. He reached the balcony, then watched as a relentless stream of walking, reeking meat surged forward toward the altar.

Yes, Elton Jones and the women and men with him *were* in trouble. They'd made the mistake of not retreating up onto the altar platform while they could. Now the golems had them cornered down by their weapons cache.

The only way to accurately pinpoint Elton's location was by noting the roughly circular area at the front of the church that the golems hadn't yet occupied.

And then, just as Malone figured that out, a fusillade of rockets streaked up out of the circular space toward the cathedral ceiling. Other rockets demolished support pillars.

Malone looked at Clair. All the color had now drained from her face.

"He's going to bring the roof down on the golems," she said as the ceiling vanished amidst a rain of smoke and plaster.

After a short pause, another upward fusillade of rockets confirmed her suspicions. In desperation, Elton Jones was going for broke.

Krakakakkk!!!!

The cathedral ceiling came down, covering the helicopter, the golems, and the pews in a wide swathe of shattered concrete. Following suit, both of the church's side walls collapsed inward. Orphaned support pillars stood like sentries amidst the wreckage.

Everything and everyone seemed to have been flattened; there was no sign of either the golems or of Elton and his unit. Malone and Clair were staring across a wide expanse of rusty church roof dotted with bird nests and bird shit, at the altar platform, the shrines with Madonna and Savior, and the rooms beyond. Above and outside, to the left and right of them, the late evening world looked in. Underneath the balcony, Malone heard the rumbling of those golems that had survived the falling roof.

Clair tugged his sleeve. "We're screwed, Malone," she said in a horrified voice.

He realized what she meant. They'd set their two bombs with one minute countdowns. One bomb was outside near the base of the OD, but the first one he'd thrown out was stuck in a golem's body . . . and that creature had to be inside the church now . . . at least partly inside. The fallen roof would have blocked off the bomb-bearing golem's advance, the pressure of newly-arrived monstrosities behind it meant it wouldn't be getting out again. And it could be anywhere under them.

Malone and Clair were trapped up on the balcony with nowhere to run and a bomb about to detonate under them.

Clair began staring at her watch.

"How long?" Malone asked. "How long!?"

"Five . . . four . . . three . . . two . . . one . . ."

Boom!!!

The balcony blew up around them. Still standing, Malone and Clair Stevens were flung through the air on a portion of balcony floor that had separated from the rest.

Malone held Clair tight as they shot forward over the fallen cathedral roof toward the wall behind the altar. He looked back once, saw that the entire balcony had been pulverized, then, looking forward again, said a silent prayer for the forgiveness of his sins as the approaching wall grew horribly close. He knew there was utterly no chance in hell of either of them surviving this. The chunk of balcony floor they stood on was already tilting under them, preparing to break their necks against the wall.

Hugging Clair tight to his chest, trying against all hope to shield her from death, Malone shut his eyes.

Next thing, the world went black. The last thing Malone heard was Clair exclaiming, "What the fuck!?"

CHAPTER 27

Lilith / Le Bleach

"Oh, you should have seen the fear on their faces," Le Bleach enthused. "Their fright was so delicious, I got wet between the legs."

Lilith Nightfall laughed. "Duke Norgem assured me that would be the case. His Macabre Army hasn't failed yet."

"But . . . there were *so many* golems."

"The duke has a endless supply of source material for his infernal workshops. He sacrifices his own citizens—their livestock and pets too—by the thousands and converts them into meat puppets."

"But that's utterly evil."

"I too approve entirely, Diana darling. Duke Norgem simply seeks to live up to his reputation in Hedaye."

"What do we now, Lilith?"

"We take our time. Once everyone's dead, the duke will personally desecrate St. Peter's for us and then we'll go look for the white ring among the ruins."

"But what if . . . ?"

"Enough talk, Diana. Take a good look at my vagina. See how wet and dripping it is? This pussy of mine is your church and your God, its secretion your holy water. Your God wants your reverence; now get on your knees like a faithful supplicant and worship it."

CHAPTER 28

Malone

Slowly the blackness cleared out of Malone's head. Surprised that he was still alive, he opened his eyes.

He was alone in a room, lying in a bed with his shirt off. The lights were off.

What the . . . ?

Memory exploded in his mind: he and Clair being flung through the air; the approaching wall of death . . . impact and blackout . . .

Death? *But no, I'm not dead, am I? So Clair and I must have escaped somehow. Some freak accident must have saved us . . . but . . . but where's Clair?*

Groggy, and with the beginning of what threatened to be a bad headache, Malone sat up and looked around at his surroundings.

The room was small and dirty, a wooden shanty with a rusted tin roof. What dim lighting there was at the moment came from the myriads of pin pricks dotting the roof. A rickety chair stood in one corner; the opposite corner held a bucket of water. The room had a barred window and two doors, one locked, the other ajar and revealing a crack of dawn.

The really odd thing about the room, however, was that it had been built directly against a rock surface, and in that rock surface (somehow clearly visible even in the dim light) was a deep arm-shaped indent, one complete with hand and finger hollows.

It was now that Malone looked at his right arm. Since waking it had felt numb, and he'd thought he'd injured or slept on it. But now on closer inspection . . .

Is this some kind of insane joke?

It took him five minutes of testing (the final test being fitting his arm into the arm-shaped indent in the wall, where it fit perfectly) to accept the fact that his right arm was now made out of stone.

He was still wondering what had happened to him and where Clair Stevens was when the front door burst open and a woman dashed in and flicked on the lights.

"Thank heavens you're awake now," she gasped. "The berserkers are hot on my trail."

Bemused by her sudden appearance, Malone quickly looked the woman over. She was tall, with bright pink hair and lipstick and flashing green eyes. Her attractive face radiated intensity, like her life was burning.

Her clothes? Boots, blue jeans, and topping those, a black leather jacket that she was now quickly unzipping.

She was nude beneath the jacket. Seeing Malone was staring, she winked back.

"Who are you?" he asked.

"Vanilla Iron." She extended her hand.

He shook it. It was dainty but calloused; a fighter's hand. He was about to question Vanilla further when her bare breasts caught his attention. Not their size (they were very large), but the fact that she had metal nipples. Vanilla's nipples were each about an inch long and made of shiny steel.

Perhaps defeated by Malone's confusion, his threatened headache had now receded. He tried to wrap his mind around his new situation. This woman here with him definitely wasn't Clair Stevens, but she seemed to know him, and also, there was the mystery of why his arm was now made of stone.

And—*shit!*—Malone now found he had an erection in his pants, courtesy of Vanilla Iron's bountiful mammary endowment.

"I've been waiting for days for you to wake up, Stonearm."

"Huh?"

She frowned as if confused. "That's your name isn't it—Stonearm Malone?"

For want of a better answer, he first nodded, then thinking better of it, he said, "Call me Malone, Vanilla. Everyone else does."

Vanilla Iron patted her pink hair and nodded. "Okay, Malone, the berserkers are here to catch you and we need to fight them off."

Malone looked over at his gun, which lay by the edge of the bed. "Yeah sure." He was now feeling very uncomfortable. It felt like someone, or something, was stroking his penis. He looked down at his pants. No, there was nothing there, just the outline of his hard-on. But it now felt like . . . like a mouth was sucking on his turgid organ. In fact, he could feel the hot lips and the wetness on his erection and the pleasure was suddenly fantastic and growing excruciating and he was about to come.

Confused, he looked across at Vanilla. She stared back at him, at first unsure what the problem was; then on noticing his erection, she giggled. "That's an afternoon log of morning wood, Malone."

Then three things happened. First, the shack door crashed open and a berserker pushed its hairy bigfoot face into the room. Second, Malone realized that Vanilla Iron had flung her jacket off and was unscrewing her metal nipples. (Unscrewing? The very idea seemed insane to Malone, but there was no doubt about it—she *was* twisting her nipples off! And why on earth would she do that with danger so close at hand?)

And third, to Malone's intense mortification, he started coming, the semen pumping from his penis.

But there was something very odd about this particular ejaculation of his:

It seemed to be occurring elsewhere.

CHAPTER 29

Malone / Clair

Malone opened his eyes again. He was lying on a dusty carpet with his fly open. Clair Stevens had her lips wrapped around his penis and was giving him a blowjob.

Seeing as he was already ejaculating and it felt so good, he waited for her to finish.

Clair raised her eyes from Malone's groin. Seeing he was awake, she winked at him, then dropped her head again, sucking the dregs of his orgasm deep into her throat. She swallowed, then lifted her lips off his penis. She licked her lips clean.

"Hi," she said with clear relief, "I thought you'd never wake up again." She pointed at his still stiff member. "I read somewhere once that fellatio's the best way to call a warrior's departed spirit back into his body." She gave him a very concerned look. "Are you okay?"

"I hope so." He picked himself up off the floor and tucked his penis away. While Clair watched him worriedly, Malone again took stock of himself. *I was just . . . where? That Malone with the stone arm, no, I didn't dream him up; that was me. And the woman with pink hair, Vanilla Iron? She wasn't dream or imagination either. She's real . . . somewhere.* He'd loved to have believed he'd imagined that just-concluded experience, but he knew he hadn't. *Yes, I visited someplace else before returning here. But have I actually even returned? I can still sense 'Stonearm.'*

That feeling of connection was fading though, and even if it hadn't been, Malone remembered he currently had dire matters to attend to. Judging from Clair's incessant glances at the door opposite his feet, she and he were still in grave danger.

But he was confused. They were currently in a large room full of metal and wood cabinets and lit by a hurricane lamp placed on a desk. All around was silence too, though he thought he heard an owl hoot somewhere.

"Where are we?" he asked.

Then, before Clair could reply, he worked out the answer himself. Her severed neck facing into the room, Trudi Carmen's corpse lay over by a wall, under a row of rotted ceremonial robes.

He gaped at Clair in surprise. "We're in the church vestry? How'd we get in here?"

She shrugged, then replied, "We were flying through the air, about being flattened, when a hole suddenly appeared in the wall and we fell through it. You were holding me to protect me and hit the ground head first. It knocked you out. I was okay. I looked back at the hole. I saw the balcony floor we'd been standing on slide down the wall out of sight, and then the wall closed up again."

Malone felt chilled. "What did the hole look like?"

Clair shivered. "Malone, it was really odd; it was a door with eyes all around its edges. I felt like the eyes could see me."

Malone nodded. "That's Crystal Baller watching out for me. She told me she saw an OD in my future. I just didn't think it was hers."

"What's she watching you for?"

"I think she wants a rematch."

"A rematch?"

"Goddess ego; she wants to whip my ass at basketball. She can't do that if I'm dead."

While Clair looked puzzled, Malone's gaze now hardened. He knew he had to cut Trudi open and get the white ring out of her belly. He peeked at her corpse with dread. It was going to be a horrible task, butchering up a woman he'd made love to just hours earlier, but there was no escaping it or even putting it off. The gory deed had to be done.

"Do you have a knife on you?" he asked Clair.

She shook her head. "But I recall seeing one while looking for matches to light the lamp." She tapped a box of matches on a desk. "Want me to find it for you?"

He nodded. She picked up the lamp and crossed to a nearby cabinet.

"How long was I out for?" he asked as she rummaged through its drawers.

"Two hours."

Two hours. That meant it was night outside now, which explained the owl hoot he'd heard earlier. "Is anyone else still alive?"

"Not that I can tell. We're the only survivors."

"And the golems?"

"All gone."

"Gone?"

"I peeked outside and all the meaties were vanished. Ouch! Goddam stop talking, Malone, and let me find this knife . . . ah, here it is! It's a switchblade . . . and what's *this?*"

She held 'this' up for Malone to see. It was a small blue statuette about five inches long and an inch-and-a-half wide. Malone would have thought it was a dildo but for the fact that they'd found it in a church and it was sculpted in the shape of a man.

"Hey, there's something printed on its side," Clair said.

"What's it say?"

Clair gasped, then began laughing. "It says, 'Instant Priest. Insert in warm anus to activate.'"

"You've got to be shitting me."

"No, I'm not." She stepped up to Malone's side, handed him the blue figurine (a model of a holy man in a cassock), then held the lamp up so he could read the words on it.

He saw she was right: the figurine did have 'Instant Priest. Insert in warm anus to activate' printed on its side.

Clair giggled. "Quite a dirty joke, huh?"

Malone shook his head. "It's not a joke."

"Of course it is, ha ha!" Then she saw that he was serious. "C'mon, Malone, you don't seriously think—?"

"Clair, Clair . . ." He placed firm hands on her shoulders, peered intently into her gray eyes. "This statue you just found is a *real* priest. It has to be. Crystal was specific that I'd find a priest when I really needed one, and I can't think of any time I need one more than right now."

Clair turned to put the lantern and switchblade on the desk. Then she stood regarding Malone. "Tell me something: do you still intend hunting the vampires?"

He nodded. "I've come too far to quit. So yes, I'm going up to Vampire Castle to finish them off." He gave her an understanding smile. "It's okay; you don't have to come along."

Her face set in hard, cold lines. "Oh no—we're going together. Don't try to stop me, Malone. Lilith killed my mother—I want to watch her die too." Then her expression turned puzzled. "But will this thing really work? I mean how do we know it's really a priest?"

"Only one way to tell for sure. Put in your butt?"

"Hell no!"

Malone gaped at her. "Please, Clair, this isn't the time for modesty."

She scowled. "I'm not being modest, Malone. I just gave you head, didn't I?" She shook her hands at the blue figurine. "No priests up my shitter. Put him in yours."

Malone gaped at her. "What?"

Hand folded over her breasts, she glared back adamantly. "You heard me, buddy. Stick him up *your* ass."

"Why not yours?"

"No," Clair reiterated with emphasis. "I'm Catholic; I was an altar boy once. I've got nothing against the church—lots of good honest people in there—but I don't want no priests up my ass, okay?"

Malone gaped at her again.

She nodded. "Yes, I was born male; so what? It makes no difference here: no priests is no priests."

Malone was stumped. Clair's expression was so cold, she clearly wasn't about to change her mind. He considered grabbing her and forcefully sticking the priest into her anus, but no, he couldn't rape her like that, and also, he could see her hand was very close to the switchblade she'd found in the cabinet.

He conceded defeat. "Okay, put him in *my* ass."

Clair smiled sweetly. "I simply adore a man who knows when he's ass-whipped." She tapped the desk. "Okay, Malone, pull down your pants and bend over here."

Feeling horribly vulnerable to be so exposed, Malone did so.

Thankfully, inserting the priest into his anus proved much easier than he'd feared. Clair first slobbered all over it, which made Malone uneasy (the priest figurine had an exceedingly severe expression on its old face), then she spread Malone's hairy buttocks and began licking his anus.

"What are you doing?"

"I'm getting you nice and wet and open."

"I see. What's that you're inserting?"

"My index finger. Malone, you fucking talk too much. Okay, let's try two fingers now. Relax your hole around them. Okay, I think you're ready for big daddy."

"Clair, if you dare stick your penis in me, I'll murder you."

"Ouch, Malone, that hurt. Look, if it makes you better, I completed my SRS two years ago."

"Okay, I'm sorry I hurt your feelings, but . . . Ouch! I said I was sorry, didn't I?"

"Sorry. It's just the priest's head going in. It's big. He doesn't look like he approves of the smell of your poop either. He looks angry as shit."

"Ouch! Ouch!"

"For God's sake, Malone, relax your fucking hole. It'll sting a little at first, but . . . just imagine you've a monster turd to let out . . . . Yeah, that's better. Okay, blue boy is halfway home . . . Hold on, let me spit a bit on your ring so you don't rip the hands jut out a little . . ."

"Ouch!"

"Sorry. Just the feet left . . . And . . . whoopee! All five inches of holy man are now in your rectum. Your ass hole just closed over his soles." She giggled. "The Pope would definitely disapprove of this."

She slapped Malone's buttocks. "Okay, you can straighten up again." When he'd turned to face her, she said, "I'm sorry, Malone, I just couldn't do it." She winked coquettishly at him. "You, honey, I'd gladly have in my ass any day; just no priests."

"Forget it." He checked his watch. "How long are we supposed to wait?"

"Until it activates?"

"I thought the label read 'Instant,' or is that just manufacturer hype again?" Shaking his head, Malone pulled up his pants. The figurine in his rectum was a hard unpleasant intrusion. Very uncomfortable. And unlike how he'd imagined, it made no attempt to slip out of his anus again. "Anyhow, we don't have time to wait for it to wake up. We need to get over to Vampire . . ." Then he stiffened.

"Are you okay?"

"There was a swirling sensation in my ass, and now the priest seems to have changed shape. It feels almost like it's melted or something."

"Hey, maybe it's activating. You want me to check and see?"

"No, at least it's no longer uncomfortable. It even feels somehow natural in my butt." He grabbed the knife off the desktop and released its blade. "Okay, time to get the ring." He pointed to the vestry door. "You keep watch. Someone is definitely going to come looking for the ring soon."

Clair picked her gun up off the desk and went to open the vestry door a crack.

Malone pulled Trudi's corpse out from under the hanging priestly robes. Then, after setting the hurricane lamp down on the carpet beside it, he knelt over the body, slipped Trudi's blood-splattered dress up to just under her breasts, and began cutting.

Her skin parted like soft white cheese before the blade.

It was extremely hard going for Malone, violently entering this beautiful pale form now vacant of the life that had previously given them both such pleasure. Her missing head made the task at once both easier and more difficult for him: on the one hand he was spared her reproachful dead gaze, while on the other, he wished she still had her head, so he could behold her lovely face just one last time.

(And now, for real, there looked to be no chance of burying her.)

Tears welled up in his eyes as worked. He sliced Trudi's belly open. Her viscera lay before him, cold and hard and gray and purple like painted sculpture. She was just raw meat now, utterly devoid of any sort of vitality.

After a brief calculation of the periods from when she'd swallowed the ring to when they'd had their last meal together in the Hotel Bizarre, and then to when she'd died, Malone stuck the switchblade into Trudi's small intestine and began cutting through its meat, slitting it open. He had to pull the coils of intestine out of her belly and unravel them (which brought yet more tears to his eyes), but he'd figured it out right: four feet along from her stomach, in a mess of congealed food, there lay the white ring.

Malone picked the ring up and wiped it clean on his trousers. The white stone circlet looked so mundane, unworthy of all the bloodshed it had caused. And yet . . .

"Hey, Malone!" Clair whispered then from the door. "Put out the lamp! We've got company!"

Malone quickly doused the lamp. The white ring in his palm instantly turned a bright transparent gold and those strange black letters again wavered in its metal.

Malone dropped the ring into his shirt pocket, where it glowed through the fabric. *This is its usual response to darkness,* he thought, so *I don't think it's the vamps out there.*

"Who is it?" he asked Clair. "Lilith?"

"No. I mean I don't think so. I can hear a man's voice."

Covering the glowing ring with his right palm, Malone joined her at the door. It was dark outside, with no suggestion of a moon overhead.

Together they listened.

". . . So yes, we're finished here," a thickish bombastic voice was saying down off the altar platform, out of their view. "No one could have survived this fantastic destruction."

"Very amusing how they crashed the building down on themselves, isn't it, Lord Norgem?" another male voice asked.

"Ha ha ha! Yes, human stupidity apparently knows no bounds. But now, hurry, Bolok! Fetch my necromancers and those six virgins for the sacrifice! We must defile this hallowed place before sunrise as the beautiful Lilith Nightfall asked us to. So hurry back to our realm!"

There was silence after that, and the loud sound of feet running off.

Clair turned to Malone in the darkness. "That must be the voodoo controller guy you mentioned out there. It sounds like he's alone now. Want us to off him?"

"No," Malone cautioned. "We've no idea how powerful he is. If he's anything like his golems, our bullets will have zero effect on him. We'd best just get the hell out of Dodge." He stroked her face in the darkness. "Well, now we know for sure that Lilith and Le Bleach won't be coming here tonight. Are you absolutely certain you still want to come with me to visit them at home? You can wait here and I'll come back for you."

163

"Hell no! We're both going."

"Okay, which way's Vampire Castle?"

"Just follow me."

Doing their absolute best to make no sound, Malone and Clair exited the vestry and made their way down into the front of the demolished cathedral and from there out into the nighttime street behind it.

CHAPTER 30

Malone / Clair

Vampire Castle was an ugly mass of stonework built on a low hill. It was too dark to see the building clearly, but Malone could sense its evil aura.

The gate in the stone wall circling the castle grounds was rusted shut, like it had never been opened. Malone figured that was very likely the case. He and Clair scaled it easily enough, and then he pointed out several lit windows on the castle's second floor. "Does Lilith have any servants?"

"None that we discovered. Vermyn and Zander used to do all the housework. Those lights are likely Lilith's and Le Bleach's bedrooms."

Malone now felt the ring in his pocket buzzing. He pulled it out; it had turned an alternating black/white color.

"What's it doing?" Clair asked.

"It senses its evil twin nearby," he replied grimly, slipping the zebra-striped stone circlet onto a finger. "Which means Lilith likely also knows we're here. We need to hurry up and attack them before they get over their surprise at our survival."

"We should have waited till they fall asleep."

"They're vampires. They sleep in the daytime . . . I think."

He and she picked up their metal crosses, found in the passageway through which they'd left the church. Both their guns had half-full clips. Malone however doubted bullets and energy blasts would do any good here.

The final things they each picked up were two wooden stakes apiece, whittled by Malone from the pickets of a fence they'd passed.

(Malone was ever-conscious of the blue priest figurine in his rectum. It was strange: he could feel it in there, thick and squirming and liquid, and yet it wasn't in any way uncomfortable anymore. The priest felt almost pleasant in his ass. Malone suspected he felt a lot like a close-to-term pregnant woman did on one those good days when she was bustling with health and everything was going right in her world.)

Clair leaned up and kissed Malone on the cheek. "That's for luck," she said. "Okay, I'm ready when you are."

He smiled at her in the darkness, then they hurried up the driveway to Vampire Castle.

***

The castle's front doors were open, which they hadn't expected.

They stepped inside and instantly found themselves in a large empty hall. The hall was lit by torches sputtering in regularly-spaced brackets along its rock walls.

At the far end of the hall, and walking toward them, were Lilith Nightfall and Diana Le Bleach. Both women wore broad grins on their faces.

Clair winced. "Well, so much for the element of surprise."

"Maybe not; I've still got the priest in my ass."

"Yeah, and a fat lot of good he'll do us in there. And this place is damn weird, Malone. It's like an illusion."

"It very likely *is* an illusion. Keep your guard up. These may not even be the real Lilith and Le Bleach."

They waited. Malone appraised the two approaching women, the raven-haired one and the blonde, both wearing flowing black dresses that clung to their slim bodies like they'd bathed in tar. Both abstractive vampires were undeniably beautiful. Both also had a thick, almost visible aura of primal evil about them. As they got nearer, their grins revealed long fangs.

Lilith and Le Bleach stopped ten feet away from Clair and Malone.

Le Bleach said, "Oh, I see you two escaped the burning church after all."

Lilith said, "Thanks for bringing the second dead ring to me."

Malone smirked. "I'm actually here to collect back the one you've got."

Le Bleach frowned. "Don't be foolish. Just hand the ring over and we'll let you leave unhurt."

Her eyes agleam with amusement, Lilith Nightfall extended her right hand to Malone. (He saw that her ring too was zebra-colored now.) "Let me have the dead ring," she said.

Clair spat. "Screw you, Lilith. That's not happening and you know it. We're here to lay your murdering ass to rest for good."

"Oh, we'd love to see you try," Le Bleach said, her tongue a caged pink serpent behind her long fangs. "Wouldn't we, Lilith?"

Lilith laughed mockingly then gestured at Malone and Clair's weapons. "You sad fools. You can't defeat me in my own house—you should know that. Stakes and crosses? Pah!"

Malone, however, heard uncertainty in her voice; and he'd also realized that behind her bluster, Le Bleach was definitely scared.

"We'll see about that," he said grimly, lifting his cross into the vampires' faces. Beside him, Clair did same. Quickly he intoned, "I damn you evil creatures to Hell, in the name of the Father—"

Shrieking, Lilith and Le Bleach flung up their hands to shield their eyes from the crosses, which had now both begun glowing a bright blue.

"—In the name of the Son—"

Lilith screamed out a curse and the hall was suddenly full of bats.

Large and small, gray, black, and brown, the bats emerged in their droves from the walls, from the floor, and from the ceiling.

Malone's invocation froze on his tongue; Clair gasped in horror. Both looked sideways at the gray walls. The stone surfaces were literally becoming the flying mammals, each dissolving into gray gas which then reformed itself into winged shapes. Likewise, the floor was deepening as its substance transformed into the creatures.

Through the veil of the dark swarm Malone saw Lilith and Le Bleach laughing.

The bats swamped Clair and Malone. Both were suddenly enveloped in a mass of warm furry bodies with scratching claws and sharp biting teeth. Those bats that touched either cross instantly burst into flame and roasted, but there were so many willing replacements. Malone was forced to drop both his stakes to protect his face. He was careful not to drop his cross, keeping it wedged in the crook of his elbow while defending himself.

"No, no!" Clair yelped beside him, swiping at the bats with her cross like they were baseballs. "Get off of me, you little horrors!" Her face dripped blood where she'd been bitten. On each left and right swing of hers, clumps of bats turned into airborne balls of fire.

The walls had now stopped transforming, but the hall was full of the flying creatures. Malone's and Clair's ears were full of the bats' high pitched chittering. Malone peeked through their milling number. Lilith and Le Bleach had made no attempts to flee. Both were instead watching he and Clair with delighted hungry looks on their faces.

A huge black bat landed on Malone's head and sank its fangs deep into his scalp. Howling with pain, he grabbed it with his free hand and wrenched it off his head, feeling his flesh tear and the blood flow.

He flung the bat away, then became aware that Clair was yelling, "Look out!"

He looked up and just made out Lilith Nightfall's slim figure charging at him through the furry airborne swarm. On his left, Le Bleach was similarly headed for Clair.

And suddenly, both women were altering, their bodies turning brown and heavy, their heads swelling and growing snouts and large triangular ears, their fangs becoming even longer; their legs shortening and leaving the floor.

The little bats parted to let the transformed vampires through at Clair and Malone. Then a cloud of them settled on Malone all at once, biting and nipping and scratching and beating their wings in his face, rendering him unable to focus on the advancing danger.

The only thing Malone could do as the transformed Lilith Nightfall reached him, her huge black jaws spread wide to bite off his head, was to hold the metal cross out in front of him. He was aware of her slowing down in mid lunge and changing direction to his left to avoid the holy symbol. He swung the cross left after her. As he did so, he glimpsed the other massive bat falling out of the air onto Clair, who (as coated in dark fluttering bodies as he was) was swinging her cross up at its head. Metal hit flesh in a shower of blue sparks. The winged monster howled loudly; Clair screamed. Both fell against the wall, then downward.

Malone wrenched his eyes and mind away from Clair; he had his own problems. Ignoring the cross he carried, the bat Lilith was snapping at Malone's shoulder. (Like they feared for their own safety, the little bats now fled his body.) Knowing what the creature's bite would do to his flesh, he kept well away from its snapping jaws. As his own offensive, he pushed the cross hard against the bat's side, and was instantly rewarded with the stink of burning fur and the hiss of barbequing flesh. Pulling its head back, the monster let out a shrill scream of pain. Malone yanked the cross off its sizzling flesh, then swung it at its head. The bat, however, anticipated his action and flung up its wing to cover itself. The cross burnt a big hole through the bat's left wing. Screaming again, the monster swiped at Malone with its right wing, catching him flush on the jaw and stunning him.

Malone felt stars spinning in his head. The bat hit him again and he dropped the cross. He pulled out his gun, but he was now so groggy that the bat easily swatted the firearm from his grasp.

And now the huge bat wrapped its feet around Malone's neck and began choking him out with them. He grabbed its scaly legs and tried to pry them off his neck, but it was no use.

Then suddenly, the swarm of littler bats all cleared up in the hall, and Malone could see clearly around him again. His body now ran red from a hundred little bites and scratches.

Even with the asphyxiating grip of the bat Lilith's claws around his neck, Malone's first thoughts were of Clair. *Is she okay? Did she survive?* His brain already shutting down from oxygen loss, he looked around for her.

Clair Stevens lay on the stone floor, her head at an odd angle to her body. Her neck was clearly broken. Malone at first thought she was dead, but then she blinked at him and her lips moved silently.

Paralyzed now or not, Clair had however taken out Le Bleach for good. The monster bat's carcass lay draped over her feet. The crosspiece of Clair's cross was stuck all the way through the bat's head, which, thick black smoke spilling up as from a bonfire, was burning fiercely around the glowing blue metal.

One more to go, Malone managed to think. But then, as though enraged by Diana Le Bleach's death, the bat Lilith gave a loud roar and squeezed Malone's neck harder with its feet.

Malone instantly faded to unconsciousness.

CHAPTER 31

Malone / Lilith

Malone jerked awake. His body hurt from several hundred tooth punctures. Remembering that he'd just been choked out, he instantly looked around to see where he was.

He was both naked and tied up, his ankles lashed together with rope, his hands secured behind his back. He sat propped up against a stone wall. Another rope lashed about his neck was secured to a metal hoop set into the stone overhead.

His neck hurt badly from his being strangled by the giant bat's feet. He was a mess, his body covered with bites and blood-mud. His nipped and ripped skin stung all over.

Malone thought he was still in the torch-lit hall where he and Clair had encountered the vampires, only now, the wall opposite him was missing. Instead of that surface's gray stone, the floor over there now ended at a ledge, an internal cliff from which steps led downward. (There was no sign of either Clair or Le Bleach's bodies, or of the crosses and stakes and weapons; or, for that matter, of the front castle doors.)

He felt an intense need to urinate, but ignored it.

A slow cranking sound was coming from the space below the ledge. Malone inched himself as far forward as the rope about his neck would allow and peered down.

The steps led to a lower room where a large open pine coffin sat atop a raised stone platform. Ventilation slits high up the gray walls let in wan moonlight and damp night air.

Lilith Nightfall was down there in the room. She was busy hoisting Clair's naked body up over the pine coffin. Clair was bound at the ankles, the rope then having been slipped over a hook attached to a chain descending from the ceiling. The cranking sound Malone had heard was Lilith working the winch which lifted Clair into the air. As Lilith turned the handle, Clair's paralyzed form swayed back and forth over the coffin, her arms flopping limply beside her head. She was still alive; her eyes were blinking in terror, her mouth babbling soundlessly.

Lilith was herself injured. She too was naked now and had a large skinless cross-shaped wound all the way down her left side, inside of which exposed ribs and belly muscles were clearly visible. Lilith moved like she was in agony, taking frequent rests between cranks.

Then she looked up and saw Malone watching her. She immediately stopped working the crank and trudged painfully across to him.

As she approached, Malone wondered what in the world he could do. He was Lilith's captive, completely at her mercy now. If she bit him . . .

Lilith climbed the stairs to Malone's side. Beautiful and evil, the fire of lust and sin in her eyes, she bared her fangs at him. "So I won after all, didn't I?"

Malone didn't reply. Now, of all times, the priest figurine in his ass had begun squirming. He looked down at his groin, wishing he could just shit it out. Clair was right: some damned help it had turned out to be.

"You look utterly delicious," Lilith said. Still concentrating on the weird sensation in his rectum, Malone vaguely understood that she was referring to how bloody he was.

Lilith grabbed Malone hard under the chin and lifted his face to hers. "Look at me when I'm talking, you son-of-a-bitch." Satisfied she had his attention again, she let go of his chin and showed him her hands, let him see that she now wore both dead rings on her middle fingers. He was unable to tell them apart: both were striped black and white.

"It's over," she said. "By tomorrow evening, the American people will simply be vampire cattle. Of course, that's really all you've ever been; I'm just making it official." She laughed, then stopped at the pain it caused in her gaping wound. She shot Malone a glare full of hatred. "You really hurt me, you bastard. I'll make you suffer a lot for that."

Malone ignored Lilith's glare and her threat. (Thankfully, the squirming in his backside had now quieted down again.) He nodded down at where Clair swung over the pine coffin. "What are you going to do to her?"

Lilith frowned. "Her fate is your fault." She indicated her extensive cross-shaped wound, which up close was much deeper than Malone had thought from afar—at several points he could clearly see her intestines. "Because of you, I'm too weak now to open up the Dead Sky; attempting it now would kill me. First I need to sleep, to heal in a bath of blood." She smiled evilly at Malone, then pointed down at Clair. "I mean, sleep and heal in *her* blood."

"No!" he gasped in horror, realizing what Lilith meant. "You can't do that!"

Her smile widened to a grin, her fangs gleaming brightly. "Why not? You love her? That just makes my revenge much sweeter!"

"Don't do it!" Malone pleaded. "I'll do anything you want."

She patted his cheek mockingly. "You're *already* going to do anything I want. *Everything* I want." Lilith flashed her fingers at him again. "Once I'm healed, I'll first use your blood to activate the dead rings and bring the Dead Sky to the USA, then, I'm going to feed you *my* blood and make you an abstractive vampire like me." She laughed loudly. "And then, my little human, you'll be my slave forever! And believe me, am I so going to make you suffer." She regarded his exposed genitals a moment, then added, "You know, I think I'll just hand you over to Cunt Dracula, to be her personal sex slave."

She spun on her heel and made her painful way back down the steps again to the coffin and crank.

"Stop!" Malone pleaded. "Don't do it!"

Lilith laughed. "Why stop? I've already won!"

And with those words, she raked her fingernails across Clair's neck, completely ripping her throat out.

Lilith laughed as the blood began flowing down over Clair's head into the coffin. She lifted her lithe white legs and climbed into the long pine box, lay down in it and let Clair's exiting life coat her body in its red liquid layers. Her fingers hung like pale hooks over the coffin's sides.

Malone shook with rage as he watched Clair die; the horrified look in her eyes as her blood spilled down over Lilith Nightfall was too much for him to take.

"I'll get you for this, you unholy bitch," he swore down at Lilith. "I'll send you to Hell if it's the last thing I ever do."

Lilith raised her head from the coffin and laughed. Her face and hair were slick with crimson now, her voice dreamy with almost erotic pleasure. "There's nothing you can do—I've won. In case you don't understand, this is my realm of darkness you're in now. Even if you could get free, and there's no way you possibly can, there's nothing here in Vampire Castle that can harm me. Search through this entire building and you won't find a single thing. Not even water—I don't drink it. I've disposed of all your weapons—the stupid crosses and stakes—and you can't get out of here until I wake up again, so don't try." She laughed. "And besides, you fool, once you're a vampire yourself, you'll be too consumed with bloodlust to give a shit about settling old scores."

"I'll, I'll . . ."

"Oh, shut up. I need to rest and heal. If you don't shut up, I'll come sew your lips together."

Malone shut up. He realized she was right: there was nothing he could do.

He sat and watched the last of Clair's blood drip down over the vampire in the coffin.

CHAPTER 32

Malone

Down in her coffin, Lilith Nightfall began snoring, the sounds fluttering upwards like evil birds. Clair's lifeless corpse dangled over her like a guardian angel.

Malone began struggling to get free. He tried pulling his wrists forward under his feet, but his arms were too firmly bound. He got to his feet and hopped away from the wall, checking if he could pull the rope around his neck off its fastening. It was an impossible task. (He was also supremely conscious of not making any noise that would wake Lilith up.)

The pressure in his bladder now returned magnified. Malone was about to pee against the wall when the wriggling feeling returned in his ass. The priest was moving about inside there again. The odd feeling instantly killed his desire to urinate. He stood confused, looking down over the ledge at Lilith's coffin as the discomfort in his rear increased. *What am I going to do now?* Oddly, it didn't feel like he had to defecate, but with the way his rear felt—like it was packed full of happy worms—it seemed he had to try.

And then, suddenly, he felt something wet squirming out of his anus, and slurping down between his buttocks. He stood frozen by disbelief. It felt like a set of hands were pushing his buttocks apart. How? His anus didn't feel *that* stretched. Seeing as his hands were bound behind him, his felt his ass. A thick warm liquid was slurping out of his hole and dripping down his legs. And yes, the sludge had formed fingers that were holding his buttock cheeks apart to facilitate its exit.

Instant Priest, huh?

There was nothing he could do but wait. Slowly, unhurriedly, the liquid streamed down his legs and pooled around him on the floor.

It was blue in color and there was a lot of it, several bucketfuls in fact.

After the last of it slurped from his buttocks, the whole blue mass flowed away from Malone. Six feet in front of him, it began congealing upwards into a human form.

A minute later, the blue goop had become a living human being. A bearded old priest in a cassock.

The priest looked at Malone in confusion. Malone gaped back at him. He *knew* the old man.

"*Father Andrew?* What are you doing here?" Father Andrew Flores had run a mobile soup kitchen down in Boston's Back Bay. Father Andrew (who'd been in his mid-sixties) had also died four years ago, falling out of a tree while trying to rescue a kitten stranded in it.

Father Andrew seemed to finally recognize Malone. "Bud Malone? Is it you? Who . . . who tied you up like this?"

Malone nodded. "Yes, yes, Father, it's me." He cast a quick glance down at Lilith, then added, "Shh, Father, we're in danger."

"I was just in this really dark and smelly place," Father Andrew whispered.

Malone was very perplexed as to how a dead man could possibly have become the blue figurine that Clair had forced up into his anus. But those were questions for later. For the moment, Malone felt a kindling of hope in his heart. Crystal Baller had told him he'd find a priest when he needed one. And here was one now.

"Untie me, Father," he whispered, "and I'll explain the problem. My hands first, please."

"Yes, of course." Father Andrew quickly got behind Malone and began undoing the rope binding his wrists. While he worked, Malone explained about the vampires, with the old priest interrupting him with whispered questions, his eyes darting often to the pine coffin with the drained corpse hanging over it. Father Andrew's expression quickly grew less perplexed and more troubled.

Once his hands were free, Malone rubbed circulation back into his wrists, then worked on freeing his neck while Father Andrew undid the rope around his ankles.

"No," Father Andrew replied a question, "I've nothing holy on me, not even my rosary. Has to be the first time in my life I've even been so bare."

You're actually dead, Father, Malone thought. *At least I think you are.* But he didn't say it.

Finally, they both stood on the rock ledge looking down at the sleeping Lilith Nightfall.

"I don't doubt that she told me the truth," Malone whispered, "there's really absolutely nothing in here that can harm her. But we can't afford to let her wake up again. If she does, we're both done for. America is done for. We need to kill her somehow. And for good."

"We could try to get the rings off her fingers while she's asleep," Father Andrew said. "She's kept her hands up out of the blood."

Malone nodded. "She clearly doesn't want to set off a reaction she can't control. but if we try that, we'll likely wake her up."

"We could make a cross and stake her . . ." the old man's words faltered.

Malone sighed. His eyes had just located the coffin lid, which leaned against the platform. The lid was a single thick slab of wood, utterly useless in this case. "Stake her? How? there's nothing—"

"We take Clair's body down and open her up. Use her bones."

Malone gaped at the old priest, confused by the bloodiness of the suggestion. Then an immense dread filled him as he remembered how he'd had to cut Trudi Carmen open to retrieve the white ring. *Oh, no not again.*

"No," he told the priest coldly. "Anything but that. For one thing, getting the body down might wake Lilith. And also, we've no knife to cut Clair open with."

"We could use that hook she's hanging from. It looks quite sharp."

Malone stared Father Andrew down.

"You should know I don't like this any more than you do," the priest said in a weary voice," but desperate times call for desperate measures. What else can we do with our nation's liberty at stake? Look, we should at least *try* to get her down. From what I know of vampires, they're extremely hard to rouse from slumber."

Malone grudgingly agreed that the priest had a point. "But that hook looks very sturdy," he whispered as they descended the steps to the lower room. "How do we get it off its chain?"

"I don't know. Let's get up onto the platform beside the coffin."

They did so and both stood staring down at the sleeping Lilith Nightfall.

She lay, pale and gorgeous, half-submerged in thick wet blood which, like a living thing, writhed and squirmed over her nude form. Her lips were slightly parted, showing her teeth. She still snored delicately, her nostrils occasionally twitching. (The striped rings on her fingers were a mocking countdown to endless night over the USA.)

Father Andrew crossed himself. "Holy Mother of God, save us from evil." Then he sighed heavily. "Ah, if only we had holy water now. She'd be finished."

"We don't have much time," Malone said. He pointed to Lily's injured side, where her gaping wound was already half-healed. "She'll wake up shortly." He stared down at the sleeping vampire, hating her and yet unable to figure out what to do to kill her. The crank handle (which would have made a great stake) was firmly bolted to its mechanism, and they had no tools to loosen it. Aside from the crank, the only other thing in the room was a large gold chalice that sat on a stone table opposite them, on the other side of Lilith's bed of blood; likely something the vampire used for drinking blood. The goblet looked heavy, but . . . familiar with Lilith's strength, Malone figured hitting her with it would prove a waste of time.

And time was something they clearly didn't have now. Not at the speed with which the blood squirming over Lilith's body was repairing her. Now her previously exposed ribs were all covered over with fresh skin and the burnt away muscles in her belly were regenerating.

Malone pointed to the hook on which Clair hung, her eyes staring open in death. "We're in a fix, Father. I just remembered—to get her down we need to work the crank and that makes a loud noise."

He and the old man stared moodily at each other.

"Ah," Father Andrew said, "what I wouldn't give for some holy water now."

Malone's gaze fell again to the golden chalice and something clicked in his mind. He walked around the coffin and picked it up. Returning to Father Andrew's side, he scowled at the old priest. "Holy water, huh?"

And then, while the priest watched him in shock, Malone began to urinate into the golden chalice.

When he was done, the chalice was half-full of urine. He held the bowl out. "Here's your water, Father. Now bless it and let's get this over with."

Father Andrew instantly cringed, his old face indignant. "Malone, you can't honestly expect me to do *that*. God will be mad."

"God will be delighted that we're saving the United States, Father." He looked pleadingly at Father Andrew. "Father, it's the *only* water we have. This is our *only* chance. Look at her, her body's almost fully repaired. She'll wake up any minute now."

Then nodding down at the chalice," Malone grinned. "Bless it, Father, for she *has* sinned."

His face grim, Father Andrew nodded and began making the sign of the cross over the chalice full of piss, his mouth whispering holy invocations.

***

Once the urine was blessed, Malone tiptoed over to stand beside Lilith Nightfall's head. Holding the chalice in his right hand, he slowly spread her jaws wider with his left. He took great care not to cut himself on her fangs. (He felt no qualms over what he was about doing. Directly and indirectly, Lilith had caused the deaths of three women he'd had feelings for . . . she had to die too.)

"No need for that, Malone," Father Andrew said, "just pour it over her."

"I've already gotten her mouth open." And with that, Malone poured the 'holy piss' down Lilith's throat. Then, for good measure, he doused her head with it and then drenched the rest of her body.

The results were very impressive.

With a scream that sounded like it came from the depths of Hell itself, Lilith Nightfall abruptly sat bolt upright in the bloody coffin. For a moment she sat there screaming, her eyes staring a bright red straight ahead of her. Then she burst into flame. The fire spurted from her mouth, from her nostrils, from her ears . . . from the healing wound in her side . . . from between her legs . . .

Then her flesh began falling off and the flames poured out of her body. Her face peeled off and fire popped her eyeballs, her breasts shriveled and turned black, her chest skin all burnt to ash. Tongues of flame spurted out between her blackened ribs like her chest was a barbeque grill.

Malone and Father Andrew quickly distanced themselves from her. The coffin caught fire. Its flames leapt up, caught on Clair's hair, and set her ablaze too.

Lilith began screaming again and beating at herself, trying to put herself out. But it was no good, she was fast deteriorating to a mere skeleton.

Above Lilith, the flames consuming Clair's corpse now ate through the rope securing her ankles to the hook. Her freed body crashed down on the screaming, faceless vampire.

The impact exploded Lilith like a bomb. Her bones sprayed out of the coffin and flew everywhere, continuing to burn fiercely where they landed.

Soon, all that remained of Lilith Nightfall were lots of little piles of ash dotted about the room. The coffin had also been completely reduced to ash. Clair's now skinless body lay sizzling and smoking on the stone platform.

Malone and Father Andrew had sat on the steps to watch Lilith's passing.

Father Andrew shook his head. "Killing a vampire with sanctified urine? I'd never have expected that to work in a thousand years."

"Me neither," Malone admitted. Leaving the priest still shaking his head he walked down the steps and began searching among Lilith's ashes for the two dead rings.

"Hey, Padre," he called after a bit, "I've found one of them. Did you notice where her other hand flew off to?"

CHAPTER 33

Malone

The second Malone's fingers touched the second dead ring, the stone walls around him and Father Andrew vanished. There was a moment when they were outside on a grassy hilltop, staring out over the city of Genesis, and then that too disappeared.

After experiencing the dizzying rush of space-time transition, Malone and Father Andrew both found themselves back in Malone's living room.

It was morning outside, the air replete with the smells of the waking city and the noise of Boston traffic.

"Well, that's ended well," Malone said. He regarded his filthy, bloody, naked body for a long moment. "I don't know about you, Father, but I really need a bath."

"I'll wait. I feel a bit tired; I'll have a little nap."

"Come with me, Father. The bedroom's this way."

***

Malone soaked in his bathtub, scrubbing off the blood and dirt. His bitten body stung like hell, and it wasn't just the pain: *Damn those bats—now I need to get a rabies shot!*

Malone was bothered. His main worry was what to do with the dead rings. He regarded the pair of them on his ring fingers. Both were still zebra-striped, though neither buzzed on his hands. He wondered what would happen to them now if he turned off the bathroom light, but wasn't tempted enough to find out.

Then he sighed. He felt another, deeper, dissatisfaction. Three women he knew had died during his quest, one of whom he'd been in love with.

Malone suddenly became aware that he wasn't alone in the bathroom.

He looked up in alarm; his spare gun was outside in the bedroom. Then, seeing who it was, he relaxed.

Crystal Baller stood by his bathroom door bouncing her transparent basketball. The black goddess (who seemed normal-sized) was smiling.

"Just checking to see that you got home okay," she said, dropping her magic basketball into the bathwater, where it floated, its myriad eyes staring at Malone. She sat on the edge of the bathtub, its water wetting her tracksuit.

He said, "I never knew goddesses made house calls."

She laughed, the bathroom lights reflecting off her dusky shaven head. Then her expression sobered. "You did a great job back there, Malone. It's all over now. America is safe again."

"Thanks for saving me from dying like a bug splattered on a windshield."

She waved it off. "No problem."

"And thanks too for the priest." He jabbed a finger towards the bedroom where Father Andrew slept. "But . . . is he alive? I mean, he died four years ago, didn't he?"

Crystal laughed again, showing her huge white teeth. "Life and death are often matters of perspective. The real question is: does he *seem* to be alive?"

Malone let it pass. He was grateful to the goddess for bringing him back home without danger. But he also felt he'd left unfinished business back in Genesis.

"I wanted to bury Trudi Carmen with love and respect," he said bitterly. "She deserved that; she was a wonderful woman."

"You *will* bury her." The goddess's smile was now a compassionate one. "Her body—with its belly sealed up and her head reattached—has just turned up in the MGH morgue. Ask Steelberg for it."

His expression instantly brightened. "And Clair Stevens? Can you do the same for her?"

"I can, but she doesn't look too good."

Malone winced on remembering how Clair had gone up in flames. "You're a goddess, lady—put a skin on her. And a pretty face, with blonde hair."

Crystal laughed. "Okay, done, Malone. She's now in the same morgue as Trudi."

"Thanks, Crystal. I'll appreciate this for a long time."

She grinned. "I just want my rematch; that'll be thanks enough."

Malone bumped his knee against her floating transparent globe, jostling its ocular contents. "You're not letting that go, are you?"

"No. We play ball again. I'll not rush you—say a week from today, when you're feeling much better."

"Alright then. You'll pick me up here?"

"Yeah, sure. Just make sure to be home at eight p.m."

"It's a date."

"Wanna do a movie first?" Then she slapped his knee and laughed. "Just teasin'."

Malone laughed too, then realized he'd forgotten something. He lifted both hands out of the bathwater. "Hey, Crystal. What do I do with these rings? I can't keep 'em."

"They'll be safe in Robopol custody. Give them to Steelberg. Explain in detail what they are and have the robot lock them away somewhere."

"Together?"

"They can ship one to say, L.A., if they like." She got off the side of the bathtub, then snapped her fingers at the see-thru basketball, which floated up to her hand. "Okay, Malone, I gotta run. Got some stuff that needs taking care of."

"Wait. I've two more questions."

"Alright, but make them quick."

"First, who's Cunt Dracula? Lilith mentioned her."

Crystal scowled with obvious distaste. "She's a problem you'll thankfully never have to deal with. The Cunt is a vampire who, along with Duke Norgem and a lot of other insane semi-divine folk, lives in the realm known as Hedaye. Your second question?"

Pointing toward the bedroom, Malone lowered his voice; Father Andrew's snoring was audible to them both. "What do I do with *him?*"

"Return him to his old parish. Have him run his mobile soup kitchen again. There's lots of poor folk who need the help he'll provide."

"But the church authorities . . . Crystal, Father Andrew is frigging *dead*. It's official—in the diocese records. He fell out of a tree; they made a death certificate; they buried him. I know where his grave is!"

The black goddess rolled her eyes. "Resurrection is one of the cornerstones of Christianity, Malone. I'm sure the Vatican will be delighted to see Father Andrew Flores again."

With that, she vanished.

After a long time spent staring at the bathroom door and considering Crystal Baller's last words, Malone began whistling. Yes, all things considered, things *had* worked out alright. Boston's sapphic population and the entire USA were now safe again. Yes, he'd do like Crystal had said, take Father Andrew over to the diocese, let Bishop Miller work out what to do with him. He grinned; the old guy would likely have a fit when the pair of them showed up in his office.

For a moment, a memory flashed through Malone's mind—of himself waking up in a strange shack with a stone arm. He smacked his palm against his head. *Damn, I should have asked Crystal about that!* Then he shrugged it off. *Whoever that guy is, even if he's a version of me, he'll have to look out for himself. I've way too much weirdness on my own plate here in Boston to go searching for more.*

He got up, drained the bathtub water, and toweled himself dry. Then, after putting on a blue bathrobe, Malone left the bathroom and padded quietly past the sleeping priest in his bed, out into the living room. There, he picked up the cordless and dialed Robopol HQ; asked to be put through to Lt. Steelberg.

"Hey, Metal Guy," he said brightly once the robot cop picked up, "I'm back . . ."

While talking, Malone stared out the window at two mating pigeons that had just landed on a TV antenna.

Yeah, it looked to be a great day.

The End

ABOUT THE AUTHOR

Wol-vriey is Nigerian, and quite tall.

He currently resides in a state of uneasy stalemate with his threatening-to-thin-beyond-redemption hair, and believes there actually are things that go bump in the night.

Wol-vriey recycles the ridiculous into reasonable reality for the reader.

His WEIRRRD philosophy?

WEIRRRD = Warp/Write Everything into Realistic Ridiculous Readable Distorted Dream Dimension Descriptions.

Wol-vriey blogs at:

http://oddityfarm.wordpress.com

WOL-VRIEY
BIZARRO AND TRANSGRESSIVE FICTION

BOSTON POSH (BUD MALONE #1)

In 2028 AD, the USA is a nation ravaged by hungry dragons and dinosaurs. In Boston, Massachusetts, private eye Bud Malone is hired to rescue a kidnapped heiress. But nothing is as it seems.

Malone works to unravel a tangled web involving Boston Chinatown, a 200-year-old woman with a 9-year-old body, white robots, a human-liver-eating psychopath, a golem, a porcelain dragon, and a snake goddess with a crush on him. There's also a woman obsessed with chicken sex. Then Malone meets Posh Lane, a gorgeous call girl who's desperate to quit her pimp.

Romantic sparks ignite between Posh and Malone, but Posh's past suddenly catches up with her in a BIG way. To save Posh, Malone agrees to run a quest for Earth's new rulers, the Forks. But, Malone has no idea that agreeing to the Fork's odd request will send him on the weirdest trip he's ever been on in his life.

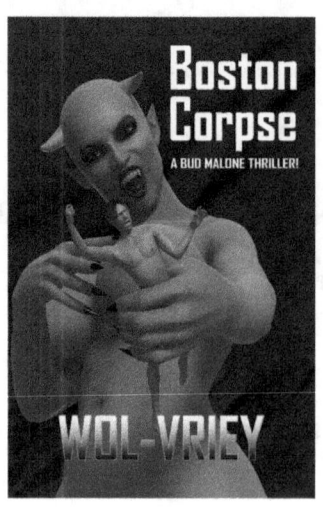

BOSTON CORPSE (BUD MALONE #2)

MAGIC CAN BE MURDER! - Drag queen Lucy Tang is back in Boston, and is hell-bent on settling her vindetta against casino owner Sookie Ling. And suddenly, Bud Malone, PI, has the case of his life to resolve.

When Boston's robot police force are baffled by a mind transfer case, they come to Malone for help. The one person who can likely help Malone out here is the witch Soledad Bathory. But Soledad seems to know a lot more than she's telling him. It's a case not made easier when Malone meets Soledad's beautiful cousin, Josephine 'Slave' Bailey. Slave has her own plans for Malone, most of which involve teaching him BDSM and making him her new Master.

Oh, and Rick Rogers owes Sookie Ling a whole lot of money, a gambling debt that's going to be literally Hell to pay!

BOSTON CORPSE - Not your average detective novel!

Burning Bulb
PUBLISHING

WOL-VRIEY
BIZARRO AND TRANSGRESSIVE FICTION

Communism = the political doctrine outlawing 'coming' (i.e. the female orgasm).

Courtney Taylor is young, intelligent, beautiful, and successful. She also has a boyfriend who loves her deeply.

The problem is, no matter what Courtney does, she can't climax during sex.

When Florence Rigid's communist forces destroy the city of Metaphor, Courtney and her friends Teresa, Highball, Miki, and Heather are cast into the midst of a quest to find the only person able to save the land of Innuendo—Dr. Carol Orgasm, wanted by the communists for developing the O-Pill, a wonder drug that grants women sexual ecstasy on demand.

The communists will do anything to get their hands on the O-Pill and prevent its reaching the millions of Innuendo's women.

But Courtney desperately wants that pill too. And so it's now a race between Courtney and the communists to find Dr. Orgasm first.

And Courtney has no choice but to win this race.

She must win it: For her own orgasm . . . and for the freedom of female sexuality everywhere.

Burning Bulb
PUBLISHING

WOL-VRIEY
BIZARRO AND TRANSGRESSIVE FICTION

VAGINA MUNDI

Rachel Risk is a professional thief with super-strong hair that can stretch like tentacles to manipulate objects. Ashley Status has both a digitally augmented brain, and 'muscle-purses' in her arms and legs in which she stores inflatable objects—cars, guns, rocket launchers, etc.

When Raye is framed as the fall girl in a jewel robbery, the pair flee Chicago's vengeful robot gangsters and take refuge in the Hotel Bizarre, where the gorgeous 'vagina singer,' Femina, is performing for a week.

But the Hotel Bizarre is even stranger than its name suggests, and very soon Raye and Ash are involved in an deadly adventure, a struggle for survival the likes of which they'd never imagined possible—with loads of deviant sex, drugs, music, and violence at every turn. And just what is the old woman in the skin desert really doing with all those cats glued to her walls?

VAGINA MUNDI—a Bizarro Hymn in praise of WOMAN!

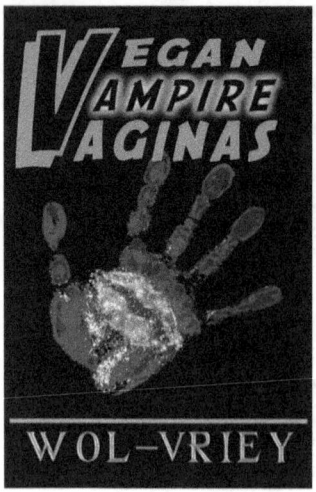

VEGAN VAMPIRE VAGINAS

The biggest bank heist in US history. And Tom Palmer can't remember pulling it off. And no, this isn't your standard case of amnesia. After a one-night-stand gone horribly wrong, Boston salesman Tom Palmer wakes up with a vagina implanted in his left hand. Then his day gets worse.

Tom is transported across space-time to a nightmare version of Boston, one where the Bizarro virus has transformed half the population into cannibals. Worst of all, Tom discovers that in this new Boston, he's the infamous gangster Pussypalm, wanted for robbing the Federal Reserve Bank of Boston a year ago. He also learns that the vagina in his hand is prophetic, i.e. it talks . . . after sex.

With 130 people left dead during his bank heist and six billion dollars missing, Tom knows he's living on borrowed time. It is in his best interests not to remember anything. Because once he does . . .

Burning Bulb
PUBLISHING

WOL-VRIEY
BIZARRO AND TRANSGRESSIVE FICTION

VEGAN ZOMBIE APOCALYPSE

In the post-apocalypse worlderness, zombies rule the earth. They're allergic to meat, and brains literally make them explode. Zombies now eat blood potatoes, parasitic tubers grown in the flesh of humancows corralled in maximum security farms. Two fugitives meet in the ancient ruins of Texas. The first is Soil 15-f, a womancow who's escaped her farm a week before she's due to be killed and her blood potato crop harvested. The second fugitive is Able Kane, former head necros food technician, now sentenced to death for heresy. But Soil is no ordinary humancow.

Unknown to herself, she's the vegan zombie agricultural revolution, and the zombies desperately want her back. And the necros equally desperately want Able Kane dead. He's fled with a forbidden discovery which will reshape the world for the worse if used. And Able is just hardheaded/misguided enough to use it.

MELANIE NEMESIS CATCHPOLE

In Springfield, Massachusetts, Melanie Catchpole is hired to fetch back a magic teddy bear worth millions of dollars from a warehouse across town. Problem is, the warehouse is down in Springfield's O-Zone-that totally weird sector of the city where Bizarro fell to Earth. The 'O' is a fairytale land, a place where dreams and nightmares literally live and breathe.

Worse still, the gingers—mutant cannibals—prowl the O. The gingers have already eaten everyone else Melanie's employers sent to get back the magic teddy bear.

Accompanied by the handsome but ruthless Doug Fisher (who she finds sexy but doesn't dare entrust her heart to), Melanie enters the O-Zone. Melanie and Doug are instantly caught up in an adventure they'd never have believed credible even if written as fiction . . . and Melanie's used to experiencing the very weird as the norm.

And now, additionally, there's a mystery to unravel: What does the dark, freezing-cold being called The Fixer want with Mary, the barkeep's daughter?

Burning Bulb
PUBLISHING

WOL-VRIEY
BIZARRO AND TRANSGRESSIVE FICTION

BIG TROUBLE IN LITTLE ASS

From Bizarro master storyteller Wol-vriey comes a truly weird western tale that will leave you awe-struck and on the edge of your seat...

In the town named Little Ass, tight-assed prostitute Rosa over-hears a gunslinger's plans to assassinate rancher Edison Bennett. Once the badass Bennett learns of the plot, he ensures there'll be hell to pay for any attempt on his life!

Yes, it's going to take all of gunslinger Jude's shooting prowess, his eclectic collection of strange firearms, a trusty horse that requires an owners' manual, and the help of the lovely and invigorating Nell (who's EXTREMELY odd when the going gets weird), to survive the Bizarro hell that Edison Bennett unleashes in order to hold onto the land that he'd stolen from Madam Zizi.

BIZARRO 101 (A BASIC PRIMER)

Welcome to the strange place:

A collection of 37 flash fiction stories designed to introduce one to the Bizarro/New Weird Genre.

Weird, dreamy, nightmarish, absurd, sad, surreal, humorous . . . this collection of tales is all this and more.

***

"This primer is the very essence of any and all styles and types of Bizarro writing. Wol-vriey collects, distills, and bottles up these 37 tiny stories for your sensory enjoyment. This is an absolute must-read for anyone new to the genre, because it demonstrates the scope of what Bizarro is, and what it can be."
　　　　　　　　　　　　　–Teresa Pollack, Bizarro commentator and blogger

Burning Bulb
PUBLISHING

OTHER GREAT TITLES FROM

Burning Bulb
PUBLISHING

WWW.BURNINGBULBPUBLISHING.COM

BELLY TIMBER

From the writers of Darkened Hills, Detour to Armageddon and Night of the Living Dead comes a novel unlike any other...

In the 1800's, ordinary people learned the secret of the Kala and undertook extraordinary measures to rid the earth of this evil. This is their story.

For John McCormick, life on the Indiana frontier held nothing but promise. His settlement along the White River would soon become the crossroads of America. Friends and family from back in Ohio and other points east were all making plans to see what all the fuss was about in the newly-formed city of Indianapolis. Yes, things were good. John had his general store and his friend George Pogue had his blacksmith business. Claims were being staked and relations with the native Indians were amicable. The town was growing and nothing could be better... or so he thought.

In Ohio, an evil was brewing. The Lecky Family, a group of ruthless Mongolian nomads, had made their way to America and were practicing their cannibalistic religion of Kala with reckless abandon. No one was safe, not even John McCormick's family.

Burning Bulb
PUBLISHING

BOB GRAY'S ATTACK OF THE MELONHEADS

"Melonheads is what I love. Give me a body count and gore, but don't forget the laughs. Anytime that I can be reminded of what makes Horror great it is a good thing. Melonheads does that and is something we should all support. Consider it highly recommended."
—*Screamsine.us*

Fifty years ago, a doctor sought to cure a terrible disease. Hidden from the world, Doctor Malcolm Crowe toiled in the dead of night while the world was sleeping, creating a new breed of mutant—all in the name of science.

Yes, he thought he could cure the sick children. But he was wrong.

Today, the results of his cruel and unconventional experiments have manifested into an evil never before seen.

Now, in Kirtland, Ohio, the town's unsuspecting residents are about to encounter the full onslaught of this unimaginable terror.

Can something be done before it's too late?

Burning Bulb
PUBLISHING

EVERYTHING HERE IS A NIGHTMARE
Collected Works Vol 1.

"Pyles makes it look easy. His characters come instantly alive with the cocksure verve and swagger of rock stars."
- Daniel Knauf, creator of HBO's "Carnivale,"
Executive Producer/Writer, ABC's "The Blacklist."

The critically acclaimed author of Demons, Dolls and Milkshakes returns with fifteen tales of horror and suspense with Everything Here is a Nightmare.

From zombies in the old west, to a young boy tempted by the Devil. From vampires with romantic longing, to an abandoned lighthouse haunted by vengeful spirits. From a serial killer getting unholy justice, to a haunted English race car, Nelson W Pyles invites you to explore a landscape of fear, suspense and horror.

Take his hand and hold on tight. Remember that whatever you find here, whatever you see, no matter what you might think it could be... know this: Everything Here is a Nightmare.

Burning Bulb
PUBLISHING

ANTHOLOGIES
BIZARRO AND TRANSGRESSIVE FICTION

THE BIG BOOK OF BIZARRO SPECIAL KINDLE EDITIONS

OTHER AWESOME COLLECTIONS

ANTHOLOGIES
BIZARRO AND TRANSGRESSIVE FICTION

THE BIG BOOK OF BIZARRO

The Big Book of Bizarro brings together the peculiar prose of an international cast of the most grotesquely-gonzo, genre-grinding modern writers who ever put pen to paper (or mouse to pad), including:

NIGHT OF THE LIVING DEAD horror writers John Russo & George Kosana; HUSTLER MAGAZINE erotica contributors Eva Hore, Andrée Lachapelle, & J. Troy Seate and established Bizarro genre authors D. Harlan Wilson, William Pauley III, Wol-vriey, Laird Long, Richard Godwin and so many more!

From Alien abductions to Zombie sex, The Big Book of Bizarro contains OVER FIFTY STORIES of the most outrélandish transgressive fiction that you'll ever lay your capricious and curious hands upon!

WESTWARD HOES

Nine outlaw writers rode into town from obscurity to pen nine tantalizing tales of horror and fantasy, and leaving once they branded their own personal marks on the weird western genre and became living legends of the American Frontier experience.

Like drunken Indian scouts, the writers fervidly tracked down and captured the Western genre, tore off its fashionable veneer and ravished its exposed essence.

So belly up to the bar with your favorite soiled dove and enjoy perusing these thrilling tales of Old West debauchery, danger and desire; compiled by the publisher of The Big Book of Bizarro and featuring the bizarro novella *Big Trouble in Little Ass* by Wol-vriey.

Burning Bulb
PUBLISHING

GARY LEE VINCENT'S
DARKENED
THE WEST VIRGINIA VAMPIRE SERIES

DARKENED HILLS

When evil descends on a small West Virginia town, who will survive?

Jonathan did not start out his life to become a rambler, it justworked out that way. William was a troubled youth with something to hide. Both were from Melas, a small town tucked away in the West Virginia hills... a town where disappearances are happening more and more frequently.

After the suicide of a wanted serial killer, the townsfolk thought the nightmare was over. But when a centuries-old vampire is discovered they find out the hard way it's just getting started. Dark secrets can only stay hidden for so long and when the devil comes to collect, there will be hell to pay. Can Jonathan and William find a way to stop the vampire before it's too late? Find out in *Darkened Hills!*

DARKENED HOLLOWS

In the heart-stopping sequel to the award-winning *Darkened Hills*, Jonathan and William must return to West Virginia to face possible criminal charges stemming from their last visit to the damned town of Melas, where both had narrowly escaped the clutches of a vampire seethe.

And as livestock start mysteriously getting murdered with all of their blood drained, worried farmers are searching for answers - leaving the local Sheriff and his deputy racing against time to learn the cause before a more violent crime is committed.

Burning Bulb
PUBLISHING

WWW.DARKENEDHILLS.COM

GARY LEE VINCENT'S
DARKENED
THE WEST VIRGINIA VAMPIRE SERIES

DARKENED WATERS

When the world goes to hell, the chosen must arise!

As Talman Cane orchestrates a flood of epic proportions in this third installment of the *Darkened* series the towns of Melas and Tarklin are caught completely off guard by the deluge. Hell-bent on finishing what they started, the evil brothers return to the lunatic asylum to take care of the witnesses and add to the ever-growing army of the undead.

Aided by Lucifer himself and the insane vampire demon Legion, the stage is set to channel all of the forces of hell to come forth. In an all-out race to survive, Jonathan, William, and Amanda soon discover they are up against impossible odds as Lucifer opens the Gateway to Hell, ushering in the zombie apocalypse and the End Times.

Find out who will survive this cosmic battle of the ages in *Darkened Waters*!

DARKENED SOULS

Melas and the Madison House are about to be rebuilt.
True evil is about to be reborne!

Young ex-priest and vampire-killer William is drawn back to the West Virginian town that almost killed him, where his vampire arch-enemy Victor Rothenstein still stalks the earth.

The town of Melas lies destroyed after the battle of the End of Days. But why is wealthy Jackie Nixon so eager to rebuild it using the bone dust of murdered souls?

Terrible evil has visited before, but the Gateway to Hell is about to be reopened in a horrific climax. And this time – it's personal.

WWW.DARKENEDHILLS.COM

Burning Bulb
PUBLISHING

DAVID J. FAIRHEAD

"David Fairhead writes compelling stories that offer very human characters and very inhuman monsters. There is no subtlety in Fairhead's imagination - he is simply dying to scare the hell out of you." - Nelson W Pyles author of DEMONS, DOLLS AND MILKSHAKES

THE FALL

Hopelessness... How do you protect your loved ones when Hell itself opens its insidious mouth?

Horror... Nightmarish Creatures invade your world and there is nowhere to hide.

Blood... How long can you hold out before they come for you?

Pain... Where do you run to avoid being eaten alive by monsters with a voracious appetite for your flesh?

Screams... While you selfishly run for your own life.

Questions... Who is to blame? Where did they come from? How many people survived...and how does the human race find the means to fight back?

THE FALL OF TOMORROW is man's last tale of desperation told by those that are striving to salvage some hope against a ravenous bastion of evil beasts bent on ruling our world.

DWELLING IN THE DARK

From David J. Fairhead, author of the FALL OF TOMORROW, comes DWELLING IN THE DARK- A soulful anthology of creeping terror to keep you up in the small hours with horror set in the past, present and future. Overlapping bits of puzzle fitting each other, before and after The Fall of Tomorrow.

A place where three children facing a monstrous foe can only pray that their bloody summer would just come to an end. Go back to the 1960's- THE COMMUNE where overindulging hippies use a mage's diary to control the end of the world, only to see first-hand that their drug induced visions have horrific ramifications. Where a young boy's visit to a haunted house becomes a lesson in RESIDUAL morality. The story, DEEPER- plunges two brothers into a sinkhole only to find they were being hunted by an insidious creature from its depths. Visit the old west as hero Dekker Collins battles evil gunslingers in DEMONEYE.

And so much more...!

Burning Bulb
PUBLISHING

WWW.FAIRLYDARKPRODUCTIONS.COM

ZAKARY MCGAHA
BIZARRO AND TRANSGRESSIVE FICTION

SEA OF MEDIUM-TO-HIGH PITCHED NOISES

The zombie apocalypse is changing; the world is coming to an odd demise; and a serial killer tries to change his ways and redeem himself before it all goes away. Now, Crabby has entered the world he left behind; the world of the undead. And things are changing. Everything will come to an end. In this new wave of the apocalypse, everything changes every five minutes. And death would be an absolute luxury. Psychological torment meets physical bloodletting in Sea of Medium-to-High Pitched Noises.

PARK MASTERS

Bad breakups, Bigfoot costumes, ghost bears, and more. Park Masters is a wacky, intelligent, quirky comedy about the power relationships have on people, good or bad. Also, it's just plain fun!

Burning Bulb
PUBLISHING

WEST VIRGINIA-THEMED HUMORROROTICA

BY RICH BOTTLES JR.

HELLHOLE WEST VIRGINIA

From the heights of Mothman's perch high atop the Silver Bridge in Point Pleasant to the depths of Hellhole Cavern in Pendleton County, evil lurks within the shadows as the sun sets upon the haunted hills and hollows of West Virginia.

Bizarro author Rich Bottles Jr. blows the coffin lid off horror genre clichés with this tour de force cast of Eco-friendly vampires, beach-yearning zombies and sex-starved she-devils.

LUMBERJACKED

If you are easily offended or do not possess a truly depraved sense of humor, this story may not be the light summer reading fare you desire. As for the four feisty female freshmen stranded on top of West Virginia's third highest mountain, they have no choice but to experience the sick, twisted debauchery and perverted mayhem described deep inside the tight unbroken bindings of this horrific missive.

Lumberjacked takes the reader to a nightmarish world where character development and aesthetic integrity are prematurely cut short by the swinging axes of maniacal lumberjacks, who are hell bent on death and destruction in the remote forests of Appalachia. And at the climax, when paranoia crosses over to the paranormal, Lumberjacked makes Deliverance look like a family raft trip down the Lower Gauley.

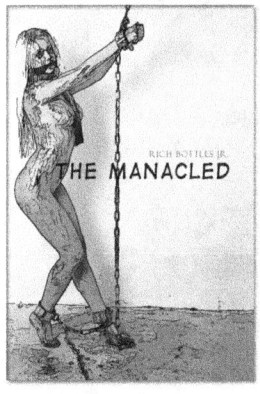

THE MANACLED

What happens when twin brothers lease out the former West Virginia State Penitentiary with the false purpose of filming a documentary on supernatural phenomena, but their true intention is to make a pornographic movie?

Chaos ensues as the disturbed spirits of murdered convicts, along with the reanimated dead from the neighboring Indian Burial Mound, take their vengeance on the unwary and undressed trespassers.

Zombies, ghosts, mobsters and porn collide in this bizarro tale from horror author Rich Bottles Jr.

Burning Bulb
PUBLISHING

NIGHT OF THE LIVING DEAD

Why does Night of the Living Dead hit with such chilling impact?

Is it because everyday people in a commonplace house are suddenly the victims of a monstrous invasion? Or is it because the ghouls who surround the house with grasping claws were once ordinary people, too?

Decide for yourself as you read, and the horror grips you.

All the cannibalism, suspense and frenzy of the smash-hit move are here in the novel.

www.TheJohnRusso.com

"THE BLAZING SADDLES OF SEX SATIRES!" - GEORGINA SPELVIN

THE BOOBY HATCH

It's a Zany Love Lab where
Looney Professors Measure Pleasure!

From Legendary Horror Writer
JOHN A. RUSSO

THE BOOBY HATCH

With NIGHT OF THE LIVING DEAD, John Russo helped
blaze a path in the horror genre that has never been equalled.
In this hillarious erotic novel, he blazes a path through the
wild, zany Sex Revolution of the 1970s.

Sweet, innocent Cherry Jankowski works for Joyful Novelties,
where she tests sex toys ranging from the ridiculous to the
sublime. But she can't find love or peace of mind and her
efforts are hampered by a Peeping Tom, an exhibitionist, a
cross-dressing boyfriend, a quack psychiatrist, and even her
own product-testing partner, Marcello Fettucini, who can't
get it up anymore and is scared of losing his job!

www.TheJohnRusso.com

Burning Bulb
PUBLISHING

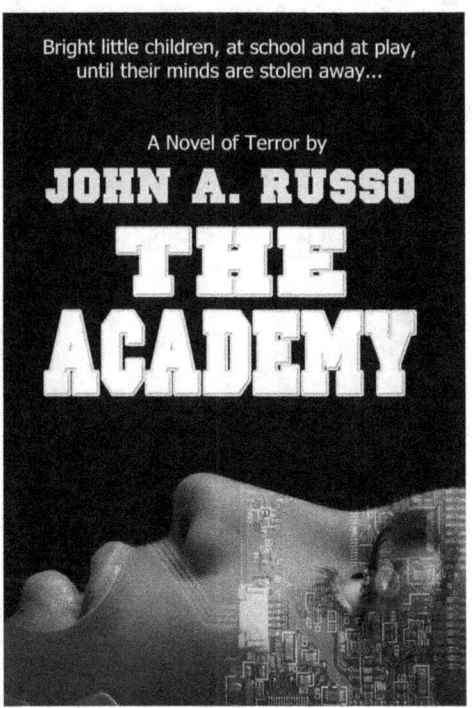

Bright little children, at school and at play,
until their minds are stolen away...

A Novel of Terror by

JOHN A. RUSSO

THE ACADEMY

THE ACADEMY

The Academy. It's every parent's dream, turning their little
darlings into geniuses, superachievers, perfect little
children.

And if there's a problem, the Academy fixes that too. It's a
simple operation. Just a little device. Then a teeny pink scar
on a tender little skull . . .

One boy knows the secret. Now he wants his mind back.
But it's much, much too late. Too late for anything but the
ugly feelings. The bad feelings. The messy sexy feelings. The
knife-cold hatred, the murderous rage, for total, screaming,
blood-drenching revenge . . .

www.TheJohnRusso.com

Burning Bulb
PUBLISHING

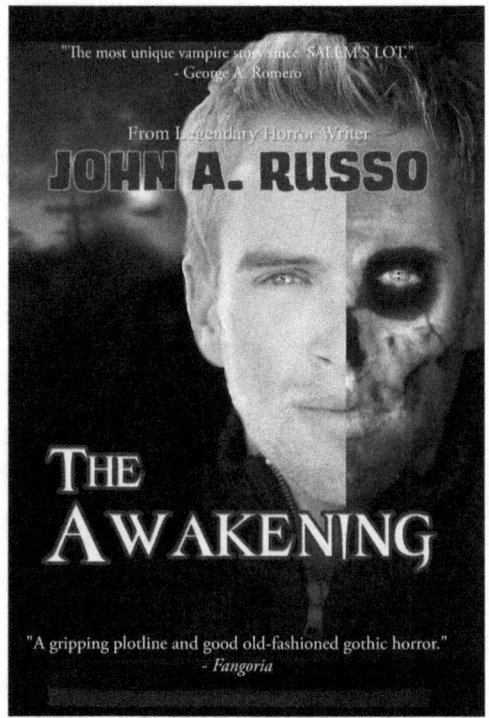

THE AWAKENING

For two hundred years, he has rested. Now he rises. Now he will be satisfied. Nothing can stop him. No one can resist him.

Benjamin Latham is young and handsome, his eighteenth-century mind wakened to a bizarre twentieth-century world. And there is the need deep within . . . an animal need, frightening, murderous, unholy . . . a vital need that must be fed.

And with his need comes a power over men and women to do his bidding, to quiet his dark craving . . .

Until the murders begin. And the inquiries. All suggesting the same hideous truth.

Now Benjamin must find a sanctuary: a lover, a partner, a friend. Someone who can share his darkness. Someone he can lead to . . . The Awakening.

www.TheJohnRusso.com

Burning Bulb
PUBLISHING

DEALEY PLAZA

From legendary horror and suspense writer JOHN RUSSO comes a harrowing tale where no one is safe!

Dealey Plaza is one of the most notorious places in America, and when youthful conspiracy buffs go there in 1964 to stage their own reenactment of the Kennedy Assassination, four of them are brutally murdered ~ the first victims of a hate-filled legacy that continues for four more decades.

The survivors of that long-ago Dallas trip, each of them now icons of the American way of life, are about to be honored ~ or killed.

Who will live and who will die? Will it be country-western star Lori McCoy? Her loving husband? Her scheming ex-husband? Or the case-hardened FBI agent and longtime friend who risks his life trying to protect them?

www.DealeyPlazaBook.com

Burning Bulb
PUBLISHING

From Legendary Horror Writer
JOHN A. RUSSO

L I M B
to
L I M B

LIMB TO LIMB

SUCH A PRETTY GIRL . . .
Tiffany Blake was a beautiful long-limbed dancer with a glorious future and the backing of a rich benefactor. Then a monstrous accident severed her leg at the hip.

SUCH A COLD, CRUEL KNIFE . . .
And now her fellow dancers are disappearing without a trace. One by one they fall victim to a dark and deadly pattern of evil – caught by the bloody, brutal logic that would have them pay with their lovely bodies for the cruel fate of another . . .victims of the sadistic madman whose flashing knife will make them writhe a gruesome new dance.

www.TheJohnRusso.com

Burning Bulb
PUBLISHING

"A sense of infectious fun, straight from the author's pen."
– Nightmare Library

From Legendary Horror Writer
JOHN A. RUSSO

LIVING THINGS

"Russo carries his talent for the horrific neatly over into the novel form."
– West Coast Review of Books

LIVING THINGS

Beneath the shimmering Miami sun sprawls one of the Mafia's biggest empires, a glittering worldof lavish beachfront mansions, neon-painted nightclubs, beautiful women, expensive cars—and absolute control over the state's billion-dollar drug trade. But, one by one, its ganglords and henchmen are falling prey to a new rival. His powers are fueled by monstrous ancient rituals; his hellish undead legions slaughter mobsters and innocent citizens alike, his unholylust for power is virtually unstoppable.

Now a burned-out ex-detective and a brilliant anthropologist must enter a gruesome, nightmare world to fight this master of malevolence and illusion. Their time is short, their weapons few, and they face an ultimate, terrifying choice - annihilation or the loss of their souls to the eternal torment of those who never die. . .

www.TheJohnRusso.com

Burning Bulb
PUBLISHING

ELVIS PRESLEY, CIA ASSASSIN BY ANDY RAUSCH

"I can guarantee you. Read this book and you'll never look at Elvis the same way again!"
~ Douglas Brode, author of ELVIS CINEMA AND POPULAR CULTURE

SOON TO BE A MAJOR MOTION PICTURE

In 1970, singer Elvis Presley secretly met with President Richard Nixon. This new comedic novel imagines that Presley became a Central Intelligence Agency operative, eventually moving up through the ranks to become a skilled assassin.

Presented in an oral history fashion, the book tells us about Presley's secret transformation by the people who knew him best.

Did he fake his death in 1977? Was Presley involved with the Watergate scandal? The Iran hostage crisis? Communicating with aliens?

Read this book to find out the answers to these and many more questions.

Burning Bulb
PUBLISHING

MAD WORLD BY ANDY RAUSCH

"*Mad World* is dark, twisted, no-holds-barred fun."
—Jason Starr, author of *Bust*, *Slide*, and *The Max*

EVERYONE'S PLAYING AN ANGLE IN THE CITY OF ANGELS

Mad World tells the stories of a black hitman who doubles as a university professor, a Catholic priest who longs to be a gangster, a would-be author from Kansas, a gay phone sex operator who claims he's straight, a group of rich twentysomethings playing a deadly game of life and death, a vicious Mafia boss, and a sleazy Hollywood movie director. As each of their stories intersect, the body count piles up and the action comes nonstop in this tense, white-knuckle thriller by first-time author Andy Rausch.

"A wild ride. If you like it gangster, *Mad World* delivers."
—Daniel Birch, author of *Get Some*

Burning Bulb
PUBLISHING

BLOODLETTING: A TALE OF REVENGE BY ANDY RAUSCH

"Relentless… Addictive… The kind of nightmare you don't want
to wake up from."
—Heywood Gould, screenwriter of *Rolling Thunder*

He was just an average Joe. But when he finds his family held at
gunpoint by merciless thugs, he's told he must murder a Mafia
chieftain if he ever wishes to see his loved ones again.

Against all odds, Joe keeps his end of the bargain, but the criminals
don't. Now at his wits end, Joe is pushed beyond his breaking point
and forced to exact bloody revenge against those who've done him
and his family wrong in this powerful and violent novella by author
Andy Rausch (*Mad World*).

"Andy Rausch has a tight noir style that combines gritty, realistic drama
with a cinematic flair that makes for a powerful, compelling (somewhat
Stephen Kingesque), authentically visual reading experience."
—Stephen Spignesi, author of *Dialogues*

Burning Bulb
PUBLISHING

THE TAILSMAN

From the creators of *The Big Book of Bizarro* and *Westward Hoes* comes a new comic unlike anything you have ever seen!

He's hot on the trail, looking for some *tail...*

Sly Franko was a man of the West, a forger of the wild frontier. Like the Country Western song that would be written years after he died, the words, "Faster horses, younger women, and more money," seemed to be the anthem of this horn dog cowboy.

Franko would ride into town on a blazing saddle, find the closest saloon to wet the whistle, belly up to a good card game, and find him a hot-loving hussy to get his cowpoke on with.

However, Sly might have met his match when a visit to bathroom leads to terror and death. Can Sly and his poker buddies solve the mystery before more of the townsfolk are murdered? Find out in this exciting premier issue of *The Tailsman!*

WWW.BURNINGBULBCOMICS.COM

THE HAGS OF BLACK COUNTY

by Michelle Bowser

Ruled by a committee of Hags, and fueled by toothless rivalries, Black County lurks just far enough out of the way to be completely unnoticed by the rest of civilization. Its inhabitants have been mentally warped for generations and the land itself seems to have the power to drive anyone unlucky enough to visit into ridiculous hillbilly madness. When a construction Company needs to bury a pipeline through its ludicrous hills and valleys, a twisted charm goes to work and every aspect of already bizarre Black County life takes a gory turn for the hysterical. Take a preposterous trip along with its citizens, both native and new, through escapades such as the Hag parade, the grand opening of Madame Skunk's House of Ill Repute, the demolition derby riot and the rabid, zombie clown apocalypse.

THE ABANDONED SOUL

by Daniel Sellers

After spending most of his 20s in a drug and alcohol fueled daze, a young man finally hits rock bottom. Having used up his friends and their good graces, he ends up squatting in an abandoned house. Forcibly sobering he begins to realize that he is not alone in this abandoned house. Left with one last friend and a mountain of regrets, he must decide if this presence is a guilty conscience, or a malicious hunter.

WE WISH YOU A HAPPY KILLDAY

by Jason Heroux

"We Wish You a Happy Killday" is the story of an international b eloved holiday called "Killday" where one day a year everyone over the age of fifteen is permitted to register for a license allowing them to kill one other person. But this year Chad Ovenstock doesn't feel like killing anyone. His friends and family urge him to participate in the festivities, but he can't seem to get into the holiday spirit. On the day before Killday Chad comes in contact with Ambrose, an old friend who suffered a nervous breakdown and is now part of The One Ant Army, a mysterious cult dedicated to making the future disappear. When the holiday finally arrives Chad refuses to participate and tries to survive on his own, surrounded by constant gunfire, countless corpses, and the nagging suspicion that Ambrose may have secretly brainwashed him into becoming a member of The One Ant Army cult.

Burning Bulb
PUBLISHING